ALSO BY KIRU TAYE

The Essien Series
Keeping Secrets
Making Scandal
Riding Rebel
Kola
A Very Essien Christmas
Freddie Entangled
Freddie Untangled

Bound Series
Bound to Fate
Bound to Ransom
Bound to Passion
Bound to Favor
Bound to Liberty

The Challenge Series
Valentine
Engaged
Worthy
Captive

The Ben & Selina Trilogy
Scars
Secrets
Scores

Men of Valor Series
His Treasure
His Strength
His Princess

Enders Series
Duke: Prince of Hearts
Xandra: Killer of Kings

Osagie: Bad Santa

Royal House of Saene Series
His Captive Princess
The Tainted Prince
The Future King
Saving Her Guard
Screwdriver

Viva City FC Series
Tapping Up
Against the Run of Play

Others
Haunted
Outcast
Sacrifice
Black Soul
Scar's Redemption

Kiru Taye

Engaged
CHALLENGE #2

First Published in Great Britain in 2021 by
LOVE AFRICA PRESS
103 Reaver House, 12 East Street, Epsom KT17 1HX
www.loveafricapress.com

Home of African Love Stories

Text copyright © Kiru Taye, 2016

ISBN: 978-1-914226-56-4
Also available in eBook

Blurb

Three friends. Three challenges. Are they willing to risk everything for love?

When savvy PR consultant Ijay Amadi meets successful Industrialist Paul Arinze, the only things on her mind are to forget the pain of her failed relationship and enjoy the delights his branding touch and soul-searing kiss promise. It's a one-time only event. Perfect.

However, Paul is annoyed to wake up and find her gone the next morning. He isn't ready to forget the dark-haired beauty or their scorching night together just yet. So he plans to have Ijay right where he wants her—in Abuja, working on his latest business project by day and enjoying the pleasure of his bed by night.

Except when Ijay arrives, she's wearing another man's engagement ring. With the explosive desire between them threatening their priorities and loyalties, the stakes get higher by the minute. Who'll be left standing at the altar when Ijay walks down the aisle?

Chapter One

You'll die a lonely man.

With ease Paul Arinze navigated the throng of people gathered at the party. He ignored the dire phrase echoing in his mind—words that had plagued him in the past few weeks. Instead, he keyed into the thrumming vibe of the urban music thumping out of hidden loudspeakers in the shiny black glass walls of the nightclub.

Paul's back prickled with sensation, the hairs standing erect. Someone was watching him. His gaze dragged across the dance floor, searching. People were dancing, chatting, drinking. A lady brushed past him—long blonde hair and a dress that showcased her full unshackled breasts. She smiled at him, the eager inviting message in her green eyes unmistakeable. She'd accommodate his desires.

Yet nothing stirred within him. No spark. No passion. Just emptiness. He gave her a reluctant smile in return and moved on. He was exhausted, mentally.

As a waiter walked by, his silver tray laden with drinks, Paul stopped him and replaced his empty glass with another full glass of champagne. It wasn't his poison of choice. For tonight, it would have to do. He took a sip from the crystal glass and allowed the fizzing crisp dry liquid down his throat. The light intoxicant didn't do much to settle his soul's restlessness, but it took the edge off his body alertness.

Spotting the sliding doors leading to a balcony, he walked toward it. Once outside, he inhaled deeply, enjoying the fresh night air in his lungs and on his face, cooling his hot skin. He slid the door shut, the sounds of music and loud conversation muffled by the reinforced glass. His gaze travelled across the blue-black night sky, the lights on the London Eye and other landmarks reflecting in the dark water of the Thames.

Slowly, a reflective smile tugged his lips as he took in the view. It was evidence of his hectic lifestyle that whenever he was in London, he never got the chance to really see London. The closest he got to any of the tourist landmarks were either from a London cab window or via his hotel room view.

Many years ago, he'd lived in the city while he'd attended university to complete his MBA. He'd loved his time here and the freedom that had come from being away from Nigeria and his father. He spent two years after his program working for a British firm to build his experience. In the end he'd returned to Nigeria. His home country was in his blood. While he was away he missed the place. Where ever else he visited—in his recent trip it'd been Singapore and New York—he never got the same peace of mind as he had when he was on Nigerian soil.

It was home to his family, closest friends and businesses—his life as he wanted it.

Yet in the past few weeks, a roiling restlessness had settled over him since he'd broken up with his last girlfriend, Kate. Letting out a resigned sigh, Paul leaned his back against the cool brick wall and allowed the memory of their conversation on the fateful night replay itself.

***

"The wedding was great fun. When are we going to set our own date?" Kate asked as she flung her clutch bag on the low round glass-top centre table.

Paul pretended he didn't hear her. They'd just returned from the wedding of an old school friend and a socialite. The couple's families were heavily involved in the Nigerian political scene—his friend's father was an ex-senator and the girl's father, an ex-minister. Socially arranged marriages were common place for the political elite. While Paul didn't mind attending other people's weddings, he certainly didn't want to discuss his own.

Silently, he shut his apartment door behind him and walked past Kate. He stood still, staring out of the floor-to-ceiling windows that overlooked the mountains in the distance. In the inky darkness, all he could make out were the outlines of the rocks. In the daytime, the view was breathtaking; part of the reason he'd bought the Abuja home.

"Paul?" Kate's probing voice broke into his thoughts.

"Our own date for what?" Paul asked, nonchalantly loosening and pulling off his blue embroidered silk tie. Painstakingly slow, he rolled it in his hands before undoing his top button. Then, he turned around to face her.

"Wedding date, of course," She purred; her smile a sultry invitation. Seductively and easily, she swayed her hips, coming toward him. When she stopped, she moved his jacket lapels apart, brushing his shirt with her palms in a sensuous movement that should've excited him. Instead, suspicion spiked his blood and tensed his muscles. "We've been dating for so long and I'm getting tired of attending other people's weddings without planning my own."

"Kate, I told you I wasn't ready to get married when we met. I'm not interested in wedding bells."

"Yes, that was over a year ago. I didn't expect you to marry me then. I do now."

Her eyes flashed angrily at him. He didn't notice. He wasn't interested. Her full bosoms heaved, nearly spilling out of her figure-hugging long black dress. To think that when he'd seen her earlier in it all he'd wanted to do was bring her here and take the dress off her body. Now he couldn't even stand to look at her.

Bile rose in his stomach. The mention of the word marriage always spoiled his mood. He wanted the smooth fiery taste of a drink to quash the bitterness in his mouth. Instead of moving over to the small bar in the corner of his living room, he allowed his gaze to meet Kate's.

"Nothing's changed for me, Kate. I still don't want to get married. I've never pretended otherwise," he replied coolly.

He should've seen this coming and done something to prevent it. Perhaps he should've broken off the relationship months ago. He'd become complacent, partially hoping that with Kate it would be different. That she understood his need for no-strings attached relationships.

She was a high-flying career girl and worked as head of department for a retail bank. He'd met her at a function right here in Abuja. He'd liked her because she was career-focused and they lived in separate towns – she in Lagos, while he spent most of his time split between Abuja and Enugu. She'd come up to Abuja for the weekends when she was available. It'd suited him fine to see her occasionally.

Emotions chased their way across Kate's face. Frustration, pain, anger. None of them touched him.

"If I wait, can you promise me we'll get married say in another year?" she asked calmly, her eyes watching him expectantly.

For some people, a year might make a difference. For Paul it didn't. He'd already spent that much time with Kate. His feelings for her today were no different from how he'd felt twelve months ago. Except now, he was disappointed she'd behaved like every other woman before her. By asking him for something he couldn't give her.

Paul pulled his face in a tight grimace. "There's no need to wait. I won't marry you."

"Then there's no point hanging around. It's over," she said in a shrill voice. With jerky angry movements, she picked up her bag.

"Listen. Why not wait until the morning," Paul said in a placating manner. Stifling the smile threatening to lift his lips in buoyant relief, he kept his face expressionless. It was best to let Kate think she'd ended their relationship, providing him with an easy way out.

"What would be the point of that, Paul? I'll pack my things and stay the night at the Hilton. I can head back to Lagos in the morning."

He nodded as she walked into the bedroom and grabbed her overnight bag. He called his chauffeur and asked the man to drop her off. When Kate came of out his bedroom, she stood glaring at him for a moment before shaking her head.

"You'll die a lonely man," she said and walked out the door.

***

Though it had done nothing to change his mind about asking her back, the words had plagued his mind ever since.

Paul let out a sigh as he took a sip of his drink. Perhaps it was time to call it a night. He was due to catch a flight out of London tomorrow afternoon. A good night's sleep wouldn't go amiss.

As he turned, the door to the balcony opened, letting out the noise from the bar and along with it, a sexy goddess.

Long dark tresses framed an oval face of flawless buttery cream, her curvaceous body in a beautiful navy lace dress that stopped just above the knees exposing satiny legs and feet in wedge sandals. For a moment she stood still, one leg paused over the threshold, the other already outside. In the pose she looked breathtaking with the dim lights from inside framing her in a silhouette.

"Sorry, I didn't mean to disturb you. I just wanted some fresh air. I'll come back later," she rattled out, the chant of her velvety voice set the blood in his veins alight.

She lowered her gaze, pulling the corner of her lower lip with her teeth in a nervous smile. Her diffident expression had his heart hammering in his chest, sending pulses of granite need down his body.

For the first time in weeks, his body responded to the sight of a woman with desire. An instant overwhelming craving. Perhaps he wasn't fatigued. He just needed the right woman.

This woman.

"No. Stay. There's plenty of fresh air to share." He straightened languorously and lifted his lips in a rapacious grin, all thought of leaving early, fizzled into the cool night air.

Stepping out fully, she closed the door behind her, leaving them in near silence. She moved to the end of the balcony away from him and put her hands against the railing.

"I love this view of London. I love coming out here whenever I'm in this building," she said, her tone conversational. Yet her soft voice sent spikes of heat into his veins.

"I have to say I like this view too. I don't see much of London when I'm here. So it's great to see it all lit up at night," Paul replied, glad that she was talking. For some reason he wanted to listen to sound of her voice.

He turned back to look out over the balcony, placing his palms on the cold metal. Even from the distance of about six feet, he could sense her. He pictured her leaning across to brush his hand with hers. A warm shiver travelled down his spine.

"You don't live in the city?" she asked, turning to face him in the near darkness.

From this angle, her face was a contrast of light and shade. Still, he could make out the gentle contour of her almond-shaped eyes, staring at him with curiosity. He wondered at their colour. He wanted to find out.

"No."

"I guessed as much."

"Why do you say that?" Paul leaned on the railing, turning his body and giving her his undivided attention. The pleasure of watching the bright city lights paled in comparison to the excitement in his blood at watching her luminous skin and graceful curves.

"I don't know. There was just something about you that didn't seem like a local."

Her lips curved wider in a luscious smile. He fought the urge to taste her lips, tightening his grip on the railing instead. It was too soon. He didn't want her skittering away in fright.

"You're good then. I'm only in London for tonight. Tomorrow, I'm off to Abuja."

"Oh. That's a shame." Was that disappointment in her voice? Did she feel this flaming hunger he felt too? "You won't get to see much of London in just one day."

"I guess not." The urge to touch her skin drew him closer. "I'm Paul Arinze."

He stopped at arm's length and extended his arm. Without hesitation, she placed her hand in his, her stare bold and holding his. On connection, a warm tingle spread from his hand down his back. Her hand was soft and warm. Yet she held his hand firmly. Confidently.

"I'm Ijay Amadi." Her voice was sultry, like a soft caress on his skin.

The throbbing of his arousal increased. The heady mix of her timidity and trust made him want to crush her soft curves against his hardness. If she had this effect on him just holding his hand, what would it feel like on the rest of his body? He wanted to find out. Shame he only had tonight.

"So are you here as a guest?" Reluctantly, he released her hand, missing its heat already.

"No. I work for Havers & Child PR Agency. I organised the product launch event earlier and this party."

Paul didn't return to his original position. He stood close to Ijay. She didn't move away. He took that as a good sign. "That's great. Congratulations, you did a splendid job. If I ever want to plan a party, you're the lady to know."

"I sure am." She laughed, dug in her purse, and handed him a business card. He took it and slipped it into his pocket. "And if you need to know the best places and people to have at your party, I'm the girl to know too."

"I wonder, are you the girl to know if I need a personal guide to show me around the best spots in London tonight?"

His question hung in the air for a moment. She didn't reply immediately. In the shadows of the balcony, he couldn't read the expression on her face. He wondered if he'd pushed the boundaries too hard too quickly. There was something about this woman that soothed his edgy feeling. Somehow he knew she felt the combustible arc of desire between them.

"I could be."

"But?"

"No buts. Give me ten minutes to make sure someone covers for me and I'll be all yours." The suggestive, sensual tone of her voice got his blood fizzing out of control.

Damn, he wanted her. He'd never thought himself the one-night-stand kind of man. Yet he was impatient with anticipation. The rush of blood southward, swelling his already aching shaft.

He nodded. "I can't wait."

She walked to the door, paused and looked at him. "I'll hurry." She beamed him another sexy smile and disappeared through the door.

***

"You're doing what?" Sonia asked, her mouth opened and eyes widened with incredulity.

"I told you already." Ijay shrugged. She'd expected a similar response from her colleague and best friend when she'd shared the news that she picked up a man at the party and was about to head off into the night with him.

"Yes, you did. But the idea sounded so crazy, so unlike you I thought I'd misheard you." Sonia waved her hand in the air to emphasis her point before reapplying her lipstick in the mirror of the ladies room. "You don't know him from Adam. He could be an axe murderer for all you know."

"Perhaps. I doubt it though. He's Frederick's friend."

Though she hadn't said it to him, she'd seen Paul earlier at the Product launch chatting with Frederick Conte whose firm was a client of Havers & Child. She'd watched him even closer when he'd arrived at the bar.

By default, she shouldn't trust any friend of Frederick's.

Still, something about Paul had attracted her attention. It was partly the self-assured way he moved across the floor, the engaging way he spoke to people and perceptive way he surveyed his surroundings. The way the navy silk shirt clung to his chest and the charcoal trousers to his thighs, there was no hiding the power and lithe of the body beneath the fabrics.

And of course the richness and depth of his voice had been pure sinful decadence to listen to. It was as if he was strumming her body with their enticing eloquent cords.

"Oh, that makes it alright then." Sonia rolled her eyes upwards in mock exasperation. "Seriously, I've heard about people doing crazy things on the rebound...this is taking the biscuit, Ijay. Come on. It's not like you at all."

"Perhaps that's the problem. I need to do something unlike me. I'm tired of being treated like a foot mat. I played safe with Frederick yet now he's engaged to Tamara; not me. I really am tired of moping around."

"You're not moping around." Her friend grabbed her shoulders and hugged her. "It's Frederick's loss."

It might be Frederick's loss. Still, it didn't feel that way from where Ijay was standing. After three years of dating Frederick on and off, all it had taken was for Tamara to show up and he'd had no problems proposing to her. They were all set for a spring wedding.

Ijay was the one who'd given him three years of her devotion. Where had that taken her? *Nowhere.* Except alone. She saw the way people looked at her with pity in their eyes and she hated it. They thought she couldn't keep a man's attention.

However, when Paul had looked at her, it'd been as if he'd really seen her. Not as rejected Ijay but as a sexy beautiful woman in her own right.

"Seriously, I just want to stop being the good, organised, reliable girl for an evening," she said reflectively. "I want to be carefree and spontaneous for a change and enjoy some time with a man who actually seems to find me attractive. I'm not asking for anything else. Is that too much to ask for?"

Tears pooled in her eyes blurring her view of the mirror. She blinked a couple of times, stopping them from dropping.

"No, it's not." Her friend's cheeks dimpled as she smiled cheerily. "Go. I'll hold the fort for you."

Ijay pulled out Paul's business card and gave it to Sonia. "Here are his contact details just in case. I'll see you back at the apartment. Don't wait up."

Ijay smiled, the words making her feel reckless. Staying out all night was never really her thing. It felt good to be doing something unlike her for a change. Ijay picked up her purse and jacket to leave.

"And you know what? Make his night unforgettable," Sonia said giving her a big grin and a wink.

Ijay felt a smile spread on her face as she walked back to the balcony and the hunk of a man waiting there. It felt great to know someone was looking forward to her company. Even if it was just for one night.

Tonight she needed someone to take away the aching loneliness she felt inside. A few minutes with Paul on the balcony had dulled that ache. A whole night of his presence would act like a sedative ensuring when she eventually slept there would be no more tears.

For nights after the split with Frederick she'd cried, wondering what was wrong with her. Why she wasn't the one happily engaged. Tonight there'd be none of that. Just the bliss of sleep.

Chapter Two

The ten minutes wait for Ijay dragged on interminably.

The air around Paul suddenly felt closed in. A cold sweat broke on his skin. His heart rate fluctuated from rapid to skipping. For a man who usually enjoyed his own company and was known for his fortitude, he now found he neither liked being alone, nor having to wait.

When it came to this one woman, his usual tolerance levels were shod and threatening to destroy his usual composure. He contemplated going back into the bar and soaking up the atmosphere to take the edge off. Yet he knew instantly that wouldn't be the solution. He also contemplated ordering a much stronger drink. That too wouldn't cut it, he decided. There was only one thing that could satisfy his craving—only one person he wanted.

Ijay Amadi.

With his hand he massaged the back of his neck. He paced the enclosed space of the balcony like a tiger in a cage. Occasionally, he stopped and looked at the crowd through the glass doors expectantly hoping for Ijay to appear any moment.

A thought occurred to him. Perhaps she'd changed her mind. She'd decided that spending the night with him wasn't such a good idea. He wouldn't blame her if she did. It wasn't as if he lived in London. He didn't do long distance relationships.

And he wasn't the kind of man that kept a woman at every port. He was purely a one-woman man. He could never tolerate men who kept more than one sexual partner at a time, no matter how discrete. Men like his father thought it was their God-given right to have multiple partners and illegitimate children all over Nigeria.

Yes, Ijay was probably right to snub him. He didn't do one-night stands and wouldn't be offering her more than tonight anyway. She was better off without him. He'd get over the snub with a good night sleep.

Resigned and ready to give up the waiting, his nerves wound tight, he froze for the briefest of moments when the sliding door opened again.

"I'm back."

Ijay stood there with a bold smile. The bolt of hunger that hit his solar plexus nearly buckled his knees. His body's need for her was simple yet primal, a new and yet age-old desire. It gave him a single-minded objective squashing all his previous doubts about getting together with her.

This was all wrong. Yet she was all right.

He couldn't stop his legs from moving forward as if of their own will toward her. His hands reached for her, pulling her against his body. He moved one hand to the nape of her neck while the other wrapped around her waist. Tilting her head up, he claimed her lips hungrily.

He heard her soft surprised gasp. Still, she didn't resist his lips' onslaught. Instead she wrapped her arms around his neck, her body clinging to his in seemingly wanton supplication.

Suddenly the world was right and yet off kilter at the same time. Her warm and gentle cuddle was like a hand wrapped around his heart, squeezing it tenderly. He hadn't been prepared for her affection. He'd expected their encounter to be that of cool strangers satisfying a pure need and moving on.

Yet in the moments of their kiss, as she opened her yielding lips for the voracious sweep of his tongue and he tasted her eager submission, it occurred to him that their encounter could be more than he'd initially thought.

With that realisation, he pulled back his head, breaking the kiss. He heard the pounding pulse of his heart rate above the sounds of the night. He inhaled rapidly, his breath coming out in puffs of steam; the air around him thinned and cold. Closing his eyes, he leaned his forehead against hers. Her essence seeped into his body through his nostrils saturating every pore and nerve ending.

"I want you..." he let the words trail off in a whisper, his throat jammed with emotion he was sure he shouldn't be feeling—couldn't be feeling.

It was Ijay's turn to pull back her head. She opened her eyes and for a brief moment he could've sworn he saw pain reflected in the profundity of her chocolate eyes.

"I can hear a 'but' in that statement," she said, staring into his eyes as if searching for answers in their depths. "Don't tell me you've changed your mind." She looked away from his face into the distant night sky, lowering her hands from his neck until they dropped beside her.

He caught the hint of disappointment in her voice and his gut tightened with guilt he couldn't quite understand. It was strange that earlier he'd been worried that she'd changed her mind about being with him. Yet now it seemed she was undergoing the same misgivings he'd had. He felt remorseful for making her feel that way.

He put his fingers under her chin turning her head to face him, while he pulled her body until it was flush with his again. "I haven't changed my mind. I just want to be sure that you want to do this. I'll be leaving the city tomorrow. I don't know when I'll be back and I don't believe in long distance relationships."

She beamed a warm smile at him, her lips lifting at the corners, her cheeks dimpling. "I understand totally. I've just come out of a long term relationship. Truthfully, I'm not interested in starting a new one."

She lifted her right hand and caressed his cheek. A warm quiver spread from his face, as her palm rubbed against the stubble on his face. "I need you...this...for tonight. Just tonight," her voice dropped to a sultry velvet whisper.

He shivered in warm expectation. Her straightforward and bold honesty appealed to him on so many levels. His plentiful experiences with women had taught him to read them with relative ease. One thing was guaranteed. They all had agendas. Even before they said hello to him, they were already calculating what they wanted out of him. And it was usually more than one night in his bed. Most wanted the ultimate prize—his ring on their fingers.

With Ijay, his suspicion radar seemed to be malfunctioning because Paul detected no ulterior motive. No calculating move to ensnare him for better or worse. The idea of a woman who only wanted him for one night should be freeing. Liberating. Yet he took her words with a pinch of salt.

She was a woman after all. And he was still Paul Arinze—distrustful of those outside his close circle of family and friends.

Yet in her confession, Ijay had laid herself bare and vulnerable, though he felt she was a strong capable woman. It amazed him she was willing to be so open, as if they were lifelong friends and she trusted him.

Her assured actions transcended his physical need, reaching the emotional side of him. The rush of primal protective need through his veins caught him unguarded. He shoved the feeling aside and brushed his lips against hers quickly.

"In that case, let's get out of here," he said, before stepping toward the door. When he opened it, he turned back and stretched out his hand. With a willing smile and sure steps, she placed her hand in his.

Hand in hand, they waded through the crowds to the lift lobby. While in the lift, he pulled her closer, their bodies pressed against each others. The silence between them was comfortable and companionable. He found that he didn't need to say anything to her. Just having her warmth seep into his skin was enough for now. The connection between them seemed so intimate and relaxing, it felt like spoken words would ruin the moment.

Outside the building there was a light drizzle of rain. The doorman with his big umbrella quickly ushered them into a waiting black cab. As if sensing their need for solitude, the cab driver said nothing after Paul gave him the name of his hotel. They rode the cab in silence, huddled together, their eyes barely registering the London landmarks as they drove past them. With Ijay's head leaning against his shoulder, he stroked her arms up and down.

After a while he realised that his nerves had lost some of the restless energy he'd had for so long. The agitation that had plagued him for months was now muted. The person responsible for his relative state of serenity—Ijay. Before he could analyse the implication of that knowledge, the taxi pulled up in front of his hotel.

With the same trusting composure, Ijay took his hand after he'd paid the cab driver and walked into the hotel lobby. In the lift Paul sensed Ijay's body tense up as he pulled her closer.

He turned to look at her, his eyes searching her face worriedly. "What's the matter?" he asked, his palms rubbing down her arms as he sought to quell her disquiet.

"I've never done this before," Ijay said, her earlier confidence deserting her now that she was in

Paul's hotel and the reality of what she was about to do became a strong possibility.

It was one thing to stand in an anonymous bar with a crowd of people not too far away and chat up a stranger. That required boldness she could easily tap into. Working and interacting with people even strangers was part of her daily life. She could do that with relative ease without worry of any consequences.

Still, picking up said stranger and ending up in his hotel room for the night, was a new event. A new adventure through uncharted territory. The possibilities of things going wrong were huge. For one she wasn't a sexy seductress used to charming scores of men. She could count the number of sexual partners she'd ever had in less than one hand. And none of them had ever been a one-night stand.

"You've never kissed a man in a lift?" he asked jovially, his black eyes twinkling with mischief.

Ijay couldn't help the smile that tugged her lips lifting her spirits. She loved the easy relaxing way they interacted with each other. As if they'd known each other for a lifetime instead of for just a little over an hour.

"Stop it," she said, swatting his chest before sliding her hand upwards. "You know that's not what I meant. I've never picked up a man before and ended up in his hotel for hot sex." She nearly cringed as soon as the words were out of her mouth. The gentle chuckle from Paul set her at ease again.

"I know it's your first time doing this. And I'm glad you picked me," his voice rumbled with a husky timbre and his hand palmed her face.

The effect on her body was a warm shiver travelling down her spine and melting her insides. She inhaled sharply taking in a lungful of a mix of his cologne and his masculine spice.

"You know it's my first time? How?" she asked, curious as to how he could read her so easily especially something she'd barely been able to articulate.

He lifted his shoulders in a casual shrug. "I sensed it. You didn't look like someone who prowled the bars looking for a man to take home. Trust me I've seen a few of those women in action and you're not it."

For a brief moment, she didn't know whether to be glad that he didn't think she was a hussy or whether to be worried because he read her so easily. Meaning he already knew she was inexperienced at this sort of thing. Before she could contemplate her next course of action, the lift doors pinged and opened.

Paul led her out of the lifts, down the corridor before opening his hotel room door. She walked in when he opened the door and held it open for her. It turned out it wasn't just a room. It was a modern luxury suite of rooms. He must be doing very well for himself because she knew rooms like this cost a small fortune especially for a hotel in the middle of Mayfair; one of the pricier areas of London.

She stood in the main sitting area with embroidered upholstered sofas, a reading desk and chair with matching cover all in earthy browns and off-white complementary colours. A door led off the space to what she assumed was the bedroom.

She heard the door shut behind her. A sense of finality overcame her. This was it. There was no turning back now. Not that she wanted to change her mind. Her decision still stood. She wanted a way to finally get rid of Frederick in her mind and move on with her life. Tonight will provide that.

Luckily, Paul wasn't staying around long enough for her to mistakenly fall in love with him. Nobody fell in love with a stranger from a one night stand. Yes, she was attracted to him. He was a good-looking, intelligent man. Perhaps if he lived in London and they dated a few times there was a chance that she could fall in love with him.

He'd be gone by tomorrow. Just the way she wanted it. There would be no time to lose her heart. There would be no resulting heart break. Boldly, she turned around and faced him, taking her jacket off in the process. She laid it on the arm of the sofa.

"What would you like to eat and drink? Let me order some room service," he said as he pulled off his jacket and tossed it over hers. There was something about the way he did that that seemed like they were already living in domesticated bliss.

"You don't have to order anything on my account," she replied, eager to get on with the night before she lost her nerve totally. From her purse, she took the pack of condoms she'd bought from the vending machine at the nightclub, placing it on the table. She might be having a one-night stand but she wasn't totally reckless.

"I hope they're the right size." She turned her back to him again before asking in a low voice she hoped was sexy, "Can you unzip me, please?"

She felt the tingle of his body's heat on her back before she felt the rough graze of his fingers on her nape as he swept her hair aside on one shoulder. The slow sound of the zipper had her enthralled. She stood still in anticipation. Then the feathery touch of his lips on her back as he kissed her skin gently on several spots. Slowly he pushed her dress off her shoulders until it dropped on the oriental carpet, leaving her in her black lace bra, thong and wedge sandals.

She heard the soft sharp intake of his breath and turned around to face him worried that something was wrong. Instead the look of pure intense admiration in his dark fiery eyes had her inhaling sharply too.

"You have a perfect body. And I'm going to enjoy each second of exploring every inch of it."

Chapter Three

Overcome by emotion, Ijay stood still, frozen to the spot. Her ribs took a battering as her heart raced. Paul's compliment boosted her confidence. It wasn't as if she ever really paid any attention to her body shape. She loved her food too much to ever diet. Her only concession was eating some yoghurt and fruits for breakfast sometimes.

Thanks to her paternal Nigerian genes, she'd inherited full bosoms and flared hips, which meant she could never become Britain's Next Top Model. On the other hand, her maternal English genes had gifted her with a narrow waist and long legs. So as far as she was concerned she got the best from both parents packed into her hourglass figure.

However, in the years she dated Frederick he'd never said any compliment close to Paul's words about her body. At best he'd mentioned she looked nice in an outfit. Praising her wasn't Vincent's thing.

At least it was what she'd thought at the time. Until he'd turned around and told her he didn't love her any more. Her world as she'd known it had shattered in an instant.

Shaking her head so she didn't get sucked into the depressive feeling threatening to blanket her, she focused her attention back on Paul. He moved closer to her, bent his head and inhaled deeply with his eyes closed.

An excited thrill went through her body and she trembled slightly. Though he wasn't touching her at the moment, just being this close to him, having captivated his attention was sexy and liberating. To know this man wanted her was a new high for her.

Boldly she reached across placing her palms on his chest. Beneath the smooth silk shirt, his body heat singed her palms. She felt his chest rise as he inhaled sharply before opening his eyes. In their dark depths she saw hunger so raw her mouth dried out. Yet there was also tenderness so gentle her heart flipped over. Nobody had ever looked at her that way; like she was the sole focus of their existence at that moment.

He slid his hand behind her shoulder and pulled her into him, claiming her lips. This kiss lacked the ravenous nature of their first kiss, still it was more intense. Slowly his firm lips grazed hers from corner to corner. She couldn't help the soft moan that escaped her lips as she clung onto his shirt, closing her eyes to savour the sweet delight that swept through her body. Gently coaxing her lips apart, his tongue swept into her welcoming mouth, her instincts yielded to the mastery of his movements. Tingle after tingle, sensation after sensation flooded her body. Instantly she lost herself, swept up in the feverish heat rushing through her body.

Seeking more of him, she pressed her body closer to him, her nipples through her bra squashed on his chest, her hips pressed to his. The hardened evidence of his arousal, pushed against his trousers, pressing into her belly. Warmth and excitement rushed through her. If her lips weren't currently being crushed by the firmness of his, they'd be curved up in a victorious smile. Paul was aroused by her. It was a powerful heady realisation that she could have that effect on him.

She felt a growl rumble through his body before he broke the kiss and swept her up in his arms. She yelped as he carried her toward the bedroom. "I'm not a lightweight, you know. Don't go breaking anything," she said jokingly.

This was another first for her; being literally swept up into the arms of a man. She found that she liked the sensation of being high up, close to his heart. It made her feel cared for and sheltered. For a thirty year old independent woman who was jilted by the man she thought loved her, it was a refreshing feeling.

Paul chuckled as he kicked the door open with his feet. "You're a featherweight," he said.

Her heart leapt from yet another compliment. He laid her down on the large bed with calm finesse, looking unruffled as if he hadn't been carrying anything. His handsome face creased into a toe-curling smile when he stood back and surveyed her body. His dark eyes shone with the promise of what the rest of him would do to the rest of her. Her body and face warmed up with lustful expectation. She wanted all the things his eyes promised and more.

"A girl could fall in love with you so easily with all these flattering remarks. I bet half the girls in Nigeria are in love with you already." She lifted her lips in a becoming smile.

Paul laughed softly, his eyes sparkling with warm humour before kneeling beside the bed and taking one of her feet in his hand. "Only half? Now, who's singing praises?" he asked as he unstrapped the buckle of her wedge sandal and slipped the shoe from her foot.

He placed a soft kiss on the topside of her foot. Her toes curled involuntarily as the tingle shot straight up her leg to her core. She'd never known her feet were erogenous zones.

From the wet heat threatening to overflow her thong, she'd say Paul had found a sexy spot on her body without even trying very hard. He touched her with the skill of an expert and the familiarity of a long term lover. He brushed his lips against the spot again, one of his hands travelling up her leg in an excruciatingly slow caress.

It seemed her entire body was sensitised, her nerve endings on hyper alert.

Oh boy!

Biting back a whimper, Ijay sank into the crisp cotton sheet as she fought to control the urge to moan out loud. She heard the sound of distant drums. It took her a while to realise it was the erratic beat of her own heart.

Paul moved to the other foot, removing the straps and releasing her feet from the sandal. "I haven't said anything which wasn't true tonight," he said, the warm air from his lips feathering her receptive foot.

Ijay creased her face in a frown, trying to get her hazy brain to function. *What was he talking about? What were they discussing?* All her brain could process was the feel of his hands and mouth on her legs.

"You're a beautiful, intelligent woman. You have a sexy body I can't seem to keep my hands off," he continued in a low husky voice in between brushing his lips against her feet.

As if everything else he was doing wasn't enticing her into pleasurable heights, his words broke down the last dam of resistance. Any control she had over her body's response fizzled away. He moved, kissing his way up her legs in alternate brushes. His large hands followed the trail of his lips.

Her body trembled in response, her fingers clawing at the sheet beneath her. The effect of his touch was electrifying. There was no other sensation like it. She'd been aroused before. Not like this. As if her life depended on him stoking and quenching the fire raging within her body.

When his lips grazed the inside of her hip, she nearly shot off the bed with the intense pleasure. Clamping her hips back down on the bed with his firm hand, he set about nipping and licking the insides of her thighs and hips. Exquisite pain pleasure shot through her body. She felt wet heat soaking her thong.

"Please," she moaned out shamelessly. To blazes with holding back. If she didn't get some respite from the fever sweeping through her body, she'd certainly burn up.

In response, Paul shook his head. "I'm not done yet," he whispered against her scorching skin. Moving up her body, he carried on with the torturous and delightful nipping and licking on her belly. Then her breasts. First he caressed them with both palms in a gentle squeeze, making them feel heavy. Then he pinched the nipples through the lace until they stood erect. The graze of the lace sending more tingles through her body.

Ijay debated removing her bra completely. She wanted to feel the lash of Paul's tongue directly on her soft skin. Yet her fingers clung on to the bedding to stop her body leaping off the bed. She was already jerking and quivering with each touch.

Oh, what the hell.

She moved her hands. Instead of going to unhook her bra, they travelled to Paul's chest and started undoing his shirt buttons. He paused from his nurturing, leaning back to give her more access. Silently he watched her actions, his dark gaze missing nothing. That she managed to get the buttons off was a miracle considering her fingers trembled.

She parted the shirt and he let it fall off his shoulders and arms, flinging it aside. She ran her palms in awe up and down his chest, enjoying the feel of the short springy hairs and the firm muscles beneath. He wasn't bulky like a body builder. Just fit and well-toned like an athlete.

She heard his breath hitch when her hands moved over his nipples. She played with them the same way he'd played with hers. He leaned his head back and closed his eyes, his breath increasing in rapid rates. Feeling emboldened by his encouraging response, she leaned up on her elbows and latched her lips onto his nipple, her palm sliding down to palm the stiff bulge straining in his trousers.

Paul let out a tortured groan. Ijay's lips widened in a triumphant smile. He opened his eyes and caught her smile.

"Oh, you're enjoying this, aren't you?" he teased with a wicked smile before moving back to remove his trousers and shoes.

Seeing him standing in short stretchy boxers that clung to his hips and toned butt had her salivating. She rolled her tongue along her bottom lip. The urge to get her hands on him again overwhelmed her, the last of her inhibitions melting with her body.

"If you look at me like that again, we'll be going fast and furious in record time," he said with a devious smile.

"That sounds like a plan to me," Ijay replied, reaching behind to unhook her bra.

"Don't you dare touch that bra. It's mine to remove, just like you're mine for the rest of the night," he commanded before he walked out of the room into the lounge. The serious tone of his voice made her shiver with need. The way he said the word *mine* was so sexy. She realised she was happy to be his to pleasure even if it was just one night. The mischievous side of her wondered what the consequence of disobeying him would be. It was a night of adventure for her. She wanted to find out.

In his absence, she unhooked the bra. "Oops. I did it already," she grinned sheepishly as the bra fell off her shoulders.

Paul returned to the bedroom, the pack of condoms in his hand. "Oh uh. Someone needs a little lesson in controlling her hands and obeying instructions." He placed the opened box on the bedside table and strode to the wardrobe with a wolfish smile. Her heart raced as he removed a blue silk tie from the drawer. She wondered what he planned to do with it when he turned and walked back to the bed. Her eyes widened with surprised when he stretch the tie out between his hands.

"What are you going to do with that?" she asked when he sat on the edge of the bed.

He dangled the edge of the tie over her stomach, trailing the tip along her skin. It tickled and tingled all at the same time.

"Do you trust me?" he asked in a slow drawl as he continued dragging the silk along her skin.

Her eyes widened again in surprise at the question. She wondered where it was leading. She looked into his eyes trying to read his thoughts. They reminded her of the midnight sky, starry and tranquil, positive and intense. The way he made her feel confident and relaxed; the way she connected with him, she'd never bonded that way with any other man.

Within a few minutes of meeting him, she knew she wanted to be with him intimately and not just physically too. Shame it was only going to be for one night. She didn't have to worry, though. At this moment, she wanted to experience being with him fully whatever it entailed.

"I wouldn't be here with you if I didn't trust you," she replied, reaching out to him.

He took her hand in his, stopping her from touching his chest. "I'm going to tie your hands and keep them above your head against the bedposts. If you don't want me to, just say so." He played a tattoo on the back on her hand with his finger, his gaze stayed up watching her face.

"I've never been tied up before," she said, pausing to bite her lip worriedly. She'd never done any sort of role play when it came to sex. The most adventurous she'd ever been was being on top of her partner. "Why do you want to do that?"

"Restraining your hands will heighten the pleasure sensation for you. I want to give you the best night of your life. So will you let me?" His lips widened in an encouraging smile, his black eyes so intense she couldn't look away.

"And you won't do anything crazy?" It felt immature asking but what the heck. He was about to bind her hands with his tie.

"Like what?" His dark eyes held sparkling amusement as if he could read her thoughts.

"I don't know. Like chop me up into pieces and stuff me in the back of your car." She giggled at ridiculous pictures her words painted in her head. If she even thought Paul was that crazy, she'd never have followed him out of the nightclub.

His deep chuckle resounded in the room. "As you know already, my vehicle of choice is a black cab and the sharpest thing around me seems to be your wit. If you're not comfortable with the idea of being bound I'll put the tie away"

"No, don't. I'm curious and as I said I trust you so go ahead." She was here already. She might as well go the whole nine yards.

"If you want me to stop at any point just say the word *blue*. Can you remember that?" he said without making any move toward her.

"Blue. Sure I can remember it." She nodded.

"Good," he said, quickly brushing her lips with his. He straddled her body, his knees on either side of her waist and moved her hands above her head. She felt as he wound and knotted the tie around her wrists against one of the bedposts. It was tight enough to hold her wrists together but not too tight that it stopped blood flow. She assumed he must be some kind of expert with tying ropes because she felt truly bound.

"Okay?" he asked when he leaned back and studied her curiously, his expression filled with tenderness.

She was at his mercy. He could take advantage of her vulnerability. If he was some kind of loony, she'd be in big trouble right now. Yet he was still concerned about her wellbeing. Her heart flipped over with compassion.

If she wasn't careful she'd fall in love with him. She was already half-way there, surrendering her body to him with such careless abandon. That was only a fine line away from giving up her heart to him. She couldn't afford to love someone else again. She couldn't afford another heart break. Not so soon after Frederick. Not right now.

Mentally, she shook her head. She had to stop being emotional and focus on the purpose of the night. This was just about sex. Nothing more. It wasn't a relationship. Just a hook up. Tomorrow Paul would be gone and she'd get back to her normal life—being sensible Ijay. There was no point getting sentimental about it.

"Of course I'm okay." She wriggled her hips wantonly beneath Paul. "Now where's the hot sex you promised me."

Chapter Four

The sensuous movement of Ijay's hips beneath Paul's thighs kindled the slow burning desire in his body. From the moment he'd set eyes on Ijay, he'd ached for her; at first a dull throbbing ache in his groin. Now it roared into a rampant inferno, threatening his self control.

The drive to his hotel and his sheer will power had subdued the urge when his body had wanted him to find the nearest enclosed space and claim her hard and fast against any flat surface. He would've sated his body's need as well as hers and their encounter could've ended there. He hadn't needed to bring her back here.

Yet there was something about the way she'd kissed him, the way she'd given herself over to him. With such confidence and total trust that had gripped his heart in a clenching vice squeezing it until he was out of breath. Now he was overwhelmed with the need to give her much more than just his body except he didn't know how to. He'd never done it before; never had to.

Like now she lay under him in nothing more than the sheer scrap of a black lace thong, all of her exposed to his attentive gaze and his yearning touch. She was his to command, her hands bound above her head. Yet she did not cower. Neither was she afraid. In the depths of her brown eyes, he saw curiosity, lust and the same conviction she seemed to have every time she looked into his eyes.

He wondered what she saw in him that gave her so much confidence. He didn't trust himself. Yet it seemed she trusted him enough to put herself and the delivery of her pleasure in his hands. That he could do. He could give her the bliss she sought for tonight. He leaned forward; his hands braced either side of her chest, his body not touching hers. Yet her body heat surrounded him in a convivial embrace.

"You're going to get hot sex when I say so," he whispered close to her ear, blowing warm air along the sensitive skin on her neck. He sensed her body vibrate in a sharp shudder.

A satisfied smile tugged at the corners of his lips. He banked it down. He loved the way she responded to him. So eager. So passionate. It pulled at the tight control he was holding over his own desires. For now he wanted to focus on her. He wanted to see her come apart with fulfilment.

Closing his eyes he inhaled deeply, taking in her light fragrance—the floral scent of irises mixed with the musk of her arousal. Warm blood left his head and headed south. It swelled his erection even further and left him lightheaded with exhilaration; its pulsing motion in tune with his overactive heart rate. Giving in to the itch to taste Ijay's skin, he licked the dip in her collar bone, feeling her pulse jump at the contact. She tasted salty and sweet, a delightful combination.

"Oh," she gasped out in a sensual excited voice.

He slid lower and leaned back, marvelling at the perfection of smooth round breasts. They were neither big nor small. Their dark areolas looked like dark chocolate drizzled over caramel cream scoops. When he clasped them in his hands, they fit completely.

Bending over, he took the under-swell of one between his lips, sucking at the soft satiny skin and loving the feel of it. He heard what sounded like a whimper from Ijay and she pushed her chest upwards encouraging him. He needed little encouragement with her. He wanted her. All of her.

With her, he wrestled with a jumble of contradicting emotions; his mind was at peace, devoid of worries. Yet his body was ablaze with lust, at the same time. He sucked the fleshy spot harder before licking it. His fingers played with the other nipple, kneading and tweaking it to hardness. Then he swapped over and repeated the same thing on the other breast.

Ijay panted, her skin hot to the touch, scorching his palms. Her body jerked with each caress he gave as he moved lower to her stomach. He loved that he was the one doing this to her. The one making her respond so fervently.

When you're gone, there'll be someone else here in your place.

His body froze. His lips hovered above her belly button, not touching her skin. A cold sweat broke down his back. For some reason that thought had his gut twisted in repugnance. A bitter bilious taste overwhelmed the salty taste of Ijay.

That he didn't like the thought puzzled him and annoyed him at the same time. He'd never worried about his exes moving on and finding new lovers before. And he'd been in longer term relationships with them. Ijay was only going to be in his life—his bed—for one night.

Yet he was having a pang of conscience over her?

It wasn't as if he was going to ask her to wait for him. He wasn't coming back this way in a long time, unless some emergency came up. So maybe he could look her up when he was in London next time. That could be months away. He wasn't going to tell her to wait. He wasn't going to wait either. Cold rage iced his blood blurring his view of Ijay's flawless curves. His hands curled into fists.

Damn it! He wasn't like his father. He wasn't going to make a woman a promise he couldn't keep. So what the hell was the matter with him?

"Paul, are you okay?" Ijay's melodious concerned voice roused him from his torturous musings.

He took a deep calming breath, inhaling her stirring scent. It refocused his attention on her, his hunger for her returning. He tongued her belly button. Her stomach muscles contracted in response.

Giving her a sexy smile, he lifted his head and looked up at her face. Her brown eyes were still hazy with lust but her face was creased in a frown. He hated that his own misgivings were making her worry. He'd promised her hot sex and he was failing her. He was going to remedy that straight away.

He reached down and palmed the vee between her thighs. Slipping his fingers into her thong, he pulled it down her legs and tossed it to the floor.

"Just savouring you, sweet Ijay," he said, parting her lower lips and swiping his tongue on blossoming bud. She let out a long pleased moan as her hips jolted off the bed.

"You are as sweet as cherry pie," he whispered against her skin before taking her velvety bud into his mouth again. He sucked and nibbled. She bucked and wriggled, canting her hips upwards. He slipped his fingers into her wet heat. Her inner walls clenched, coating his digits in her syrupy juices.

He barely held it together, the need to be inside her warring with his need to fulfil her first. Feeling her body coil with tension, he worked her body with his mouth and hands.

"Come for me, sweet Ijay." He looked up at her passion-filled face, her brown irises rolled up.

She didn't wait for him to finish his sentence before she screamed and shuddered intensely. Holding onto her hip, he lapped up her juices, not letting go until her body's trembling calmed. Inexplicably, a sense of satisfaction swept through him as he rose up on his arms and watched her sexy replete form stretched out against the white sheets.

He leaned forward and kissed her swollen lips, letting her taste her own sweet flavour. She kissed him back passionately. Lifting his head, he grinned widely at her.

"You do something wicked with your tongue. That was..." She trailed off, her face breaking into a glorious smile. His heart flipped over with pleasure. "Sorry, I can't even find the right words. Just know that you blew my mind. If I walk around like a zombie for the rest of the weekend, it's your fault." She giggled, the light-hearted sound thrilling him.

He had no explanation for the warmth that spread through his body at her compliment. He'd received admiring comments before. Yet he'd never quite believed them. He didn't like it when people praised him. It made him suspicious about their motives as it always turned out they wanted favours from him. This time around he took Ijay's words at face value. She really meant them. And she wanted nothing more in return. It set his mind a-buzz with elation. He could live with her praise.

"I don't want any zombies near me tonight. I'd rather have a warm passionate woman writhing beneath me all night long. Are you up for that?" His lips widened in a grin as he thought about all the ecstasy they could rouse together.

"Yeah, I think I can live with that." Her laughter was soft and tinkled with joyous warmth that rumbled through his body.

He reached across and picked up condom, ripped the foil pack before rolling it on. He moved to roll Ijay onto her belly and stopped. Something inside him wanted to see her face when he was inside her. He wanted to watch her expression and her skin colour when it was flushed with the heat of pleasure.

So he lifted her legs, hooking them over his arms as he knelt between them. Gently, slowly, he pushed himself into her wet heat. A soft moan escaped from her lips and she lifted her hips encouraging him further within her. He felt her inner walls stretch to accommodate his girth. He slid out leisurely and thrust in until he could go no further, his balls sitting in the valley between her round bottoms. She was hot and tight and gripping his thick shaft like a satin glove. A groan rumbled through his body escaping from his lips unhindered.

"Oh, sweet Ijay," he growled, his pounding heart whooshing hot blood through him. He thrust in and withdrew. "You feel so good...So good."

Bracing his arms on either side of her body, he kissed her ravenously, thrusting his tongue into her mouth in mirror movements to his shaft in her wet heat. He held onto the heady sensation swarming his body as he sought to drive her to bliss again. The sound of their panting breaths and smacking bodies echoed in the room. He returned to lavishing his attention on her breasts. Sensing her body tightening with need, he slipped his hand between their bodies and pinched her bud.

"*Paul. Oh,*" she shouted, her body quivering as she climaxed. Her inner walls convulsed around him pulling him over the edge and he spilled into the sheath. He stopped himself from collapsing onto her body by taking his weight on bent elbows. Her eyes stayed closed when he brushed his lips gently over hers, moving her riotous mass of hair out of the way. Then he rolled onto his back, taking her with him.

***

"Paul! Where's that boy?"

Paul ran out of the kitchen where he'd been washing the dishes, using the kitchen napkin to wipe the soap suds off his hands. He rushed into the living room, struggled to keep from slipping on the glossy marble floor he'd buffed earlier.

"Yes, mother," he said when he stood in front of the woman who'd been yelling out his name.

"Who's your mother, you stupid boy? Do I look like that dead whore who slept with married men and had a bastard like you?" his father's wife shouted at him from the sofa where she lounged with a glass of brandy in her hand.

"No, ma," Paul replied as he cowered his ten year old body. He'd learned early to keep his distance from her especially when she was drinking. She had no problems taking out whatever frustration she felt on him.

"'No, ma,'" she mimicked his words. "Peel two oranges and bring them to me quickly. Don't make me wait."

"Yes, ma" he replied and raced off back into the kitchen to peel the oranges before he got into trouble for being late.

His hands trembled as he peeled the oranges and tried not to cut himself. He put the peel oranges on a small porcelain plate and took them out to the living room. As he put the dish on the side table, one of the oranges rolled off, onto the floor.

A hard slap connected with his face, knocking him back onto the floor. His head hit the stone floor making him feel dizzy.

"You stupid boy, can you not do anything correctly?" A foot connected to his side. Pain rocketed through his body. He raised his hands to fend off the blows.

"No!"

Paul sat up in bed abruptly, waking from his nightmare. He looked around the dim room, trying to get his bearings. He noticed the woman sitting up beside him. It took him a moment to recall her name. She had her hand against his arm, her face creased with a frown.

"What's going on?" he asked looking down to find his body slick with sweat.

"I think you were having a dream. You were moving around as if fighting someone off. Are you okay?" she asked, caressing his face.

"I'm fine," he said gruffly, turning away and pushing off the bed. He took out a bottle of water from the fridge and poured himself a glass, downing most of it. Then, he walked into the bathroom and looked at his face in the mirror. For a moment, the bruised face of the teary ten year old Paul stared back at him.

Anger welled in his veins. He balled his hands into fists and fought the urge to smash them into the mirror. Instead he swivelled around and turned on the shower faucet. He stepped under the warm spray, glad to have it massage and sluice his tense muscles. He closed his eyes and leaned against the tiles, hoping the pounding water on his back would wash away the tormenting memories of his childhood.

"Can I join you?" Ijay's sultry voice roused him.

49

He turned to find her standing outside the shower cubicle, her full round curves bare to his all-consuming gaze, her dark hair wild and tousled, her full lips pulled in a tentative smile. In her hand she held up a wrap of condom. He gulped in air as he leaned back. Perhaps she was what he needed to forget the nightmare.

Reaching across he pulled her in, crushing her to his chest. He kissed her ferociously, seeking to lose himself in her. He wanted to forget the agony and pain of his childhood. He just wanted the pleasure of here and now. Breaking off the kiss to catch his breath he tore the foil with his teeth and rolled it on. He grabbed Ijay again, lifting her up.

When she wrapped her legs around his waist, he backed her up to the wall and sank into her warm depth. The rage in his veins drove him as he thrust fast and furious into her slick heat. She clung on to his shoulders, his hands holding her hips as he drove into her. As her body coiled with tension, she moaned out his name. He thrust into her a couple more times before joining her in ecstasy.

He shut off the shower and stepped out of the cubicle with Ijay still slumped on his shoulders. Guilt gnawed at his gut. He'd let his anger seep into their passion. Letting her down gently he wrapped her in the bath towel and carried her to the bed. He laid her under the sheets before drying his body. Tossing the towel away, he joined her under the sheet. He spooned her into his body, kissed her brow and drifted back to sleep.

He woke with a jolt later. Looking up, he noted the sunlight filtering through the curtains. He glanced over at the table clock. It was seven-thirty. Stretching he reached for Ijay. She wasn't there. He sat up in bed, thinking he should join her if she was in the shower. He noticed the notepad with a scrawled note on top. Lifting it, he read the note.

Paul,

Sorry, I'm not good with goodbyes. I didn't want to just leave without telling you how much I enjoyed last night. It was the best I've ever had. Have a safe journey back.

Ijay

Stunned, Paul stood up and paced the room, scrubbing his hand on his head. He couldn't believe that she left him and just written a note. Why had he been bothered about moving on when it was obvious she was eager to move on with her life?

If she'd enjoyed the night so much, why didn't she ask him to call? Or write that she'd call him. It was obvious she didn't want any future contact from him. If that's what she wanted he'd oblige her. Angrily, he crumpled the piece of paper in his hand and tossed it in the bin.

Chapter Five

"Gosh, this is so exciting. I wish I was the one going to Abuja," Sonia raved as she stirred her mug of tea.

Ijay rolled her eyes upward at her friend's comment. They were in the staff room of Havers & Childs offices in Soho. It was a moderate space with white kitchen units against one wall with kettle, coffee machine, small microwave oven and large fridge-freezer. At the other end were small round tables and chairs. It was empty at the moment, except for the two of them. She hugged her mug of coffee as she leaned against the kitchen counter.

"Anyone would think my trip was all fun and games, the way you're going on about it," Ijay replied before taking a sip. The sweet taste of hot coffee and chocolate rolled down her tongue, warming her body up. She loved her mochaccino drink—the sweet blend of aromatic coffee and decadent chocolate—the best of both worlds as far as she was concerned.

"If I was the one going to Nigeria for six weeks, I can guarantee you it'll be fun and games for me. All that sunshine, the beaches, loads of family and of course my pick of hot men," Sonia explained, her hazel eyes taking on the dreamy quality as if she was actually picturing herself there already, her head cocked to one side.

Ijay burst out laughing, putting her mug on the worktop so it didn't spill over as her hand shook. Her friend had a way of over-exaggerating that left her in stitches. "I didn't know Nigeria was known for its selection of hot men."

"Look who's talking. As if your fiancé is not a 'hot man' from Nigeria," Sonia said, flicking her fingers in the air to emphasis hot man. "Vincent is smart, good-looking and a medical doctor. If that isn't hot, what is? I have to get in on the action, seriously."

At the mention of Vincent, Ijay stopped laughing and nodded. Sonia had a point. She was engaged to a gorgeous man who was everything a dream fiancé should be. Without thinking, she fingered the sparkling diamond ring on her finger. A ring he'd given her within only a few weeks of their meeting. Getting a proposal of her own after the fiasco that was Frederick certainly made her finally feel like a lucky woman. Sometimes she had to pinch herself just to make sure she wasn't in a dream.

The corners of her lips lifted in a reflective smile as memory swept into the present. It seemed her luck turned in just one night. One blissful night in the arms of a man she hasn't seen or spoken to since. She'd earned a new promotion at work for her efforts in the products launch event and most importantly Frederick had been wiped off her radar by the enigma that was Paul Arinze.

Heat rose on her skin as the memory of what he'd—they'd—done that night came back in a full force. Full high-definition images flashed through her mind. Her nipples pebbled, her breasts getting heavier. Biting her lower lip, she suppressed a pleasurable moan. She turned her back to Sonia in the pretence of picking up her mug. She didn't want her friend to notice how flustered she felt.

It had been that way since that night—thinking about Paul daily, her body coming alive with lust each time. When Vincent came on the scene she pushed Paul to the back of her mind, choosing instead to focus her attention on the new man in her life. Still Paul plagued her. Sometimes at night in her dreams, he visited her and re-enacted their night of passion.

Frustrated that he could still have such an effect on her after so long, she let out a sigh and took a sip from her drink. *What's the matter with me?* The man hadn't called her or sent her a message since their encounter.

Okay, so she hadn't called him either. She'd left a note for him. Surely that counted. He could've sent her a text message to say *Goodbye* or something. She really needed to forget him. There was no point in dwelling on the past. She had to focus on her future—Vincent.

Like Sonia said Vincent was the perfect fiancé; so perfect everyone of her friends or family who met him, loved him. Her parents cooed over him. Of course her traditional father, a university lecturer loved that he was Nigerian, a doctor and from a nice

family. Apparently his hometown was not far off
from hers.

Her mother, a romantic European, loved that
Vincent was a charming gentleman and worked in
London. She was happy that Ijay didn't have to
relocate to Nigeria after the wedding. Still, Ijay
couldn't shake the doubt that worried her
sometimes.

"I am looking forward to the trip...it's just," she
trailed off not sure she wanted to discuss her doubts
out here in the staff room where anyone could walk
in any minute.

Sonia looked up, a line of frown creasing her
normally smooth forehead. "I know that look Ijay.
Something is wrong. Talk to me," she said in a low
tone, flicking a strand of braided hair off her face
before moving closer to Ijay.

"Not here."

"Okay, let's find an empty meeting room."

Ijay nodded, picking up her mug to follow Sonia
out into the corridor. They found a small unused
meeting room with a white board and flip chart
easel in the corner. She walked in behind her friend
and closed the door. They sat down near each other.

"You're not worried about seeing Paul again, are
you?" Sonia asked, widening her eyes with
curiosity. She lowered her gaze and took a sip of her
drink.

"Of course I'm not," Ijay replied sharply before
she could bite her tongue.

Her friend must've sensed the tension rolling off
her stiffened shoulders immediately. Sonia rarely

missed anything. Her brow arched high with suspicion.

"Really? You're not bothered that you're going to work professionally with a man you had a one-night stand with?" Her friend was nothing if not blunt and direct.

Ijay exhaled in a resigned sigh, tapping her finger nails nervously on the table top. She'd avoided facing this problem. Sonia bringing it up now meant there was no escaping it. She was anxious about meeting Paul again. Especially as she was the lead in the project her company had bid and won to run a PR campaign for Paul's manufacturing firm.

She'd be in Nigeria working closely with Paul for six weeks. It would be her first major project since her promotion. She couldn't afford personal sentiments to come into it. She'd have to be totally professional with her dealings with Paul. He'd surely moved on.

So have I.

"Okay, maybe a part of me worries about it a little but that's not my major concern. I can handle it." She paused and straightened in her seat. "It's probably just me being silly...Vincent and I haven't slept together," she said in a low flat voice.

"Sorry, I don't get it. Which Vincent? Your fiancé?" Sonia looked even more puzzled.

"Yes, my fiancé of course. Who did you think I was talking about?" Ijay rolled her eyes upwards, waving her hand in exasperation.

"Seriously, you haven't had sex with him? Why not?" Her friend still looked nonplussed. Ijay couldn't blame her. She was still trying to get used to it herself.

She lifted her shoulders in a shrug. "He said he wants to wait until we get married."

Sonia leaned back in her seat, her eyes and mouth widened in surprise. "Wow. I didn't know there were still men like that," she gawped.

"I know. I couldn't believe it at first. It's been six months and he hasn't touched me." She leaned forward and whispered conspiratorially, "I've never seen him naked even."

"OMG!" her friend gasped. "You're going to marry this man and you've never seen him naked? Hang on a minute. He doesn't think you're a virgin, does he?"

"No. Of course not. I told him when he started talking about purity and waiting for our wedding night," Ijay said in exasperation.

She was glad she wasn't the only one who didn't think it was a little peculiar. She hadn't wanted to discuss this previously as she'd been thinking she'd get used to it when Vincent has stated they wouldn't be having sex before marriage.

Now that their traditional marriage was looming, her worry was increasing. She couldn't even discuss with her parents because they would tell her it was a good thing that he wanted to wait.

"And how did he take that?" Sonia's querying voice brought her back to the meeting room.

She scrunched her face as she thought for a moment. "I think he took the news well. Though, afterwards, he did seem to go cold on me for a little while. Hey he still wants to marry me so that's good, right?"

"Of course it's good. But is it to do with his faith or just a personal preference?"

"Well, his mother is a devout Catholic so I guess his upbringing was quite strict. Still...I don't know...Don't you think it's kind of strange that he doesn't want to get intimate. I'm worried that there'll be no passion when we eventually do it."

"I guess that could be a problem. You guys get on very well at the moment, don't you? I mean, you're attracted to him, right?"

"Sure. Things are great otherwise."

"So there shouldn't be a problem later. I personally believe you can tell how hot love-making is going to be by how hot the guy kisses."

Ijay sighed in exasperation. "That's exactly my worry. He barely ever kisses me. When he does it's so chaste. No more that a brush of the lips. It's so infuriating because I want more. I want my heart to pound with excitement and my skin to flush with heat. And he doesn't seem to care about that at all."

The room echoed with Sonia's laughter, her eyes shining with tears.

"You think it's funny?" Ijay asked glaring at her friend and fighting the smile that threatened to widen her lips. Her friend's laughter was always infectious.

"You can't be serious," Sonia finally said when she'd calmed down. "Maybe you should try seducing him. Wear something sexy and kiss him passionately and see what happens."

"Yeah, I tried that and earned myself a lecture on keeping my body pure for the marriage bed. Seriously, I don't know what to do anymore." Ijay slumped her shoulders in resignation.

"He gave you a lecture? This is serious...maybe it isn't such a bad idea to wait. I mean you've waited this long already and you only have a few weeks to your *Igbankwu* traditional marriage ceremony. After that you're technically married so you guys can get down and dirty."

"I know. That's what I keep telling myself. I guess I'll have to," she acknowledged.

Still six weeks suddenly seemed like a long time, especially since she was going to see Paul again. It didn't help that she remembered every detail of their night together. She just didn't want to be swarmed by those memories any more. Not now she had Vincent. She loved him.

So it wasn't a fiery passionate love. Her body didn't tremble every time Vincent was around. Though, he was kind and caring. And he loved and respected her. Those attributes were good enough for her. All she wanted now was for them to make their own hot and sweaty memories. As a result, Paul's image would dim into the background. She wouldn't have to wake up in the middle of the night craving his touch.

She couldn't do it if Vincent wouldn't even kiss her, let alone touch her to ignite any passion. Sighing, she stood up. "I need to get back. I've got calls to make this morning."

"Sure. I've got a list of things to sort out before lunchtime," Sonia said behind her. They walked back to the staff room.

"Thank you so much for listening. I'll catch up with you later," she said, giving her friend a brief hug.

"No worries. I'm only happy to help. I'll e-mail you the details of your flight and hotel booking once I get the confirmation from the travel agent." Sonia was the Office Manager and was in charge of organising business travel for the staff. Ijay was always grateful for her help.

"Okay. Thanks. See you later," she said before walking out of the meeting room. When she got back to her desk, she found a text message on her phone from Vincent telling her he had to cancel their dinner date for tonight. He worked as a temporary cover doctor and was sometimes required to work on short notice.

Ijay was slowly getting used to the fact that his job required long odd hours and also some travel. As much as she was disappointed she had to live with it. She hoped he'd eventually settle for a permanent role once they were married. Of course, how soon that would happen, was anyone's guess.

Picking up her phone she sent a reply telling him not to worry. They could rearrange for another day. With the text sent, she turned her focus on the work at hand—preparing for the trip to Nigeria and facing Paul.

Chapter Six

She's coming to Abuja.

The words swirled in Paul's mind as he stared at his computer screen. The open page was of the e-mail he'd received from Havers & Child detailing the names of the people who'd be working on the PR awareness project for his food processing business.

POD Foods had been processing food products for other fast-moving consumer goods businesses in Africa for years. Recently, they started producing their own branded packaged food items.

He'd put out an invitation to tender for a team to help with boosting their brand with consumers. Havers & Child had won the bid. It helped that one of the owners was an old school friend.

Paul, Frederick Conte and Charles Havers had all studied for their MBA at London Business School. However, the decision had been purely business driven. The bid team from H&C had presented the best package for his fledgling business requirements.

So it had nothing to do with a certain Ms. Amadi working for the firm, then?

Exhaling deeply to calm his racing pulse, he turned away from his desk and the source of his excitement, momentarily ignoring the question that flashed in his mind. His top-floor office was very modern with its clean lines and sleek surfaces—a minimalist's dream office.

Much like in his life, he hated clutter in his work environment. In an ideal world, he'd have glass walls everywhere. In this case he'd settled for a mix of style and functionality. The stark white opaque walls offered him much needed privacy, offset by the stylish black burnished steel of his desk top and leather chair. There was a small round table at the corner and two black leather sofas facing each other on the far end. The floor was covered in hardwearing grey carpets.

Swivelling his black soft leather executive chair, he stared out of the glass windows of his high-rise office block overlooking Independence Avenue. The mid-morning traffic was light. He paid to little attention to it. He stood up, his gaze stretching north to the lush greenery of Millennium Park in the distance.

Some days when he needed some space to think with clarity, he'd stroll through the park. On other days, he loved just watching it from this vantage point. It was one of the reasons he loved working up here. He had one of the best views of Abuja City Centre although he was bang in the middle of the business district.

Today, though, the beautiful scenery was superseded by a more urgent one. The name he had seen on his screen scrolled through his mind like one of those ticker-style headline flashers he saw in airports or train stations. It was a name he'd tried not to remember in the past six months. Yet there seemed to be no escaping it.

Wanting to confirm what he'd seen the first time, he glanced back at his laptop on his desk. The name Ijay Amadi stood out bold and black against the flickering white background.

Instantly an image flaunted in his head—of her sumptuous body spread-eagled across the crisp white cotton sheets of his hotel bed—lush lips slightly parted with expectation, intelligent brown eyes smoky with lust, willing body curvy and delightful. A pulse of desire flared in his veins, heat skimming his skin at the rate of electric currents, hardening his body in the blink of an eye.

He could never argue with her effect on his eager body. Even as a memory, he still responded as if she was here in his office with her spread-eagle on his desk. As if he could smell her sweet fragrance and feel her body heat in every pore of his skin. His ache pulsed in tune with his pulse rate.

Okay, maybe he hadn't exactly forgotten about Ijay. He'd sworn he'd after he'd woken up that morning six months earlier in his hotel room to find her gone, a quickly written note in her stead. He should've been happy that she'd kept to her words.

"I need you...this...for tonight. Just tonight."

He remembered Ijay's sultry velvet whisper. She really hadn't wanted anything more from him, apparently. Yet he'd gotten angry because that night at the back of his mind, he'd held on to a little hope that there was more to them. That they could work something out.

Seeing her note had killed that hope and inflamed his exasperation. If he didn't know himself too well, he would've given heed to the thought that he wanted to do away with his policy of a lifetime—Stay clear of distance relationships. Usually if a woman wasn't within an hour's commuting flight of him, he'd never consider her. Yet in his darkest moment that night, he'd considered giving Ijay a shot.

Eventually, the initial anger he'd felt had fizzled away. In its wake his restlessness returned. Ijay's presence had subdued it. Now it was back with a vengeance. Nothing seemed to shake it. Not even the company of other women.

The fact that he'd dated other women yet hadn't made love with any of them wasn't helping either.

It wasn't that his body wasn't able. It was that his mind wasn't willing. His mind was on Ijay. The only reason he could come up with was that they'd only had one night together. He'd had a taste of her. It wasn't enough.

Usually his relationships lasted months. With Kate it had been over a year. So by the time they'd broken up he'd been ready to move on.

With Ijay he wasn't ready to move on yet. He needed a bit more than one night for that to happen. He should've known one night with her was never going to be enough.

The opportunity to return to London hadn't come up. He'd been busy working practically all waking hours on his new business, shuttling between the factories and his head office.

Even if he'd had the time, he certainly didn't have the inclination to go to London just to chase after a woman. He hadn't been reduced to that. He wouldn't be reduced to that. He might share a genetic makeup with his father but he certainly wasn't ruled by his dick. He'd never allow it to rule him.

Blowing out a frustrated sigh, he returned to his desk and sat down. He typed his password to log back in via his screen saver scrolling across the screen.

So maybe he'd secretly hoped Havers & Child would win the bid to work on his project. And that they'd send Ijay as part of the project team. While he would've never allowed the lure of a woman, let him chase across the Atlantic Ocean to seek her out, there was no reason why he couldn't manipulate matters to suit him. He'd done his bit by offering the project and letting fate determine the rest. At the moment, it seemed fate was on his side and wanted him to see Ijay again.

He'd requested to see a list of those travelling from London to Abuja, although he hadn't needed to. Pamela, his personal assistant, was liaising with Havers & Child for any visa requirements and travel arrangements.

However, seeing Ijay's name on the list, he couldn't quell the excitement that bubbled under his skin. Nor the pounding beat of his heart against his ribs. He'd see her again. She wasn't just a member of the team. She'd manage the project.

This meant he was going to be working closely with her for six weeks while she was in Nigeria. Very closely.

The possibilities!

A big wide predatory grin spread across his face. A thrilling warm shiver ran down his spine. This time around he'd have her in his territory. To command. To seduce. To pleasure. It seemed sweet Ijay could play hardball. She'd walked away from their glorious night together without looking back.

Well, she'll soon find out I can play hardball too. I'm so looking forward to it.

She wouldn't be able to run like she'd done in London. He'd have her attention Mondays to Fridays and even weekends when necessary. They'd get to re-enact their time together, get to create new gratifying encounters.

It wouldn't be just for one night, too.

Oh no. He had six whole weeks to fulfil her fantasies as well as his. Every craving he'd ever envisioned involving her would be realised. When she returned to London he'd finally move on without craving her any longer. Ijay would be flushed from his system. At last.

And if she doesn't want you?

"I'll make her want me, damn it!" he spoke out loud, smashing his fist on the steel table top, finally letting his frustration get the better of him.

The items on the table rattled and jumped. The phone of his desk buzzed.

Breathing in through his nostril first, he slowly exhaled from his mouth to calm himself. He was in his office. He shouldn't let anything upset him.

Definitely not for a woman who was only going to be in his life temporarily. Just like every other woman he'd ever had any dealings with. Yet, six months of keeping a lid on his disappointment disintegrated all because he opened an e-mail and saw Ijay's name on the list.

Feeling calmer, he reached out and picked up the phone receiver. "Yes, Pamela," he spoke into the phone.

"Michael Ede is on line one for you," she replied in her usual calm efficient voice.

"I'll take that, thank you," he replied before pressing the button to connect to line one. "Hello, old boy. How are you?"

"I'm doing great, thank you," Michael replied jovially.

Along with Peter Oranye, Michael was one of his closest friends. They'd all met when they both attended College of Immaculate Conception in Enugu as teenagers. In those days, if one of them got into trouble, they all invariably were in trouble too. They'd had each other's backs.

In some of his darkest days as a young man, his friendship with Michael and Peter had ensured he stayed on the right track. Their friendship had remained fast in all the years though they'd gone on to different Universities. Eventually they'd come back to settle in Enugu and had some joint business ventures. He didn't trust people easily. He trusted those two with his life.

"When are you getting to Enugu this week? There's something I want us to discuss," his friend continued, his voice still calm. Michael had a great poker face. He was one of those people who were always cool under fire. Yet they'd been friends for so long that Paul could detect the even merest inflection in his voice when nobody else could. He sensed all wasn't right.

"I'm not in Enugu this week," Paul replied remembering that he hadn't called to inform his friends he wouldn't be available for their usual game night on Wednesdays. It was really a time for them to catch up with each other rather than any serious gambling. And sometimes the idea of new business ventures sprang from their time together.

"I have some consultants coming in from London for POD. I want to be here to help them settle in before we come down for factory visit. Is there something wrong?"

"Nothing's wrong. That's good news about the POD project." Paul sensed his friend changing the subject. He let it slide. "I didn't realise they were coming so soon. How's the project going overall?"

"It's going very well. We've finally confirmed and sourced the materials for the packaging. Part of what I want the team to do is confirm the branding for the packaging before we place the orders, which is why I want them here sooner rather than later."

Also because a certain sexy lady will be here soon too.

Heat flared to his face and Paul shifted uncomfortably in his chair as his trousers felt tighter. He was glad his friend was on the phone and not sitting in front of him right now so he couldn't see Paul's disquiet in his body's blatant arousal. Michael had the keen sight of a hawk and wouldn't have missed a thing. That's why he'd done so well working security details and intelligence gathering during his stint in the army.

"No worries. I hope all goes well with that. I'll let Peter know about Wednesday," Michael said.

"What did you want to discuss? Can we chat about it over the phone?" Paul asked wanting to get more details of what was bothering Michael.

"It's nothing that can't wait. We can chat about it some other time," Paul could sense Michael's dismissive shrug but he wasn't giving up yet.

"How are things between you and Kasie? I noticed you are spending more time in Lagos these days."

Michael chuckled. "That's how I find things. While she still works partially in Enugu, majority of her time is spent in Lagos. As they say the bee has to fly to the nectar, not the other way round."

Paul shook his head as he laughed too. He'd never believed his friend would fall hard for Kasie when they'd initially challenged him to date the girl for a bet. Yet within a few days of meeting Kasie Bosa, Michael had fallen head over heels in love with her and had even wanted to forfeit his plane that he'd bet in the challenge just to win the lady over. It had been love at first sight.

Yet he couldn't understand that kind of love. Couldn't understand how a man would want to give up something of importance to him just to keep a woman. He'd never allow himself to care that deeply for a woman. He didn't even know how he could.

"So it seems, my friend," Paul replied in jest.

As they chatted and later ended their conversation, in his mind he knew differently. He didn't have to go to the nectar. He could work things to suit himself. And he had. In his case he was getting the nectar to come to him. When he'd sapped as much as he wanted, he'd send it back. It was that simple. He wouldn't have it any other way.

Chapter Seven

It's good to be back on African soil.

Ijay inhaled deeply to quell the nervous energy making her body tremble as she stepped out of the lift into the lobby of the Hilton Abuja hotel. Having only just got off her flight from London less than five hours ago, she should be feeling naturally exhausted. Yet the butterflies in her stomach were not from tiredness but from excitement. She was going to see Paul Arinze again after six months.

Blowing out the breath through her lips, she reminded herself that she was here on business and focused on the matter at hand. Her boss, Charles Havers was waiting for her in the lobby so that they could head off to POD Head Office. She walked through the lobby covered in marble to the lounge. The opulence of the hotel matched the other Hilton hotels she'd been in. Charles was already there, seated on one of the sofas. He stood when he saw her.

"There you are," he said, giving her a broad smile when she approached. "How do you feel? I know we pre-arranged to meet at POD this morning. But it was a long flight. I can arrange the meeting for later if you prefer."

Charles was a typical English gentleman. For a Harrow School old boy he was very congenial and his concern for his staff's well-being always showed. Ijay always preferred working with him compared to Philip Child the other co-owner of the agency. Philip was more task-orientated. Charles was a people person. This was why he always headed any bid teams and was more client-facing than Philip.

"I'm fine. I thought I was going to be more exhausted but the shower, change of clothes and light breakfast seemed to have done the trick. I'm ready to go," Ijay said.

Even if she was feeling exhausted, she was hardly going to admit it to her boss on the first day of a new project when they were supposed to be meeting the client. She couldn't give Charles any reason to think she couldn't deliver this project.

This was an important initiative for Havers & Child since it would be their first project in Africa. It could open the door for more projects out here, if she successfully delivered. So it wasn't just her reputation at stake, it was the company's reputation too.

"In that case, let's go. The car is waiting." Charles picked up his briefcase and headed toward the hotel entrance. Ijay followed him with her laptop case and bag.

The wall of heat hit her body as she stepped outside in the sunshine. She'd forgotten how warm it was outside because of the coolness of the hotel. The temperature had to be close to the hottest day in a London summer and it was only ten am. Compared to the mild spring temperature in

London when she'd departed, it was baking hot in Abuja.

Luckily the Mercedes GL car that had been used to drive them from the airport was parked just outside the entrance. The driver stood outside it, holding the back door open for them. She quickly got into the air-conditioned space before Charles joined her.

"Phew. It's hot today, isn't it," Charles said when he shut the car door.

"It sure is. We're no longer in London," Ijay laughed. "Is this your first time in Nigeria?" she asked as the car left the hotel premises and joined the mid-morning traffic.

"Yes. First time in Africa, I have to confess. I'm more of the ski holiday kind of person, I'm afraid."

"Really? So you've never even been to Marrakesh or Sharma el Sheikh as most of British holiday makers enjoy?"

"No. Sad, isn't it? I'm happy to spend winter in the Ice Hotel in Sweden but summer in a hot climate and I end up looking like a lobster. At least that's what Fiona calls me. She always insists we book a vacation in the Caribbean to compensate for all the ski trips I take her on." Charles chuckled.

Ijay smiled. "I don't blame her," she replied.

Fiona was Charles wife and a high powered lawyer in London. Apparently they'd been childhood sweethearts. Ijay had met Fiona a few times and she always came across as hard-nosed which was such an opposite of Charles who was a gentle soul. Fiona was petite, slim and blonde-haired. Charles was tall, pale-skinned and ginger-haired. Yet despite their differences, they seemed to have been in love forever.

She glanced out of the car window, her mind turning to her own personal relationships. Despite the differences she had with Vincent, could their relationship withstand the test of time? She really didn't know the answer to that question.

As the scenery whizzed by, the car taking her closer to her destination—and Paul—her anxiety returned. Her palms felt clammy, her skin breaking out in a sweat. She smoothed her hand against her skirt and tried not to fidget. She couldn't blame her clammy skin on the heat of the sun. She was sitting in the freezing coolness of a fully air-conditioned car. It was her rising fears overtaking her body.

For one, she'd found out Vincent wasn't altogether happy that she was going to work in Nigeria while he wasn't there. She'd never thought of him as controlling.

Still, his reaction when she'd told him about being assigned the POD project had been less than congratulatory. He'd told her to request a reassignment to another project instead of going to Nigeria. She'd had to explain that this was a major project for her, the first since her promotion. She couldn't afford not to do it. She couldn't afford to mess it up either.

They'd fallen out over it and hadn't spoken for a few days. It had been their first major argument. In the end, he'd called her to say he'd accepted she could go. Angry about his initial stance, she'd insisted he explain his irrational behaviour. He'd said he was concerned about her wellbeing in Abuja given the recent security issues. He'd been worried about the danger she'd be putting herself into.

His explanation made sense to her, his concern for her wellbeing melting her initial anger. She promised that she'd be careful and they soon made up. It seemed his concern for her absence hadn't persuaded him to change his mind about their physical intimacy. Her attempt to spend the night in his bed was again rebuffed. As usual he dropped her off to the apartment she shared with Sonia later that night.

She exhaled in frustration, her hands clenching on her lap. All her attempts at seducing Vincent had failed. It seemed she wouldn't get to feel any passion in their relationship until they finally said "I do."

She had to wait. There was nothing else to do.

Except she felt edgy, unfulfilled and lonely. She hadn't realised one could be in a relationship and feel that way.

Is it just me? Is there something fundamentally wrong with me? How can I have a great man like Vincent and still feel unfulfilled?

Vincent was still a good catch. They'd met when a friend had invited her to watch a play at the National Theatre. After the show, they'd had drinks in one of the bars along the Southbank. She'd discovered they shared so much together—a love for music and drama.

So they didn't agree on everything, their sexual relationship being one of them. Yet, it wasn't insurmountable. All they needed was that one night together and that problem would be solved. He was a really good doctor with a passion for his job, just like she had a passion for her job. He was successful and driven. Just as she was. So there were plenty of pluses in their relationship.

All she had to do was get through the next few weeks of work. Vincent was coming to Nigeria in a month's time. They would spend the last two weeks together as they conclude the plans for their traditional wedding. So there shouldn't be any reason for her to worry.

Yet as the car pulled into the business premises for POD Foods, the butterflies in her stomach took flight again.

Paul is in there. He's waiting for you.

Annoyed at the stray thoughts that crept into her mind, she tightened her grip on her bag as she readied to step out of the car. It didn't stop her heart rate from increasing. Whether it was apprehension or excitement driving her reaction, she didn't want to dwell on analysing it. Instead she reminded herself of the reason she was there. Business.

The chauffeur opened her car door. Inhaling a few calming breaths, she stepped out. Quickly she followed Charles into the building to get out of the blazing sunshine. The security man greeted them as they walked past. At the reception desk, they signed the visitor's book as the receptionist called Pamela to inform her of their arrival.

Before long, a tall skinny girl with skin like dark chocolate and long jet-black hair strode out of the lifts in a pink shirt and navy pencil skirt and navy high-heeled shoes.

"Mr. Havers, I'm Pamela. It's nice to finally meet you," she said, her mocha lips lifted in a welcoming smile as she stretched her hand out.

"Hi Pamela, it's nice to be here. Please call me Charles," Charles said as he shook her hand. "This is Ijay Amadi." He introduced Ijay with a wave of his other hand.

Ijay stepped forward, smiling and extending her hand. "It's great to finally put a face to a name, Pamela." They both shook hands. Ijay liked Pamela instantly. She radiated warmth and intelligence.

"Likewise, Ijay. You're both welcome to POD Foods. Let me take you upstairs. Paul is waiting in his office," Pamela replied.

At the mention of Paul's name, Ijay's heart jumped with unease, her skin temperature rising rapidly. Suddenly she wasn't so sure she wanted to see him. Wasn't so sure that she could look at him without the memories of what they'd done together invading her mind.

Surely it was much better not to see him at all. Not to rehash something that had been beautiful and yet so temporary. Despite the heat that unfurled in her belly every time she thought about him, she belonged to someone else now. There could be no going back.

Absentmindedly, she rubbed the ring on her finger as she followed Pamela and Charles into the lift. The ring acted as a talisman for her. It was there as a source of reassurance and reminder.

"How was your flight to Abuja?" Pamela asked when the lift started its journey upward.

"It was a good flight. I managed to sleep most of the way," Charles replied.

"Yes, that's one of the reasons I was glad it was an overnight flight. Although I'm quite surprised I'm still functioning well after less than four hours sleep," Ijay answered. "I think most of it is probably adrenaline and excitement. It's my first time in Abuja."

"Same here," Charles added, nodding his head as he turned back to Pamela. "From what I can see so far, it's a really nice city."

"It is. I enjoy living and working here. While you're here, if there's anything you need at all just ask me," Pamela said just before the lift doors beeped and opened.

"Thank you," Ijay and Charles said almost together.

"You're welcome. This way, please," Pamela declared before leading then down a hallway flanked on either side by offices.

Ijay realised that each step of her stride took her closer to Paul. Wanting to distract herself from the mix of excitement and apprehension churning in her stomach and making her hands tremble, she watched the space around her.

Tentatively, she smiled as she walked along, impressed by what she'd seen so far: modern furnished offices, people working on PCs or laptops, people in meeting rooms with round tables and flipcharts. It was no different from any office environment in London. It was strange because she hadn't known what to expect. She hadn't lived in Nigeria for over ten years. And the way the media portrayed Africa in the news, it was like the whole of Africa was still in the dark ages.

Yet this morning she'd been driven on well paved roads in relatively little traffic, sat in an expensive car with all modern conveniences, and was now in a suite of offices similar to those on Canary Wharf.

I don't see this on BBC News.

Pamela stopped in front of a brushed steel door with the name, Paul Arinze, Managing Director, tagged on it and knocked.

"Come in," the deep commanding voice was unmistakably Paul's.

The pounding of her heart against her ribs increased. Even through the disjointed barrier of the wall and door, she could still feel the effect of his silken voice deep down in her core. Just like that first night.

This is it.

Pamela opened the door and allowed Charles to go in first. Taking a deep bolstering breath, Ijay stepped into the office behind Charles.

Paul stood up and walked round his wide steel desk. Her breath caught in her throat. In the light of day, he looked even more incredible than she remembered. In navy-blue pinstripe trousers, light-grey shirt and embroidered blue silk tie, Paul looked very potent and smart.

Instantly she recognised the tie. It was the same one he'd used to bind her hands that night. Images of the two of them bombarded her mind. Paul kissing her feet, licking her breasts, filling her up until she felt like every pore of her body was saturated with him. Her body came alive, the flame of lust licking her skin with heat. Her breasts heavy and aching with need.

Transfixed, she mentally shook her head but was unable to look away from Paul as he walked toward Charles. She'd forgotten just how powerfully lithe he was. The sureness and flow of his stride reminded her of his ability to ensnare her attention. Charles was a tall man but he stood shoulder to shoulder with Paul.

"My dear Charles, welcome to Abuja," Paul said as they both shook hands and smacked each other on the back. He didn't even glance at Ijay. It was almost as if she wasn't there.

Could it be that he doesn't remember me?

Her stomach churned, her mouth tasting the bitterness. Somehow she didn't like the thought that he might have already forgotten about her in six months. Surely that was what she wanted all along. To forget and be forgotten.

No! Not when he's wearing that tie. If I'm going to be made to remember every detail of him, then I want him to remember every detail of me too!

Anger bubbled in Ijay's veins chasing the apprehension away. She stiffened her back and stood taller, focusing back her attention on the two men. It dawned on her then that Charles and Paul were friends. She hadn't realised before and had thought the two were acquainted through Frederick. Perhaps not, by the way they had just hugged each other.

If her boss was very good friends with Paul, how would that affect her work and career if things went wrong? She didn't know. It was more reason she had to keep her relationship with Paul professional for the duration of this project. She couldn't jeopardise her work.

"It's good to be here, my old friend," Charles said confirming Ijay's fear. I want to introduce you to Ijay. She'll be working directly with you on the project on this end and feeding into the team in London."

For the first time since they walked into his office, Paul turned his attention on her. His lips were lifted in a lopsided grin. Yet his black eyes were hard as granite. She sensed anger radiating from him, somehow. His smile was for the benefit of the audience. *Is he angry at me? Why?* She inhaled deeply, confused.

"Of course, I remember Ms. Amadi. She's the wonderful lady that organised Frederick's product launch event, right? I met her in London on my last visit," his tone was light and still jovial.

Ijay stepped forward, extending her right hand to meet his. "That's correct, Mr. Arinze," she responded, happy that her legs didn't wobble under Paul's close observant gaze, forcing a cool smile on her face.

He took her hand into his firm calloused hand. A burst of electric energy travelled up her arm, pooling heat in her belly. Her eyes widened with surprise. She pulled at her hand. Slowly, he released it, his eyes sparkling with a knowing glint, his lips lifted in a half-amused smile.

Immediately, she knew he remembered everything. He'd worn that tie on purpose to remind her of their night together. Agitated, she bit her lower lip and looked away quickly, her heart fluttering wildly.

Why is he doing this when he hasn't bothered to contact me in six months? Why now?

Chapter Eight

You can't run forever. I've got you, now.

Paul held Ijay's wild gaze, her brown eyes flickering with a mixture of confusion and desire. Inhaling deeply, he quelled a smug smile from breaking out on his face. Anticipation thrummed in his veins. He was one step closer to having Ijay again. He hadn't known how much that would thrill him until he'd seen her standing in the middle of his office, looking even more radiant in the morning than she'd done that night, months ago.

In her alluring plum skirt suit that flattered her feminine curves, she looked sharp and confident. With her matching high-heeled pumps, she looked tall and sexy, her straight legs elongated.

He inhaled deeply. The sweet fragrance of lilies invaded his nostrils. The sweet scent of Ijay. He watched as her buttery-coloured skin darkened on her smooth cheeks. It wasn't quite a rosy blush. More a plum colour like her suit.

He knew that response. He'd seen her satiny skin take on that hue before, when she was sexually stimulated. She was aroused now. He'd bet on it. This close to her, he could smell it. Almost taste the syrupy sweetness of her essence.

It was good to know he still affected her. Just like she affected him. He schooled his expression and moved back, needing the distance to tamper down his body's response to her presence.

"Please have a seat," Paul said. Turning away from Ijay, he ushered his guests to the small round table. Sitting on the sofas would be a bad idea, though their meeting would be relatively informal since they'd only arrived in Nigeria this morning. It was purely for meet-and-greet purposes. The real hard work would start the next day. But he needed the height of the table to cover his body's growing response to Ijay.

The both muttered their thanks and walked past him toward the table. From the corner of his eyes he watched Ijay stride to the table, her wide hips swaying gently, her round behind hugged tightly by her plum six-panelled A-line skirt.

When she pulled out a chair, she took off her matching jacket and hung it over the back of the chair, revealing her fitted sleeveless white cotton shirt. From her body's demeanour, she appeared serene as she sat down. She sat with her shoulders straight and hands on her lap. Charles sat next to her.

Paul moved to the other side of the table and sat down. A vantage position to watch Ijay from. He wanted to observe her face, her expressions. Yet it gave him some distance from her. If he sat next to her, he might be unable to keep his hands off her body.

When she looked up at him, her gaze hardened in a furious glare, her lips pursed in a straight line.

Unprepared for her fury, his breath caught in his throat, his heart hitting his chest with force.

She knows!

Stifling a self-satisfied smile on his lips, he reached for his tie deliberately, in the pretence of adjusting it. Her stare followed his hands' movement to the tie. The skin on the back of his hand prickled under the intensity of her glare. He didn't care. He was getting the response from her that he wanted. He'd worn the tie today, especially for her. His frustration at her disappearing act that night drove him. He wanted her to remember that night, him and everything they'd done.

The blue embroidered silk tie was the best symbol of their encounter. He hadn't worn it since that night because each time he'd picked it up, Ijay's scent filled his lungs with yearning. Recollections of their time together would come flooding back, leaving him aching and frustrated.

Just like the tie had been a symbol of his power over her body that night, it had since become a symbol of her memories' power over his body. Wearing it today was a way of shifting that power base again. Wearing it was putting control right back into his hands. Exactly where he wanted it.

The sound of crockery rattling on a laden trolley full of refreshments being wheeled in by Pamela distracted him for a moment.

"Ah. Refreshments are here. Please help yourselves. I know you Europeans love your coffee. We have the best of Kenyan coffee here," he said, pointing to the trolley laden with drinks and pastries. One of the reasons he was grateful for

Pamela. She always did her best to make sure they catered for their visitors' tastes.

"Thank you. That's quite a selection just for us," Charles said, pouring himself a cup of coffee from the flask before loading his porcelain plate.

"You know we Africans don't joke with our bellies. I personally can't function well without a decent breakfast," he joked.

Charles laughed. Paul saw a tentative smile break on Ijay's face. His heart lifted momentarily. Without saying anything, she reached out and poured herself a drink. Something on her finger caught the light and sparkled. It drew his attention and his gaze narrowed to her hand. On her engagement finger was a small diamond stone sitting on a gold band.

No...She's engaged?

His heart dropped into his churning stomach. With a frown on his face, he glanced back up to her face. Their gazes met. Her brown eyes glittered with cold humour, her lips in a haughty smile confirming his fear.

The impact was like a full body blow—painful and crushing. It was unexpected. Something he hadn't planned for. Cornered, he had to retreat and think. Pushing back his chair, he stood up.

"Please excuse me for a minute. I'll give you some time to enjoy the refreshments and settle in. We'll start the meeting in about five minutes."

"No problem, Paul. I'm rather enjoying these cinnamon rolls," Charles said, before taking a sip of his coffee.

Paul nodded to Charles. Without giving Ijay another glance he walked out of his office choosing to walk to the gents down the hallway near the lifts. He needed the walk and the distance from Ijay to clear his head. Luckily when he got in, there was no one in the cubicles. He paced the floor, confused, his face scrunched in a frown.

When did Ijay get engaged? How did it happen so soon? They'd been together only six months ago. Yes, he hadn't called her in that time. He'd been bidding his time waiting for the right opportunity. Perhaps he was a tad arrogant to still expect her to be single.

But this? An engagement?

When did she meet someone new? He'd known she'd been on the rebound that night. She'd confessed to him that she'd been dating Frederick before his fellow LBS alumni had broken off their relationship to get engaged to someone else. She'd been in love with Frederick. Was she still in love with him? Ijay couldn't possibly be engaged to Frederick, could she? Frederick was due to marry another woman soon.

When has that stopped anyone before?

He paused from pacing and scrubbed his head roughly. *It's true.* Marriage wasn't sacred to people these days. He read all the time about couple getting married and divorcing in very short timescales, about people breaking their vows with infidelity. All he had to do was drive past magazine vendors and he could read the headline splashed on gossip rags. He didn't even have to look too far away to see it happen. In fact he was born and bred in the bedrock of adultery. His father was never faithful to one woman.

Was that what Ijay was doing? Was she seeing Frederick again? She couldn't have met someone else and become engaged in such a short time. Surely, it had to be Frederick.

Letting out a low growl, he gripped the corners of a sink tightly as his vision became clouded in red. Jealousy pulsed through his mind. Hate made his body tremble with rage. He despised cheaters. He'd witnessed the ugly consequences of cheating. He'd seen the results first hand and had borne the brunt of it.

How could he sit back and let two people he knew live such a lie? He wasn't going to let it happen. He wasn't going to let Ijay marry Frederick. If Frederick had cheated on his fiancée with Ijay, then nothing stopped him from doing so to Ijay when someone else came along. Moreover he'd thought a woman like Ijay would be wiser and know not to get involved with someone who was already engaged regardless of her feelings.

What would happen in six months time when Frederick met another girl and dumped Ijay? Would she end up in a bar picking up another man for a one-night stand? He disliked the idea even more than he disliked the idea of Ijay marrying Frederick. Those two couldn't possibly be healthy for each other if they kept jumping in and out of a relationship.

Disgust clogged his throat. He wanted to scrub its bitterness off his tongue. Scrub the crazy notion of Ijay and Frederick together off his mind.

What kind of infatuation made a person blind to the realities of life?

He shook his head. No. He had to stop it from going ahead. He looked up at the mirror, watching his chest rise and fall as he panted. He was going to carry on with his seduction plan. This time the objective had changed slightly. He was going to save Ijay and Frederick from themselves. An engagement ring on her finger wasn't going to deter him.

Happy with his decision, he washed his hands, dried it patiently before striding out of the gents. This time his steps were more relaxed and confident, his mind calmer and with purpose.

"Right. Where were we?" he said when he returned to his office. His guests turned around. He could feel Ijay's gaze heating his body. He ignored her for a moment, smiling at Charles instead. He wanted to be face to face with her when he met her gaze. He needed her to understand the unspoken messages in his eyes.

"We're ready for you now. Thank you for the breakfast," Charles said as he wiped his hands with a wet wipe.

"Don't mention it. It wouldn't be African hospitality if we didn't fill our guests with food and drink," Paul asserted. He strode to the table, pulled his chair out and sat down. "As this is an informal meeting, I hope you don't mind if I take this off." Leisurely, he undid his tie and pulled it off his collar. The sound of silk sliding against cotton resonated in the room.

"No, no. Go right ahead. In fact, I think I'll join you," Charles laughed and proceeded to fiddle with his tie. "After all, when in Rome, I have to behave like the Romans. Or should I say, when in Abuja."

Paul chuckled. His affable friend was full of English humour. He focused on the woman sitting next to his old Uni mate. Meeting Ijay's gaze, Paul saw her chest rise sharply as she held her breath. He tidied his collar with one hand and undid his top button. On the other hand, he dangled the tip of the tie over the table, letting it trail over it for a few seconds.

When Ijay's high cheeks darkened in a blush, he rolled up the tie on his hand and purposefully placed it on the table midway between Ijay and him. He liked the idea that she could reach out and touch it. Mostly, it was to let her know that she'd feel it against her skin soon.

Her worried gaze flicked to the tie on the table and she bit her lower lip. She looked back up at him, her brown eyes querulous. He loved to see the fire in her eyes. Raising his brow, he flicked his eyes to the tie and winked at her. Her eyes widened immediately in astonishment.

Get ready, sweet Ijay. We're not done yet. You'll wear my bond again.

Smiling pleasantly, Paul turned his attention to Charles as Pamela took her seat beside him.

"Right. Now that we're all refreshed, let's get started so that you can get back to your hotel early and get some rest," he said, silently relishing the fierce look Ijay was giving him. "I want to start by saying I'm thoroughly looking forward to working

90

with Havers and Child on this POD venture. It's been six months in the making and I know the next six weeks will realise our dreams." He smiled inwardly as he saw Ijay's nose flare out in response to his insinuations. She understood his meanings. He knew it.

We're going to have a great time, sweet Ijay. So much more than you know.

Chapter Nine

Sonia: *So how are you getting on?*

Ijay let out a slow sigh as she tried a to get a true handle on how she felt. She was having a Skype chat with Sonia. The last few days had been tense on her nerves. A critical project, new work environment and the biggest source of distraction—Paul—were all contributing to keep her on her toes. She didn't really want to unload all that onto her friend. She didn't want to come across as if she wasn't coping well. Sonia would be supportive, but she'd ask too many questions that Ijay wasn't ready to answer. She replied choosing her words carefully.

Ijay: *Not too bad. Charles is on the flight back to London this morning. I have a meeting with Paul later to discuss the plans for when we visit the factory. Overall it's been good. Abuja is hot and I'm adjusting to it slowly. It's great that everywhere is air-conditioned though.*

Sonia: *Yes, I've arranged for a car to pick Charles up from the airport. How are things with Paul?*

Ijay: *Things are professional at the moment.* She typed in a rush. She'd hit the enter button before she realised her mistake.

Sonia: *At the moment? You expect things to become unprofessional later?* ☹ *She added a frowning face avatar.*

Ijay: *No, of course not.*

Ijay: *Well it's just that something happened on the first day. Paul did some things that made me think he wanted to get personal. Nothing's happened since and he's been very professional for the past two days.*

Sonia: *That's good. You may have read things into his actions because you were already apprehensive about seeing him again. Don't worry. You're there to work, nothing else and he knows it.*

Ijay: *You're right. I should stop worrying. He's not a big bad wolf about to gobble me up.*

A warm shiver ran through Ijay straight to her core. Perhaps thinking about Paul as the big bad wolf wasn't the best idea if she didn't want to get personal with him.

Sonia: *LOL @ Big bad wolf.*

Sonia: *How are things with Vincent?*

Ijay: *I don't know.* ☹ *I haven't spoken to him since the day I arrived. We've exchanged text messages. That's all. He's been busy with work I guess. I'm hoping we can catch up over the weekend.*

She really was trying hard not to get worried about Vincent. Considering all the fuss he made before she left London, she'd been expecting him to be more enthusiastic about speaking to her daily.

Sonia: *Well, I wouldn't worry about it. When you were in London you were hardly speaking to him every minute. So it's hardly going to change now that you're in Abuja.*

Ijay: *True. Still, I'd really like a little bit more attention from him. He was the one who was concerned about me being here.*

"Especially since I'm here on my own with Paul," she said out loud. Luckily, there was no one around to hear her reflective words. Being in Abuja with Paul made her feel more sensitive. Vulnerable. She just needed the daily reassurance from Vincent. Was that too much to ask?

The meeting reminder on her laptop popped up. She had a meeting with Paul in ten minutes.

Ijay: *Anyway, you're right. There's probably nothing to worry about. I have to go now. We'll chat again soon.*

Sonia: *Cool. Don't forget to let me know if there are any hot men working in the POD offices. You know I'm relying on you to hook me up, girl.* ☺

Ijay chuckled. *No worries, girl. Later.* ☺

She glanced at her watch and shut down her Skype connection. The teams met daily for updates and plans as she got acquainted with the project. Now that Charles had returned to London, the meeting would be between just her and Paul.

It would be the first time they were alone since that night. The apprehensive knots in her stomach tightened. She took calming breaths. There was nothing to worry about. Maybe the tie thing was just to test her out. He'd seen her engagement ring. And he'd kept things professional since. He wouldn't be change things now, would he?

She picked up the items she needed for the meeting and walked to Pamela's desk with a smile fixed her face.

"Hi Pamela, is Paul ready to see me now?"

"Yes, you can go straight through," Pamela replied with a smile.

"Thank you," Ijay answered. She took a deep breath before knocking on the door.

"Come in," the timbre of Paul's voice vibrated through her body. Would she ever get used to hearing his voice?

She pushed the door open and walked in. Paul sat on the sofa, leaning back. Today, he was in a sky blue cotton shirt and charcoal trousers. His shirt sleeves were rolled up his arms showing off hard toned arms. She remembered the feel of them against her body when he'd held her. She'd felt desirable. Beautiful. Sexy.

Ijay, focus!

Fighting the nervousness in her stomach with another deep breath, she walked to the sofa and sat opposite Paul. He looked up from the file he was reading. Unhurriedly, his lips lifted in an appealing smile, his onyx eyes gleaming delightfully. Thud. Her heart rammed into her chest.

"Hi, Paul," she managed to choke out, covering her mouth with her hand as she coughed out the lump in her throat.

"Hi, Ijay," he said and straightened in his seat. "Did you get to read the market research report?" He lifted the report in his hand.

"Yes, I did." She nodded, taking the report out of the plastic folder in her pile of paperwork.

"Good. I'd like to discuss it this morning. Before that, I wanted to let you know we'll be going down to the factory next week. We'll be in Enugu for three days. Will that be okay?"

"Sure. That's no problem." In the three days she'd worked closely with Paul, she'd come to appreciate his attitude. He was direct, dedicated, and open to new ideas. He never wasted time getting to the crux of an issue or dealing with it. He was a natural leader.

"All right. Now, let's walk through the report," he said.

Once they started discussing the items in the report, Ijay relaxed. The nervous tension in her shoulders eased off, her heart rate settling to a near normal rate. This was her job and she was very good at it. Otherwise she wouldn't be here. Regardless of what was going on in her personal life, she loved her job. It was her strength. She could do it with flair. Without panicking.

As they chatted, she identified the areas she thought they needed to focus their marketing efforts on based on the report summary. She also highlighted what she saw as the brand strengths and unique selling points.

Paul listened to her attentively. He maintained eye contact when necessary, his expression always encouraging as his gaze flicked from the report in his hand to her. Though her body registered his presence with an underlying buzzing sensation, it wasn't overwhelming or distracting.

Perhaps because Paul was in business mode, she felt at ease. He nodded when he agreed with her ideas. When he had a query, his facial features creased in a frown, parallel lines appearing on his forehead. He asked questions. She answered, confidently. At the end, they also agreed a plan of action for the next week and things to focus on while they were down at the factory.

Feeling positive that working with Paul would work out just fine, she packed her things to leave his office. Perhaps she'd allowed her vivid imagination to run wild the first day at his office. He didn't really want anything more from her than for her to deliver the PR project for POD.

"Let's have dinner tonight."

Ijay's heart thudded in her chest, her hands frozen mid-air with her notepad and paper documents hanging precariously. His resolute words were unexpected, his deep voice husky with emotion.

"Pardon?" she choked out, her forehead screwed up in a frown. Was she imagining things again, perchance? Her gaze flicked up to meet his. The challenging spark from the other day was back in the vigour of his black eyes.

"You do eat dinner, don't you?" he returned with a lopsided grin. Was he mocking her?

Her frown deepened, the nervous knot in her stomach revisiting. She lowered her notepad to her lap. "Yes, but—"

"I'll pick you up from your hotel at 7pm."

Her grip on her notepad tightened in annoyance. How could he say it like it was a foregone conclusion? She hadn't agreed, yet. "Paul, I don't think going out to dinner with you is a good idea."

"Perhaps, but we need to talk. If you'd rather we did it in your hotel room?" he raised his eyebrow, his eyes sparkling with a sardonic glint. He was certainly mocking her now. The two of them in a hotel room was definitely not a good idea.

"No!" she shouted. She closed her eyes briefly, taking a deep breath. She opened her eyes and met Paul's determined gaze with resolution. She wouldn't allow him to ruffle her. Too much was at stake. "Dinner will be fine. I'll be ready at seven," she said coolly.

He nodded. "I'll see you later."

Glancing away, she calmly picked up her things and walked out of his office. She walked briskly to the ladies. Once the door shut behind her, she leaned against the wall and she blew out a deep shaky breath. This thing with Paul was doing her head in.

So he hadn't worn his tie since that first day. Neither had he said anything overtly. His insistence that they talk over dinner might be innocuous. He had something up his sleeves. She could swear it.

To think that he'd pulled that stunt with his tie. He knew what effect it would have on her. He'd been taunting her. Punishing her. But, for what?

She shook her head. She didn't know Paul's motive. She'd been hoping that he'd say something—anything—so they could finally talk properly. She couldn't confront him directly. He was a business client. She had to keep things professional on her end at all times.

She wasn't happy about meeting him for dinner. It was bad enough being alone in the office with him. Working with him so far had been purely business. So that wasn't a problem. However, a restaurant, despite the other diners, would be intimate and personal. She couldn't guarantee his behaviour or hers for that matter.

Still...what was the alternative? Him in her hotel room?

No way! That was so wrong on several counts. Warmth spread through her body, heating her cheeks and settling low in her belly, her nipples hardening painfully. Hugging her body, she groaned out loud at her body's shameless response to being in a hotel room with Paul. How was she supposed to acquire the strength to resist Paul if her body kept responding so blatantly?

The way she felt right now, if she was left in a room with him alone, and a bed within easy reach, she could be the one pouncing on him. Her body was so wound up from the pent up tension of not having any sex for over six months. It hadn't been so bad when she was in London. Yet in the three days in Abuja, she'd turned into a walking mass of hormones.

"Oh, Vincent! Just one night with you would have saved me from all this stress."

Saying his name out loud made her cheeks sting with mortification. She was engaged. Her traditional wedding was in a few weeks. Yet the memory of another man's touch was affecting her in a way no other man has. Even her soon-to-be husband. She really had to get a grip.

She walked to the mirror and looked at her reflection with determination. Dinner with Paul would be just talk. She'd make sure of it. The restaurant environment would provide a good barrier. They would hash this thing between then out finally. She'd tell him things should be purely professional between them. And that would be it.

Feeling better with her decision, Ijay returned to her desk and concentrated on work. The focus on the project was a good distraction. She didn't think about Paul again as she worked on estimates and resources she needed to deliver the plan. As she worked she became more convinced that things would go well. She just needed to get a better understanding of the key products.

The day flew by. At lunchtime, Pamela took her to a local restaurant. They'd already been out to other restaurants as Pamela tried to help her settle in Abuja. Today she settled for a plate of jollof rice, roast chicken and a side salad. It was a huge contrast to her afternoon meals in London. There she spent lunch mostly at her desk with a sandwich. Here most of the office was empty at lunchtime as people went out to lunch.

Pamela had been really helpful, showing her the local amenities and where to get a local sim-card so she didn't have to pay for roaming charges. Yesterday, Ijay found out about Millennium Park. Some people chose to have a picnic out there if they preferred.

After work, the car service dropped her back at her hotel. Her apprehension level rose as she prepared for her dinner date with Paul, the butterflies returning to her stomach. To ease her edge nerves, she focused on the fact that her meeting with Paul would be a good thing. So that she could finally flush him out of her system.

She showered. Deciding what to wear was a problem. She'd been more focused on getting out of Paul's office that she'd forgotten to ask him the dress code for the evening. Finally, she settled for a black tunic dress and peep-toe shoes. It was stylish without being over the top.

Just before seven her phone buzzed. She picked it up. It was a text message from Paul.

I'm downstairs.

Her heart jumped and raced off in agitation, her palms suddenly feeling clammy. She wiped them on a towel and looked at herself in the mirror. Her straightened hair fell on her shoulders in a layered bob, her face with a touch of light make-up.

Stay calm. You can do this, Ijay.

Taking several deep breaths, she picked her clutch purse and left her hotel room.

Chapter Ten

Paul strode into the lobby lounge of the Hilton hotel, his strides long and hasty. The restlessness that had plagued him had returned. Impatient, his blood whooshed with excitement of seeing Ijay; touching her, tasting her. He'd been tolerant by waiting three days since her arrival in Abuja.

Moreover he'd had to make sure Charles' evenings were occupied. He'd taken both of them out to dinner the second night and last night he'd hung out with Charles catching up on old times. He'd avoided asking Charles about Frederick's engagement. He wanted to speak with Ijay about it first. While Charles had been around, Paul had been careful not the get personal with her.

Not that he ever conducted any kind of personal affairs in the office environment. Whenever he stepped over the threshold of his business premises, it was always business first. Business and pleasure had always been separate entities before. He'd never been tempted to merge the two. However, he'd been tempted with Ijay. Greatly tempted.

Sitting next to her every day, trying to concentrate on work when his body ached for her had been pure torture. Her elusive scent clung to the air around him every time he inhaled. Even this morning as he sat next to her, it had taken all his will power not to reach across to her.

Whenever she was thinking, she took her bottom lip into her mouth, chewing it worriedly. He'd wanted to run his tongue along the hassled rim; wanted to pull it into his mouth and suck it like lollies. He'd ached so much he'd resorted to keeping his folder on his lap to cover the evidence of his torment.

"Hello, Paul. Fancy meeting you here."

Paul broke his stride and swivelled in the direction of the sing-song female voice he recognised. Looking tall, dark and slender in a navy blue skirt suit, Kate stood before him confirming what he'd already suspected. She sashayed in his direction and wrapped her arms around his body in a lingering hug. Her musky perfume floated around him. She lifted her lips to kiss him. He turned his face at the last moment, giving her his cheek instead.

"Hi Kate. How are you? What are you doing here?" he asked in a pleasant tone, when he stepped back out of her reach. He hadn't seen her since she moved her things out of his apartment. It was a surprise seeing her again. Not that he let that affect the way he treated her. In fact, he was in a good mood about seeing her again. If she hadn't left him, he wouldn't have gotten together with Ijay that night in London. He would've never cheated on Kate.

"I'm doing well, thanks. I'm here on a conference and this is my hotel for the week. I noticed you were headed for the lounge. Shall we grab a seat?"

"Sure," Paul agreed. Suspicion rose in his mind about Kate's motives. The last time he'd seen her she'd been in a rush to get away from him and had refused to spend the night at his place. Her sudden friendliness set alarm signals off within his highly guarded senses. However, it wouldn't hurt to have a chat with her. They'd got on quite well when they'd been together. There was no reason not to be civil with each other.

They walked to the seating area. Paul waited for Kate to sit first. She sat on a two-seater sofa and smiled invitingly at him. He chose a single-seater with arm rests. Undaunted, she scooted to the end of the sofa closer to him. Reaching across, she placed her manicured hand on his arm.

"It's been such a long time, Paul. How are you doing? What are you doing here?" She waved other hand expressively.

"I'm doing all right. I'm just here to pick someone up for dinner," he remarked nonchalantly, lifting his shoulders in a lazy shrug.

"Oh...is this your new flame?" she asked. He saw the lines around her lips tighten though she still maintained the smile. Her hard eyes told a different story. She didn't like the idea of him seeing someone else. Not that he cared, anyway.

"She's not a flame. Just a PR consultant working on the POD project," he said dismissively.

The hard lines on her face eased out. Lowering her eyelids coyly in a gesture that would've had his heart racing in the past, she leaned closer and caressed his arm through his jacket, moving her hand up and down on it. "In that case, why don't we have dinner tomorrow? I heard about a new restaurant that's just opened we could try out."

Today, Kate's calculated deference had little effect on him, except confirm his need for someone else. "Why?" he asked. "I thought you didn't want anything to do with me any longer."

"I know. I was a bit hasty in my actions that day. Blame it on my hormones or something. I wasn't thinking straight," she cajoled.

"Having dinner with you'll change nothing. I still don't want to get married." He hardened his tone so she'd understand. Nothing had changed between them. He didn't foresee it changing. Ever.

"I totally understand. Look, I'm a career girl and I love my life. Who needs marriage anyway? Come on, what do you say? We were good together." She uncrossed and parted her legs slightly. Paul couldn't miss her blatant provocation. It was a gesture he'd instructed her to adopt whenever they were together privately.

In the bedroom as well as the boardroom, Kate was very savvy. They had been good together. After an initial reluctance, she'd eventually taken to his proclivities like a duck to water. It was probably why their affair lasted longer than any other he'd had previously. That she could give head the way no other woman had been able to was an extra bonus he couldn't deny.

However, he now craved something different. Someone who's touch was tentative, yet stimulating. Someone docile, yet challenging.

Someone still willing to learn a thing or two. He didn't want a pro. He wanted Ijay.

With his peripheral vision, he saw someone approaching. He glanced up and saw Ijay. She was in a short silk black dress that skimmed her curves and stopped above her knees, exposing long legs heightened by stilettos. His heart stopped, like it'd done the first night he'd seen her standing over the threshold of the bar's balcony. His blood bubbled with enthusiasm. He moved his arm away from Kate and sat up straight.

"I'm afraid I'll have to decline your tempting offer, Kate. Have a great evening. I plan to." He stood, ignoring the frustrated glare Kate gave him. He turned his attention to Ijay and walked to her with a beaming smile.

"You look beautiful," he whispered against Ijay's skin as he brushed his lips on her silky cheek. Inhaling deeply, he allowed her enticing fragrance to rouse his body and felt the timely pulse of his need before moving back. "So beautiful, I'm persuaded to skip dinner and eat you instead." He winked at her.

She gasped in a soft voice, her chest rising rapidly. Her chocolate eyes widened with heat and surprise; her high cheeks peaking to a dark rouge colour.

Her gaze lowered to his chest demurely. "Thank you," she murmured.

She couldn't possibly know what that gesture did to him. The vice that seemed to clamp his chest whenever Ijay was around wrung tighter, adding to the rigid ache in his groin. He willed his body to relax. Otherwise he'd be walking like John Wayne.

"Shall we head off?" he asked when he got his body under control.

She nodded, biting her lower lip anxiously. He suppressed a groan and looked away from her. He had to get her out of the hotel with so many beds close by. Not that he'd be patient enough to reach a bed, if she carried on enticing him the way she was doing.

Placing his hand on the small of her back, he guided outside into the warm evening air.

***

The restaurant was busy when they walked in. They sat in a secluded corner of a moderate and friendly Nigerian restaurant. They'd been ushered to a private booth with no other diners near them by the owner who Paul said was a good friend of his.

There was low African music playing in the background, paintings of African landscapes and people hung on the walls. The atmosphere felt authentically African. She loved the vibe.

Yet somehow she hadn't expected Paul to take her to a place like this. She'd thought he'd take her somewhere more upmarket with a European menu. This was one surprise from him she liked.

Instead of sitting across from her, Paul had insisted on sitting next to her. They were so close, their thighs almost touched. They might as well be touching skins because she felt the heat exuding from his body. It spread out from her sides and wrapped her in his spice.

Concentrating on her Fish Pepper Soup starter was a chore, when her body was awakening, her breasts were getting heavier. The ache in her core was becoming more insistent.

It had started when she'd walked into the hotel lounge and saw Paul talking to a woman. The woman was seated seductively close to Paul, her hand caressing his arm. The fierce jealous pang that had swept through Ijay had surprised her. She hadn't expected to feel that way about seeing Paul with another woman.

Truthfully, she hadn't given it much thought until tonight. At the back of her mind she'd accepted that Paul would be seeing other women since he hadn't bothered contacting her in six months. Yet seeing another woman touch him in such a personal provocative way had made her want to rage at the woman.

That was so crazy considering she was engaged to someone else. Even if she wasn't, Paul had made it quite clear that he wouldn't have a relationship with her since she lived in London and he lived in Nigeria. It was never going to work. She'd accepted that, surely. That's why she was wearing another man's ring. So why was she getting hung up on Paul?

Focus on mundane things. She looked at the bowl of *Isiewu* —a delicacy made from goat head and spices—that Paul was devouring enthusiastically. It provided the inspiration to get away from her body's response to Paul.

"You know I've missed all this," she said a little bit more enthusiastically than she'd planned.

108

Paul's lips lifted in a smile, his eyes glinting with knowing amusement. "You have? But there are Nigerian restaurants in London."

"Yes, I know. It's not exactly the same. I think food cooked in Nigeria is more authentic."

Placing his fork back on the plate, Paul nodded. "You are right," he agreed. "I'm always eager to get back to Nigeria when I'm away. Despite all the lovely variety of meals I get to eat when I travel, none of them beat the ones I eat at home. Except one."

The ominous way he said 'Except one' had her stomach in a knot of excitement she shouldn't feel. It sounded as if he was referring to her. She debated asking him what the meal was. That intense gaze he fixed on her, had her skin tingling. She bit her lip and lowered her gaze, seeking to hide his effect on her from him.

"Aren't you going to ask me what the meal was?" Paul asked in a low voice, leaning closer to her. His thigh rubbed against hers. She drew in breath sharply, her mouth drying out. As her core pulsed, she shifted restlessly in her seat. He placed his hand on her thigh, the heat from his palm scorching her skin.

"Are you wet for me, sweet Ijay?"

Sweet Ijay! Two tiny words that disintegrated her resolve accompanied by five words that had her body steaming at their eroticism and directness. Lord help her, but she'd missed the way he said those words like she was rare and precious to him. Those words arrested her and kept her ensnared.

Fixated by his arousing touch, she held her breath as his hand travelled up her thigh, shifting her dress up. If she wasn't wet before, she surely was now. She felt her core weep, soaking her thong.

He was so close. So close.

His hand rested at the junction of her hip and thigh. She swallowed the lump in her throat and closed her eyes. *Touch me!* Her body screamed taking over her normally rational mind. Surely she wasn't being rational any longer. They were sitting in a restaurant where the waiter or anyone else could turn up at any moment.

"I can smell your sweet intoxicating fragrance. I want to taste you so much," he whispered in a gruff voice, his fingers skimming the edge of her lace undies. "Say the word, sweet Ijay and I'll stop. Do you remember the word?"

Automatically, she nodded while still holding her breath. Her mind screamed, *Blue!* But her body was drowning in sensation, so wound up. If he didn't touch her soon, she'd commit murder. Just this once and it wouldn't matter anymore.

Forgive me...I want him to touch me.

His fingers pushed the soaked thong aside and slid inside her. She gripped the edge of the table, her nails digging into the wood. While his fingers slid in and out of her in a painfully slow rhythm, his thumb played a thrilling tune with her swollen bud.

Feverish heat travelled through her body. Her body raced toward the edge, ecstasy only moments away. She couldn't wait to fly off the edge. To have her first climax in over six months. To relieve the tension she'd felt. Not long now. Her body coiled tighter, her breathing coming in shallow gasps.

His hand stopped moving and slipped out of her body. A desperate whimper escaped her lips. She opened her eyes just as Paul lifted hand. His fingers glistened with her juices. He put them into his mouth one after the other and licked.

"You're as tasty as ever, sweet Ijay," he drawled.

"Paul...please." She couldn't even recognise her own breathy brazen whisper. She looked up at his face, pleading with her eyes. He really wasn't just going to stop now, was he? His eyes lost their fiery spark and hardened into dark rocks.

"Soon, first I want to know why you ran," he said the words casually but his expression was brooding. It was like a splash of cold water on her hot skin. She snapped out of her lusty haze, annoyance taking precedent in her mind.

"What do you mean? I never ran," she snapped irritably.

"So what do you call leaving me with such a lousy note?"

"What? I explained my reason in the note. I didn't want an awkward moment in the morning after the great evening we'd had. I enjoyed the evening. What more did you want?"

Her body vibrated with anger. Anger at Paul for playing her body against her. Anger with herself for not having any self-control where Paul was concerned.

"I wanted you to be there when I woke up. I wanted to kiss you and make love to you in the morning."

She looked away from him, focusing on a painting on the wall. "And just prolong the inevitable? I wanted a clean break. I didn't want to have to get hung up on another man who didn't want to be with me long-term. You're the one who said you didn't want a long-distance relationship."

"I did. But..."

Something in his voice made her glance at Paul. A tortured glaze swept through his dark eyes.

"You've changed your mind?" *Dare she hope?*

"No. I'd thought about it and assumed we could come to some arrangement only to wake up and find you gone."

"What? So why didn't you call me? Or do something? It's been over six months, Paul," she said, her voice laced with her frustrations. Why was he doing this now?

"Do I really need to remind you of what you wrote in that note? It was unequivocal." He reached in his pocket and pulled out a folded piece of paper. He unfolded it and spread it on the table. "Look at it."

Ijay looked at the rumpled paper and recognised her writing. It was the note she'd written on that fateful morning. *He'd kept it!*

"Can you see what's missing from it?" his angry gaze moving from the paper to her face. She was too stunned to say anything and just shook her head.

"There's no call me or I'll call you in there. This note says quite plainly you didn't want me to contact you," he emphasised his words by stabbing his finger on the paper.

She'd looked at the piece of paper again. At the time she'd written it, she'd thought it was the end for the both of them. She'd never thought she'd see him again. She'd thought that was what he wanted. She hadn't wanted to come across as clingy or desperate. So she hadn't asked him to call her even though she'd wanted him to. It was too late now. It didn't matter anymore.

"Paul, I'm sorry if my note upset you. It changes nothing now. I'm engaged to someone else. So we have to forget it. Forget what we did, please."

"Tell me the truth. If I'd called you and asked to see you again, would you have agreed?"

"Yes, but—"

"No buts. You're here now and I want to see you again."

"Hello! Newsflash, I'm engaged." She waved her left hand angrily in the air.

He took her hand in his and stroked the back with his other hand. Tingles travelled up her arm. She tried to pull it back but he held on. Dismissing her words, he shrugged nonchalantly, his expression still stern. "You don't really want to marry Frederick. I'm saving you both the headache."

"What's Frederick got to do with anything?" she asked, frowning in confusion.

"You're wearing his ring, aren't you? I'd say he has everything to do with it."

"Where did you get such a crazy idea? Frederick is not my fiancé," she replied with exasperation.

"He's not? Then who is?" Frowning, he dropped her hand quicker than a chef drops a hot pan.

"Vincent Arinze. Do you know him?"

The expression on Paul's face turned thunderous, his features drawn tight, and his hands balled into fists. He looked like he'd just seen a ghost.

Chapter Eleven

"Vincent, please call me. I need to talk to you."

Ijay left out a frustrated sigh after leaving yet another voice message for her elusive fiancé who was getting harder to get hold of these days. It seemed whenever she wanted to talk to him, he was out of reach. Continually getting his voice-mail was disconcerting to say the least.

Gritting her teeth to stop the banked tears in her eyes from falling, she switched off her phone and dropped it on the table. The events of the night had left her feeling raw and sensitive.

She recalled Paul's expression when she'd told him about Vincent. The distressed and disgusted look on his face had left her feeling confounded. His eyes had darkened to a menacing glint and his lips twisted with repulsion.

It had left her feeling sick.

That he could be all over her one minute and the next look at her with loathing had hurt her more than anything else he'd done. The anger rising within her had put the tears on hold.

He'd promptly called the waiter's attention, paid the bill and ushered her out of the restaurant. All attempts to get him to explain the reason for his response met with stone cold silence all the way back to her hotel. He'd unceremoniously bid her good night at the entrance of the hotel. She'd stood there fuming in silence and he'd driven off into the night.

As she walked up to her room, she'd tried to work out why Paul would be in such a state about Vincent. His behaviour confirmed to her that Paul knew Vincent.

Though their surnames were the same, she knew Vincent didn't have a brother. He had a younger sister Veronica, whom Ijay had met for a few hours in London while Veronica was in transit to the United States.

Vincent's sister was about the same age as Ijay. Though there'd been an initial coolness from Veronica, which Ijay had put down to them just meeting for the first time, they'd gotten on relatively well in those hours they'd spent together.

So it was just Vincent, Veronica and their mum. Their father had died a few years back. When they'd first started dating, she'd chosen not to ask Vincent if he knew Paul. She'd tried to imagine how that conversation would have gone and changed her mind.

"By the way, Vincent, do you know a Paul Arinze? Oh, he's just a man I had a one-night stand with whom I keep dreaming about."

No biggie, right? *Wrong!* What man would have liked his future wife flaunting a one-night stand in his face? She'd quickly decided against it, choosing to forget Paul in the process. Of course, not discussing Paul was the easy part. Forgetting him was a little more difficult to achieve, to her chagrin.

So maybe Paul was a cousin of Vincent. Or some other random person who just managed to have the same last name as Vincent. It was known to happen. After all she knew of people with the last name Amadi who were not related to her family.

Either way, Paul knew Vincent. And they'd done a bad thing tonight. She only hoped Vincent would forgive her when she told him.

She had to tell him.

There was no way she could live with herself knowing what she'd done. She only wished she could see Vincent face to face when she told him. It would be better than telling him on the phone. She really couldn't wait. Not when the guilt was slowly driving her insane.

Robotically stripping off her clothes, she walked to the bathroom and turned on the shower. She didn't even bother covering her hair with the shower cap. She stepped under the shower, the warm jet pounding against her skin, plastering her hair against her face.

What have I done?

Guilt and shame wracked her mind. Her body trembled at the enormity of what she'd done.

I'm not that kind of girl.

She didn't swing from one man to the next. Once she got into someone, she committed with all her being. For her, it was all or nothing. That's why it had hurt so much when she'd split from Frederick.

For the three years she dated him, she never gave another man the time of day. Never allowed herself to get into that kind of situation. Since she'd been dating Vincent, she hadn't looked at another man.

Except Paul!

What was it about Paul that was making her lose herself—her inhibitions? On the first day she'd met him, she'd thrown caution to the wind and slept with him. Something she'd never done before. She was sensible Ijay. When it came to Paul she seemed to have no sense at all.

She certainly didn't see herself as immoral. When she'd read about other people having affairs while in relationships, she'd wondered what it was that drove them to it. Why they would jeopardise a loving relationship for the sake of a brief affair?

The consequences of these illicit affairs were devastating in some circumstances. Some people lost everything including their closest families.

In her case, she'd certainly risked more than a broken heart by allowing Paul to touch her today.

So it hadn't been full on sex. But the intent had been there.

She'd ached for him since she arrived in Abuja; had wanted much more than his touch. She'd wanted to feel him in every pore of her body. If he hadn't stopped, she'd have climaxed, shamelessly, in a restaurant where anyone could have heard or seen her.

Madness!

Disgust rolled through her, twisting her stomach in a cramp. She bent over and crouched low on the bathroom tiles, the water still hitting her back.

Tears rolled down her face unhindered, her body trembling.

Worse she still ached for Paul. She yearned for the warmth and safety of his embrace, the soothing sound of his voice, the fiery touch of his hands.

In the one night they'd spent together, he'd given her something that no other man had. He'd restored her confidence in the desirability of her body and herself as a woman.

Something that Frederick had smashed when he'd dumped her and started dating a slimmer woman. And Vincent trampled on each time by not even touching at all.

Paul was the only one who really seemed to see all of her as she was and still appreciated her.

In that one night, he'd stolen a piece of her heart. In the past months, she'd hoped that Vincent would come to replace that lost piece. That he'd make her feel wanted and sexy again.

In that one thing he'd failed her. Yes, there was a reassurance in knowing he wanted to spend the rest of his life with her. They were friends and respected each other. That's what relationships should be about. Right?

It shouldn't matter if there's little or no sex as long as they cared for each other. That's what sustained relationships in the long term. Passion would fizzle out eventually.

So why did her body not agree with her mind? Why had she been yearning for Paul to fulfil the wanton promise in his eyes? Why did she crave the bliss that came with being in his arms—the fiery soul-searing touch of his kiss?

The sting from the cold shower spray made her stand up and shut off the faucet. She hadn't realised how long she'd been crouched on the floor. She grabbed a towel and dried herself before wrapping her body in a bathrobe and her hair in a towel. She walked back into her room and sat on the bed, staring at the wall blankly.

She had already put her future marriage to Vincent in jeopardy by what she'd done tonight. The shame hitting her now would be nothing compared to the guilt she'd feel when she had to explain to her parents that the wedding would be cancelled because she couldn't control herself.

Her parents had always been supportive but this would bring disgrace to her family. The invitations to the traditional wedding had already been issued. The plans had already been made.

This was a big deal for her parents especially her father who was enthusiastic about seeing his first daughter get wedded. Any change in plans would disappoint him much more than her mother.

Bending her head, she clasped it in her hands bent on her knees. She'd never felt this stressed before. Not even when she'd split with her ex.

How was she going to cope with seeing Paul tomorrow morning at work? She couldn't call in off sick. It was unprofessional. Moreover he'd know it was because of him. She didn't want him thinking he affected her so badly that she'd hide from him. She'd have to keep a brave smile on her face and do her job as expected.

She tipped to the side on the bed and clutched her body in a foetal position.

God help me.
***

Vincent Arinze!

Paul let out a volley of punches on the punch bag dangling from the ceiling in the gymnasium on the ground floor of his apartment block in the secluded gated complex. He paid a premium in service charges but it was worth it to him living here.

One of the perks being that he could use the gym late at night after work without worrying about the drive back home. All he had to do was take the lift up to his apartment afterward. It came in handy tonight because he could take out his frustrations on the passive bag.

How had things become so complicated in such a short time? How did the woman he wanted become entangled with his half-brother? Vincent, who was only a few months older than him, shared his father's blood but was from a different mother.

Whilst married to his mother, Paul's father had several affairs one of them to Vincent's mother. Vincent's mum had been pregnant with him first. This meant that Vincent had been born a few months ahead of Paul.

When he was around eight years old, Paul's mother died. Vincent's mother and children moved into his father's house. His stepmother had mistreated him turning him into their houseboy. His father had been too busy with his external affairs to bother about what was happening to Paul in their home.

Then again, perhaps he'd known.

When Paul was eleven he was sent to boarding school at CIC Enugu. Till today, he saw it as the best thing his father had ever done for him. It got him away from their house and that woman's grip for the first time in his life. He suddenly had wings to fly.

Paul went off the rails for a while getting into trouble in school but his relationship with Michael and Peter had grounded him. In fact, Peter's parents had adopted him by default when Peter told them he had nowhere else to go during their school holidays.

Throughout that time, a kind of sibling rivalry had ensued between Paul and Vincent. Each time Vincent did something wrong he'd blame Paul for it. His stepmother had no problems punishing him for it.

It happened again and again that in the end Paul started retaliating. If he was going to be punished he wanted to be punished for doing the wrong thing.

It all came to a head one school vacation when Paul had returned home to find out there was a new teenage girl, Onome, who'd moved onto their street with her family. He'd liked the girl and asked her out. She'd agreed.

Later Vincent confronted Paul claiming that Onome was his girlfriend and that Paul should leave her alone. Paul had refused and asked Onome who denied it. She'd said that Vincent had been pestering her but she'd refused him. Enraged, Vincent had sworn he'd make both of them pay.

A few days later, Onome was raped. Paul found out about it when police turned up at his house. They searched his room and found the clothes and black hood the perpetuator had worn in his wardrobe. He'd claimed his innocence but was ignored and arrested.

His father bailed him out and paid reparations to Onome's family. They eventually dropped the charges because they didn't want Onome to face any trauma in court. His father sent him back to boarding school and to his maternal uncle's house afterwards.

Till today, no one else had been charged for the rape on Onome. Yet Paul knew there was only one person responsible though he hadn't been able to prove it.

The smug expression on Vincent's face as Paul had been led away by the Police convinced him Vincent was responsible. Who else would direct the police to his house, if the perpetuator of the crime had covered his face?

It could only be Vincent. And now the same Vincent was engaged Ijay.

Paul pounded the bag until he made himself dizzy and sat on the floor with his head on his gloved hands.

He was infuriated with himself that he'd let his arrogance rule him. That he allowed his anger with Ijay to fester for so long. Now she was engaged to Vincent, Paul had to back off. He couldn't continue their petty childish rivalry.

Despite the anger he had against Vincent for raping Onome and setting him up, Paul realised the greater responsibility lay on the head of their parents who were totally irresponsible. They were responsible for the kind of people their offspring turned into.

As far as Paul was concerned Vincent's mother was not fit to be a parent. She'd spoilt her children. The same thing could be said for his father.

Paul could easily retaliate using Ijay as a pawn against Vincent. He knew Ijay was his for the taking. Her responsiveness tonight at the restaurant showed him that if he pushed her, she'd let him do as he pleased. It would hurt Vincent and send a message to him that Paul knew what he did to Onome.

What about Ijay? You care about her.

No, I don't. It's just sex.

Pain throbbed in his head. Groaning, he rubbed his temple with his wrist.

You care about her. That's why it hurt you so much to find out she's with Vincent. Otherwise, you would have taken it the same way as when you thought it was Frederick.

Letting out a sigh, he relaxed his shoulders, conceding the thought in his mind. He cared about Ijay. He didn't want to care about her. Not that way. It seemed it was too late, anyway.

Chapter Twelve

When Ijay walked into Paul's office the next morning, the stress of the last few days had finally got her temper up. She hardly slept last night. Half of the night was spent worrying about the fact that she hadn't spoken to Vincent yet.

The other half spent worrying about how to deal with Paul. When she eventually slept her sleep was choppy. She woke up almost every hour in cold sweat plagued by nightmares. In her dreams, both Paul and Vincent hated her.

So this morning she wasn't in the best of moods. As she got dressed, she decided to take back control of her life where Paul was concerned. She hadn't been very prepared when she'd first arrived in Abuja. She hadn't known what Paul's intentions were or what he was capable of doing. He'd shown her his true colours in the last few days.

She'd speak her mind. If the result was that she got booted off the project, at least she would have stood up for herself. And hopefully she'd have peace of mind.

Paul was at his desk and barely looked up when she walked in. She strode with purpose to his desk and stopped in front of him. He looked up and leaned back in his chair. At first his eyes brightened with surprise, and then two parallel frown lines creased his forehead.

"Ijay, I didn't realise we had a meeting now," he said briskly in his usual business tone.

Her heart thumped in her chest. It was the first time she'd heard his voice since last night. Its deep note resonated within her. She ignored its effect and gripped her notepad tighter. She didn't need the notepad. Just wanted something to hold on to while in Paul's office.

"We don't. I need to talk to you," she said, glad her voice sounded calm and she was winning her battle for inner peace.

"Sit down." Paul pointed to the chair in front of his desk with the pen in his hand.

"No. I'd rather stand. I won't be long," she replied promptly, glad she was still composed.

He lifted his eyebrow, his dark eyes staring at her silently as if to say, 'Really?'

Still, she stared him down, cocking her eyebrow too in a challenge and refused to back down. After a few second of watching each other, she saw his chest lift as he let out a resigned sigh and rubbed his head with his palm.

"Okay. Let's hear it," he conceded, dropping his pen on the table.

Yeah! She celebrated silently. It was a small victory but worth celebrating where Paul was concerned. She hoped he'd continue his magnanimity.

"Do you still want me to work on this project?" she asked, her fingers crossed mentally. She'd worried last night whether he still wanted her to work on the project, after the way he'd treated her at the end of the evening. Like she had the plague.

"Yes," he answered without hesitation. The frown lines on his head deepened, his dark eyes looking worried. "Why?"

"If you want me to continue working on this project, then all your games have to stop. Right now. I came to Abuja because I wanted to work on the POD project, nothing else. I'm engaged and I want it to stay that way. I won't date you or sleep with you." She had to blow out air when she'd finished rattling out her mini-speech. Now that it was out she felt both relieved and anxious at the same time.

The lines around his mouth hardened. A muscle ticked on his forehead. He tapped his fingers on the steel table top, making a rat-tat-tat sound that drew her attention to his long fingers and short buffed nails. She remembered how he'd licked those glistening fingers the previous night.

Ijay!

She bit the inside of her lower lip hard, drawing salty metallic tasting blood. Shifting her stare away from his finger, she looked up into his eyes. They hardened to dark glinting rocks. He looked like he was going to disagree. Her heart sank thinking he'd call her bluff. She really didn't want to go home without completing this project.

"Okay."

Flabbergasted, she almost staggered backward, not sure she heard right. "Sorry?"

"I said fine. Whatever you want to do is fine by me," he said, holding her gaze intently while lifting his shoulders in a dismissive shrug.

Still amazed, Ijay tried not to gawp at him. He couldn't really be giving in so easily. This had to be another game. He had to be toying with her, letting her take her guard down before he pounced again.

"You mean that. No more insinuations. No toying with the tie?"

He nodded. "No more. In fact, I wish you the best with Vincent. I hope you're both very happy together." For someone who was wishing her well, Paul's expression was harsh. He didn't look too pleased about it. Why? When a minute ago he was telling her he was fine with her decision to keep everything professional.

"Erm, Thank you...I appreciate it," she said feeling a mix of melancholy and relief, as all the initial steam she had evaporated. "So will you explain why you reacted so badly about Vincent last night?"

A pained look passed over Paul's darkened eyes. He looked away from her briefly and inhaled deeply, his chest rising and falling. Her heart clenched at his tortured expression.

Suppressing the urge to walk over to him, to touch him and reassure him, she balled her fists and stood still. Something had upset him. Something about Vincent. She was sure of that. She wished Paul would tell her what bothered him. She really wanted to understand him better.

"I'm sorry. I can't help you with that. You'll have to talk to your fiancé about it," he said and turned to his laptop as if dismissing her.

Ijay wasn't ready to go yet without trying. She leaned closer to him. "Paul, talk to me please." She really wanted to help him. She cared about him way too much not to help, if she could.

He moved backward, as if avoiding her touch. Ijay frowned. Was he now avoiding physical contact with her?

"Ijay, I've conceded the things in my power to concede. You say you don't want any personal involvement with me, I grant it. But don't push you luck." His eyes were now back to being cold, uncompromising black rocks, his lips drawn out in a straight line. He was definitely not going to tell her anything.

"Fine," she bit out angrily finally giving up. If he wouldn't tell her then Vincent surely would. She turned to depart.

Paul stood abruptly. His chair scraped the hard carpet emitting a dull scuffing sound. He came round the table but stopped short of touching her. She held her breath, not sure of what he'd do.

"Ijay wait...If you ever need anything. I mean anything. Call me."

Where did that come from?

She narrowed her eyes into squints, her face pulled in a frown. His body radiated his tension as he held her gaze intensely. When she nodded, he relaxed, his shoulders loosening up.

"Thanks," she said and walked out of his office before exhaling.

She returned to her desk. Something in Paul demeanour had her confused. Something was definitely off with him. He had the same kind of haunted look he'd had when he'd woken up that night to a nightmare. Her heart ached for him.

She couldn't do anything about it. Going to him would have cancelled out all the agreement she'd just had with him. She'd decided to stick with Vincent, if he'd have her. That's what she was going to do.

Although, Paul had given in to her demands way too easily. She'd gone into his office prepared for an argument. Paul was demanding...in control...unyielding. Yet he'd capitulated without retorting.

Perhaps, he'd lost interest in her. So why did her heart clench painfully? Why didn't she feel relieved? He didn't mean anything to her apart from as the man she'd slept with once.

Liar!

Okay. She liked him, more than she should. She wanted more from him. Still, it was never going to happen. He'd moved on. It was much better this way. She had to get through the next few days and face up to Vincent when she eventually saw him.

Thankfully now that she'd settled the matter with Paul, she concentrated on her work for the rest of the day.

***

Ijay was at the airport on the way down to Lagos when Vincent finally called her. She took a deep gulp of air before she answered the ringing phone.

"Hi Vincent, where have you been? I've been trying to reach you for the past day." She couldn't hide the exasperation in her voice.

"Sorry, baby. I had to work and I forgot my phone at home. I'm here now. What's up?" he replied nonchalantly which wound her up even more.

"Really? You were working last night? You don't usually work at night."

"Of course I was working. I had to cover an emergency shift. What did you think I was doing?" He sounded annoyed.

She took a deep breath and told herself to back off. She didn't want him wound up before she told him the bad news. "I don't know. I'm sorry. It's just that I've been so stressed out and when I couldn't reach you I started wondering what was going on."

"Well, I'm here now. So what's on your mind?" he asked in a calmer tone.

"It's just that I miss you."

"Oh, I miss you too, baby. I really have to go shortly. Was that it?"

"Vincent, do you not even care that I'm here on my own," she exploded at him. She glanced around her, grateful there was no one standing close enough to hear her rant.

"Ijay, you were the one that insisted that you wanted to go to Abuja, remember," he came back at her. His words might be true but his shoving them back in her face didn't make her feel any better.

She groaned in anger at his offhand attitude and just blurted out the words. "I had dinner with a man last night—"

"Wait a minute! What man?"

That got his attention, she smirked silently. She could see him frozen on the spot in her mind's eye.

"He's the client, the owner of POD Foods. We'd met initially in London months ago before I met you and we had an affair. Well, last night while having dinner I let him touch me but—"

"Bitch!"

Stunned, she opened her mouth silently for a few seconds and closed them again. "Pardon?"

"So that's why you wanted to go to Abuja. So you can go fuck around," his voice was so loud, she wondered if his neighbours could hear him over in London. She cringed, her guilt making her body heat up.

"It wasn't like that at all. He started to touch me but stopped," she explained.

"You let my bastard of a brother touch you?" He yelled into the phone in agitation and let out a few more curse words. Ijay sensed he was moving around because his voice kept trailing out.

"Paul is your brother?"

"Didn't he tell you? Well, he won't be for much longer when I finish dealing with him."

The line disconnected. Still in shock, Ijay stood on the spot for several minutes without moving, as she tried to process what had just happened. When her flight was called, she slowly dragged her hand luggage to the departure gate. She boarded the flight still confused and finally settled in her seat, staring blankly at the back of the seat in front of her.

What just happened?

Vincent was enraged. That he'd used the b word was like a neon sign announcing: *Look, I'm pissed off.* It was the first time he'd ever sworn within hearing distance. He was usually such a gentleman that she'd never thought he could use expletives. He'd used several all within a few minutes.

She could understand all that. He was angry at her. Did that mean their relationship was over? He'd simply cut off the phone. She'd have to hang on to the hope that he'd reacted in anger. When he calmed down, perhaps they could talk more rationally.

He was furious at Paul too. He'd threatened Paul. Confused and worried, she bit her lower lip as she tried to figure out what was going on. Vincent had never told her that he had a brother. He'd said specifically that he only had one sister. He'd referred to Paul as '...my bastard of a brother...'

Maybe Paul had a different mother.

Suppressing a frustrated moan, she picked up the in-flight magazine and tried to concentrate on the words without much success. Her mind kept going back to Vincent's words.

Maybe they were just words said in anger but something about them still sent a disturbing cold shiver down her spine. Since Vincent was in London and Paul in Abuja, she hoped Vincent's anger would cool off by the time he saw Paul again.

She was glad she was on her way to her family home in Lagos instead of sitting on her own without anyone for support in a hotel room. Luckily her flight was only an hour, so they were taxing down to the arrival terminal at Murtala Mohammed Airport in no time. When she disembarked and picked up her luggage she found her mother waiting at the arrival lounge.

Her mother, whom she always thought was a twin sister to Annette Benning, looked so elegant in her long body-skimming blue linen boubou, her brunette hair cut in a short layered style. Her mother always looked at ease in African attire. If it wasn't for her tanned skin tone, you'd forget she was born in Loughton to Caucasian parents. She looked like any other African mother.

When she saw Ijay, her face beamed with a smile. Ijay couldn't help the tinge of sadness that swept through her mind. She'd have to deliver news that would wipe the smile off her mother's face. She planted a smile on her face and hurried toward her mother.

"Hello, darling," her mother cheered when Ijay hugged her.

Ijay held on tight for a brief moment as tears stung her eyes. After the stresses of the past few days, it was nice to see someone who loved and cared about her regardless. Someone whose arms were always comforting.

"It's great to see you again, mum," she said when she finally leaned back.

Her mother gave her a scrutinising look. "It's great to see you too, dear. Come on, let's get you home."

Their family driver, who'd been with them for years, took Ijay's suitcase when she said hello to him. They all walked down to the car park.

"How was the flight?" her mother asked.

"Uneventful." Ijay shrugged defensively.

"And Abuja?" Her mother gave her another examining look. Ijay tried not to blush under her stare. Her mother knew her children very well and rarely missed a thing.

"It's a great city. I haven't seen much of it yet. What I've see is good."

"Good," her mum nodded as the driver loaded the boot with Ijay's luggage and they got into the car.

The car left the airport headed in the slow evening traffic for Victoria Garden City where her parents lived. Sitting next to each other in the back seats, her mother took Ijay's hand.

"Ijeoma Clarissa Amadi, what is the matter?"

Her mother rarely ever addressed her using her full name. Whenever she did it was either as a reprimand or to get her attention.

She looked at her mum. The concerned expression on her mother face made Ijay blink while fighting the tears clogging her throat.

"Talk to me. I know something's wrong. You are usually more enthusiastic about coming home. You look pale, like you're dreading being here. What's going on?"

"Oh mum, it's a long story."

"Well, it's a long drive to VGC. Is it work?"

"Yes and no. I messed up. I cheated on Vincent with Paul. Now Vincent is angry and I think the wedding is off."

"Wow, wow. You did what? Who is Paul and what exactly did you do?"

Taking a deep breath and releasing it, Ijay told her mother everything. Well, almost everything.

Chapter Thirteen

"Are you sure Paul is Vincent's brother?" her mother asked, the look of unmistakable surprise on the older woman's face.

Ijay found that discussing her dilemma with her mother turned out to be therapeutic. She didn't go into the full details of her one-night stand with Paul who had been practically a stranger at the time.

No mother wanted to hear about the sexual exploits of their children, no matter how liberal their own outlook. Moreover, it was bad enough telling her mother she would've cheated on her fiancé and having to deal with the embarrassment factor too.

Luckily her mother was more interested in the fact that Paul was Vincent brother and Ijay hadn't known until today.

"Yes, definitely. As soon as I mentioned Vincent's name last night, Paul shut down faster than the Nigerian national grid cuts the power. And this afternoon, when I told Vincent about Paul, he said Paul was his brother."

"Hmmm. This is quite peculiar." The crease on her mother's face deepened.

"You can say that again. Now that I think of it, I never even mentioned Paul's name to Vincent but he knew straight away whom I was referring to. How is that possible?" Ijay lifted her hand and rubbed it against her lips as she thought about her conversation with Vincent again.

"I really think it's odd that Vincent has a brother whom he's never mentioned to you. You are supposed to be getting married in a few weeks." Her mother looked at her again with an unbelieving look.

"I've been in shock trying to process everything. Even though I can't remember mentioning Paul's name, Vincent obviously knows about him." Ijay shook her head and stared at the road through the windshield, barely seeing the traffic in front.

"You must have said something to him. Maybe when you were discussing working in Abuja," her mother persisted.

"I mentioned Havers & Child had won a bid to work for a company in Abuja but I'm not sure I mentioned the company name or the owner. I don't know. Maybe I did," Ijay conceded.

"Well, don't worry about that for now. I'm sure it'll all be sorted out when you speak to Vincent again."

"Mum, do you really think he'll ever speak to me? I'm afraid he's going to call the wedding off."

"Listen there's no need to panic. He's a man. His ego has been hurt. He probably just needs a few days to cool off, and then you both can talk again more rationally next time."

"I hope so, mum."

"So tell me about Paul. What's he like?"

"Mum?"

"Come on. I want to know about the man who lured my daughter away from her fiancé. I know you. You are as loyal as anyone I know. Once you get into something you never give up on it. As a child, once you were given a toy, you would play with that one toy until it was ragged and broken before you would turn your attention to another toy. No amount of cajoling ever made you look at another toy."

"This is different."

"No, it's not. You've carried the same attribute throughout your life. I know you would never cheat on Vincent unless Paul was more than a passing fancy. You care about this Paul, don't you?"

She let out a sigh. "I do. A lot. I never planned to," Ijay said, finally admitting it out loud. A sense of relief swept over her. "I didn't know how much I cared about him, until I saw him again. But I told myself it's too late. I've already made the commitment to Vincent. I can't back out of it now. Moreover, Paul doesn't want anything permanent with me. So why even bother?"

"How do you know he doesn't want anything more? Neither of you have given it a chance," her mother replied.

"Mum, are you saying I should've given Paul another chance?" she asked in shock. Was her mother condoning her cheating on Vincent?

"That's not what I'm saying. I'm simply trying to tell you not to beat yourself up. Vincent didn't handle things too well with you. There are ways the two of you could have explored intimacy that would've set your mind at ease and helped you resist Paul more. So Vincent is not innocent in this. That's what I'm saying."

"I feel so guilty, though."

"That's only natural. So tell me about him."

"The truth is Paul is still an enigma. I know very little about him. However, I do know that he's an astute businessman and natural leader. Working with him so far has been great. He's very attentive and encouraging. He's passionate about his business and the people that work for him. That passion also translates into his personal dealings with me. He makes me feel protected and wanted. When he looks at me, I feel like I'm the only woman on earth. Does that make sense?"

"It does, my dear. How does that compare to Vincent?" her mother probed further.

"I don't know what Vincent is like at work," Ijay explained.

"I've never really been to see him there. Recently things haven't been so great with us. He's been very busy with work. I didn't feel I was getting the attention I deserved from him. Okay, so there isn't the kind of sizzling passion I feel with Paul. But Vincent is consistent and stable. He's a doctor, so obviously he cares about people. And if it wasn't for my mess up, he'd still be here tomorrow. This is something I cannot guarantee with Paul."

"My dear, in life, you cannot guarantee anything. I know that naturally humans want to settle for the safe and comfortable. Sometimes to get the best of life, you have to take a leap into the unknown."

"Paul is such an unknown, mum. He won't even talk to me. Sometimes when I look into his eyes he looks so lost and tormented. Like there is something inside him eating him up. I hate that he won't let me close enough to help him."

A smile spread out on her mother's face, surprising Ijay. "Do you remember Lucky the dog?" Mrs. Amadi asked, her eyes twinkling with amusement.

"Of course I do, mum." Ijay remembered her pet Labrador that died five years ago.

"Remember when we found him he was lost, starved and wounded," her mother continued.

"We were afraid he was rabid. You insisted you wanted to take him home. We had to take him to the vet to get him checked out first. After treatment, we finally brought him home. I remember your face when he came home. You were ecstatic but disappointed because he was very wary of people to start with. In the end you took care of him and loved him and he became a lifelong family pet until the end."

"Yes," Ijay choked out, tears stinging her eyes. She'd loved that dog. They had all grieved for him as a member of the family when he died.

"Well, you might have to look at Paul the same way. Unfortunately there are people who are broken and wary of other people. They need patience and love to coax them into accepting your love."

"I've already told him I don't want to have anything to do with him." Ijay said, her heart clenching when she remembered the distressed look on Paul's face this morning. Why should he listen to her when she'd been quick to dismiss him?

"First things first. You have to talk with Vincent. If you believe that your heart lies with Vincent, then by all means I'll help you all I can to resolve things. But don't settle for Vincent just because he proposed to you first. That would be wrong and you'll regret it. Trust me on this." Her mother had a glazed melancholic expression.

"Mum, is there something I should know?" Ijay frowned, suddenly worried.

"I've never told you this before, but I think its pertinent now." Her mother just stared straight ahead as she spoke. "When I met your father, I was dating someone else. It was in the early eighties and there were not as many inter-racial relationships as they are now. I fell in love with your father. He was young, suave and intelligent studying for his doctorate degree at the same University I was working.

"Yet I couldn't do anything about it because I was sure my parents wouldn't approve and I didn't want to disappoint my parents. So I stuck with my boyfriend. It wasn't until your father was getting ready to return to Nigeria that I bumped into him in the faculty late one evening. He invited me out to dinner and confessed he was in love with me. He wanted to marry me and take me back to Nigeria. You can imagine the surprise. But I knew then I couldn't let him go without me. Well, the rest is history."

"Wow," Ijay gasped. "I never knew that...What happened with grandpa and grandma?"

"They weren't happy to start with but eventually came around to the idea," her mother replied. "I thought about all that time I'd wasted not doing what I wanted to do. Of course my ex-boyfriend was not happy either. He too got over it and eventually married another of my friends."

"So everything worked out for everyone?" Ijay asked tentatively.

"Yes and that's my point. You have to go with your heart, my dear. And whatever you decide, you'll have my support and your father's. I promise you."

"What about the traditional wedding and all the guests?" Ijay still wasn't convinced everything would work out fine. Paul was a huge gamble that she wasn't sure her heart could cope with if she lost. She remembered the disappointment with Frederick and how that had destroyed her confidence with men. Paul had given her back that confidence. It could be shattered again if things didn't work out.

"These days, people cancel weddings frequently. I wouldn't worry about it. Your father and I'll handle it. It's simply a question of talking to his kinsmen at home."

Well, if her mother was encouraging her to take a chance then she really owed it to herself. She really needed to talk to Vincent again first, though. Thankfully while she was in Lagos she didn't have to see or speak to Paul, so there would be no distractions. She'd give Vincent a day to cool off and call him on Sunday.

"Thank you so much mum." She hugged her mum tightly. "You don't know how much this means to me."

***

Ijay's Saturday turned out relatively uneventful. It was great just relaxing at home, hanging out with her younger sister Uloma who was twenty-seven and lived at home. Uloma worked for a big retail bank at Victoria Island. They went out to the Palms shopping mall and later that evening Silverbirds cinema.

On Sunday, the family went out to the early morning service at Church. It was always the routine so they could come back in time to prepare lunch. They were relaxing at home after lunch when they had a visitor.

Ijay and Uloma were sitting outside in the garden, under the shade of the canopy while Uloma regaled her of events at her workplace, when the bell at the gate rang. Both Ijay and Uloma went to see who the unexpected guest was at the gates.

"That's Mrs. Arinze," Uloma said, when she opened the side pedestrian gate and saw the silver Landcruiser Prado just outside their gates.

"Really? How do you know her?"

Ijay's heart thudded as she peered to have a look too. She could only make out the outline of the passenger at the back noting it was a woman. The windows had dark screens covering them. She hadn't planned on seeing her mother-in-law yet. Vincent was supposed to take her to meet his

144

mother when he arrived in Lagos in a few weeks. Why was the woman here today?

"Yes. She's been here a few times, always going on about her perfect son, Vincent who is a doctor in London," Uloma said with exaggerated irony and a huge shrug as she walked over and pulled one end of the gates while Ijay pulled back the other.

"Oh? Interesting," Ijay replied and lifted her hand to hide the laughter bubbling inside her. Uloma was the family clown and would make jokes out of every situation. If Mrs. Arinze was boastful about her son's achievements, it was no wonder.

When the car drove in and the dark-skinned woman in dark glasses, gold embroidered lace *iro* and *buba* and matching accessories stepped out of the back seat, Ijay recognised Vincent's mother from a photograph she'd seen of the woman. She looked very elegant and classy.

"Welcome, Mrs. Arinze," Ijay said and she curtsied to the woman.

The woman looked at her in surprise. "You know me?" she asked.

"Yes, I'm Ijay." She smiled shyly. Gosh, this was her future mother-in-law in the flesh. Feeling a little daunted, she swallowed the lump in her throat at seeing the woman especially now that things were rocky with Vincent.

"Oh, my daughter. I'm pleased to see you. You are more beautiful than the pictures Vincent sent me." Mrs. Arinze smiled amiably, flashing white teeth.

Ijay's face heated up and she blushed. "Thank you."

Uloma who'd been locking the gates again approached them.

"Uloma, how are you? Is your mother home?" Mrs. Arinze asked.

"I'm fine, mummy." Uloma replied with a curtsy. "Yes, she's inside."

Mrs. Arinze had already started walking to the door. Behind her, Uloma rolled her eyes and nudged her sister. Ijay waved her hand silently, gesturing that she should behave herself. She didn't want her mischievous sister getting her into trouble with her mother-in-law-to-be.

When they got inside, Ijay and Uloma brought out refreshments before leaving the two older women together. They went upstairs in their two-storey duplex and chose Uloma's room because they could listen out and see when Mrs. Arinze departed.

As they waited, Uloma volunteered to go and eavesdrop on the women's conversation. Ijay was tempted. She wanted to find out if Vincent had told his mother already about their conversation and if that meant the wedding was off. If that was the case, she didn't know whether to be happy or sad about it.

In the end she convinced Uloma not to eavesdrop. They would wait for their mother to tell them the reason for Mrs. Arinze's visit. In the meantime, Uloma tried her best to keep Ijay distracted by continuing the story they were chatting about outside. After a while, they heard the sound of a car leaving and the two girls raced downstairs to meet their mother.

Seeing the worried expression on her mother's face as the woman came back inside, Ijay's stomach knotted with apprehension.

"I need to speak to you," Ijay's mum said before sitting down gently on the sofa. She looked like she was about to deliver some horrible news.

"What's happened? Is the wedding off?" Ijay asked and sat down gingerly next to her mum. Uloma sat on the adjacent sofa.

"No. Not yet. There's something else," her mum replied, her face still pleated in worry lines. "Vincent's mother confirmed that Paul is Vincent's younger brother from his late father's former concubine."

"Okay. And?" That explained why they were brothers and Ijay didn't know. It was surprising. Yet, she didn't think that was the worst news from the worried expression on her mother's face.

"She says Paul was so disturbed and destructive, his father almost disowned him because he raped a girl."

"Gosh! No way. That's not true, mum. I can't believe that," Ijay replied instantly shaking her head even as bile rose in her throat. The Paul she knew would never force anyone to have sex.

"She says the clothes used by the assailant were found in his room, including the hood worn. That's why he was arrested. She showed me a copy of the arrest record from eighteen years ago."

"Really? Oh no," Ijay cried out, gripping her knees in her hands. Nausea rose in her throat, her head spinning. She felt like she was going to throw up.

Why, Paul? Why?

"I know, it's really bad," her mum continued. "Vincent is happy to go ahead with the wedding but they want you to be safe from Paul. So they've asked you to step down from the project. It would be best for you and give Vincent the peace of mind that Paul won't harm you."

Ijay looked up, the distress she felt slowly turning to annoyance, her hands gripping her dress. "Mum, you know that's blackmail, right. They can't tell me who to work for?"

"Well, if you want the wedding to go ahead, those are their conditions."

Chapter Fourteen

What a fool!

Paul shifted in his seat, physically adjusting and mentally willing the swell in his trousers to subside. He allowed the rage he felt to boil over in his veins. Slowly, it overtook the pulse of desire razing his body with heat, the cool air blowing from the car air-conditioner finally having an effect on his hot skin.

His body was unavoidably responding to the effect of sitting so close to Ijay on their trip to the airport. Her sweet fragrance filled the enclosed space of the car—arousing and intoxicating. A side effect of his insistence to continue working with her even when his mind wanted to send her back to London and save his body the torment of her presence.

What antiquated sense of chivalry had overcome him that he'd agreed to leave Ijay alone when she'd asked him—eyes blazing with determination, bosoms heaving from agitation—on Friday? When what he'd wanted to do was bend her over his desk and sate the ache that was now slowly driving him insane.

What sentimental poison had gotten into his veins that he considered what she said she wanted of importance compared to what he knew she wanted? When he knew she wanted him as much as he wanted her. He could stake his life on it.

As she'd stood in front of his desk on Friday morning and threatened to walk off the project if he didn't back off, she'd still been aroused by his presence. Her rouge coloured skin had told the tale even if her red lips hadn't.

He could've called her bluff. He could've shut off her protests by kissing her, pushing her to test her resolve. Instead he'd allowed the warm ache in his heart to overwhelm the pulsing need in his groin. Now he was paying the price with a raging need that coursed through his veins and refused to be satisfied by anyone else.

He lifted his line of sight from the sheaf of paper in his hand he was supposed to be reading and glanced in Ijay's direction. Her shoulders were stiff and straight. She sat tensely, her back slightly turned as she gazed out of the window.

The landscape was of arid Savannah, the scattered trees and dried out brown grass whizzing past as the car speed down the highway toward the airport on the outskirts of Abuja town.

At this time of year, the heat of the sun scorched the earth mercilessly and left everything in its wake parched and brown. The only greenery visible was patches of irrigated farmlands interspersed with fallow land. This area was sparsely populated with only a few villages and houses to be seen from the road.

"There's just so much space and so little people over here compared to Lagos," Ijay said distractedly. Her soft voice travelled through him, leaving him feeling breathless. He inhaled sharply in surprise. It was as if she'd read his thoughts.

"I know. That's the reason I prefer the relative calmness of Abuja and Enugu to Lagos," he replied with a smile on his face, hoping she'd turn around and face him.

They were the only two cities he wanted to live in. Nowhere else appealed to him. He wanted her to see it in his eyes and understand. He needed her to understand that about him.

"I have to admit Lagos can be chaotic. That's the fun of it I guess. Having lived and worked in London, I guess I can relate." Finally, she turned round, leaning back in her seat. Her full lips lifted in a reflective smile as her warm brown gaze met his and held.

It was the first time he'd seen her smile since she arrived back in the office this morning. His heart kicked against his chest in acknowledgement and gladness.

She'd been withdrawn throughout their meeting this morning, her gaze barely connecting with his. He hadn't tried being conversational and they'd dealt with the business at hand before moving on swiftly. He hadn't seen her for the rest of the day until they were ready to depart for the airport.

"So if you lived in Nigeria, would you prefer to live in Lagos?" Paul wasn't sure why he was asking. Since she was engaged to his half-brother, it shouldn't matter to him.

Somehow he needed to know. Did they have anything in common outside of the fiery chemistry between them? Because he knew she still felt it as much as he did. Even if she chose to deny it. Perhaps there was something else that would bind them. Some hope.

For a moment, he held his breath, waiting for her response.

"I have to admit that after spending a few days in Abuja, I found Lagos a bit rowdy over the weekend. Then again, it's where my family lives so I guess it would be nice to be close to them," she remarked with a nonchalant shrug.

Despite everything, her words made his heart sink with disappointment. He let out a sigh. He'd been foolish to hope—for what he wasn't even sure.

"How are your parents? I'm sure it was great seeing them again," he said, hoping to keep her talking.

He loved the effect of her voice on his body. There was something reassuring in the depths of her velvety voice. Also, maybe he'd find out why she was so standoffish this morning.

"It's always fantastic to see my family," she replied, her eyes flicking to the side slightly as she remembered the weekend. The enthusiasm in her voice put a smile on his face.

"My dad was cool as always. It was great catching up with my sister. And my mum is just the best. She picked me up from the airport. And straight away she picked up that all wasn't well."

Her eyes took on a melancholic glaze before she looked away.

His heart hit his ribs with a strong thud. "Really? What happened?" He asked in a rush of words, his curiosity getting the better of his manners.

"I can't talk about it," she said shaking her head and turning away.

He knew instantly that something was up and it was because of him. His eyes narrowed into slits as he placed his hand on her shoulder and nudged her insistently until she faced him again.

It wasn't the warm and chatty Ijay staring back at him. The smile was gone from her eyes. In its place was the reticent and cool glower. Somehow she was blaming him for whatever had gone wrong. He didn't care. He wanted her to tell him what had gone wrong.

"If Vincent has done something to you, I'll kill him," he bit out, a wave of anger clouding his vision in red.

"Funny thing is he said practically the same thing about you." She said in a harsh low voice.

The heat was back in her eyes. Not the welcoming, soul-searing kind. This time her brown eyes flashed angry fire at him, her hands balled on her lap as if she was restraining herself from hitting him.

Somehow, he welcomed her annoyance. It was an emotion he could deal with and meant she still felt something for him. Even if she hit him, it was better than the cold shoulder she'd been giving him.

"When did he say that?" He watched her through the thickness of his black lashes.

"On Friday when he called and I told him about what you and I'd done. He knew instantly who you were even before I mentioned your name. Go figure that one."

Ijay shook her head in amazement and annoyance. "Why is that Paul? How come your brother knew I was involved with you even before I'd told him about you? Can you explain that Paul?"

His heart raced as he took in her words. Something wasn't right. He couldn't pin it correctly yet.

"How should I know?" He went for nonchalance. He didn't want to alarm Ijay but something was definitely off. How could Vincent know if Ijay hadn't told him? "Didn't he tell you? What else did he say?"

"You mean apart from calling me a bitch and threatening to deal with you?" She retorted with disdain.

Paul clenched and unclenched his hands beside his thighs. A menacing growl rumbled in his stomach and he gritted his teeth to stop from letting it out.

"He called you that? Is he mad?" Paul said as he shook his head in wonder and disgust at Vincent. "I hope you told him where to get off. Tell me you've called off the engagement."

His hands trembled with rage as he suddenly felt confined. He needed some space to walk off the fury in his veins. He really wanted to get his hand on his mad brother. He couldn't stop the car. They were nearly at the airport and they still had a flight to catch.

"You would like that, wouldn't you? You want me to be single so you can have your wicked way with me with no guilt. Well, sorry to disappoint you. The wedding is still on."

Shocked, he reared back, the violent thoughts in his mind taking a back seat for a moment. "You can't be serious. You'll stay with a man who will be verbally abusive? What would he have done if you had that conversation in his presence? Hit you?" His stomach churned with outrage at the idea.

"Come on. He was only angry. Can you imagine what he felt when he received the news on the phone that his fiancée cheated on him with his brother? Of course I expected him to be angry. He'll cool off soon enough and come back to his senses. If anyone has the right to call off the wedding, he has. Not me."

Paul shook his head in disbelief, his eyes watching Ijay's face. Her chin was set stubbornly. She really meant her words.

"I can't believe you're saying this. I can't believe you're defending Vincent. He'll not let up, I promise you. Things will only get worse with him when you eventually see him. You have to cancel your engagement before it's too late. You'll cancel it."

He glared at her as he fought the urge to claim her pouting lips and end this ridiculous argument of theirs. Surely she wasn't so blind she couldn't see that Vincent was a madman. Instead, she glared at him in return, her brown eyes turning fiery amber, her jaw tightened.

"You Arinzes are very good at ordering people about, aren't you? Well, I have news for you. I do what I want, when I want."

The hardness of her tone stunned him for a moment, striking him with the storm of her anger. She turned to open the door as the car had already stopped in front of the terminal building.

Paul couldn't let her walk out of the car without letting her know they were not done yet. If he didn't have a flight to catch, he'd send the chauffeur out and lock her in this car until she conceded. Instead, he gripped her shoulders firmly, stopping her from moving away.

"This conversation isn't over," he said when she looked up at him angrily. He let her go and stepped out of the car himself.

***

Throughout the flight to Enugu, Paul fought to control the range of emotions yo-yoing in his veins. One minute he was fighting the urge to throttle Ijay each time she flashed a defiant glare at him.

At one point he had to suppress the smile that threatened to lift his lips. He didn't want her thinking he'd relented. Yet he admired her mettle and determination.

Damn, she was stubborn. He'd realised it when she hadn't even bothered to contact him even once after their night together. He hadn't been with any other woman who'd ever ignored him afterwards. Yet Ijay had done that even when she'd admitted she'd wanted to see him again.

This was more serious. Her life could be in danger if she went ahead and married Vincent. Paul could swear that Vincent was up to something. He didn't know how Ijay met Vincent. Paul knew somehow it had to do with him. It wasn't beyond Vincent to be conniving and devious.

Vincent must've found out about his night with Ijay. This whole engagement thing could be just a move to spite Paul. He didn't want to think it but it was a strong possibility.

It wasn't beyond Vincent to send someone to track Paul's activities. He'd known that his step-mother had been tracking his movements for years. This was a new extreme low for his belligerent step-mother and brother.

In the past, Paul hadn't cared about them monitoring his activities. He was getting on with his life. He could handle himself. He worried about Ijay. She might be stubborn and strong. However, he knew what Vincent was capable of doing to a woman who offended him. It wouldn't be pleasant.

By Ijay confessing their affair to Vincent, she'd condemned herself in Vincent's eyes. Paul knew that much about his unforgiving brother. Revenge and physical violence against a woman wasn't a taboo to Vincent. Paul didn't want Ijay hurt. He wouldn't stand by and let Vincent hurt her. Still, how could he help her if she insisted on marrying Vincent?

When he took another sideways glance at Ijay, she drew her bottom lip between her teeth and pulled. Inhaling deeply, he fought the groan about to erupt from his lips and gripped the arm rest tighter. If she wasn't driving him crazy with anger, she was driving him mad with lust.

He unclipped his seatbelt, stood up and took the short walk down the business class aisle to the toilet. None of the other passengers seemed to notice the disturbing bulge in his trousers. As he slid the door shut and locked the door, he gritted his teeth at the overwhelming temptation to join the mile-high club.

"What is this woman doing to me," he muttered out loud at his harassed reflection in the small mirror above the aluminium sink.

No other woman had ever appealed to his baser instincts in such a way that he was constantly battling with quelling his sexual impulses. However he'd readily admit that if Ijay walked into this cubicle he'd happily sink into her welcoming slick depth, all sense of propriety lost.

Turning on the tap, he splashed cool water on his face. Then he grabbed a paper towel and wiped his face. Feeling a tad restrained by the enclosed space, he unwound his tie, rolled it up and stuffed it into his trouser pocket. Then he tidied his collar and undid the top two buttons on his shirt. The cool air on his skin felt good. The heat in his blood cooled too now he was away from Ijay and her intoxicating fragrance.

Feeling better, he returned to his seat next to Ijay, hoping he could get some relaxing time for the rest of the flight. It seemed Ijay didn't think so. She looked up from her magazine, her eyes searching his face with concern, her beautiful face creased at the forehead.

"Are you all right?" she asked, her velvety voice washing over his skin like a bed of feathers. A hand clamped around his heart giving it a warm squeeze. When she looked at him like that, all he wanted to do was to take her into his arms and reassure her. He wanted to promise her that everything would be all right.

Their gazes met and held for a moment. The arc of sizzling tension between them returned. Her eyes widened when his stare dropped to her lips briefly. He wanted to taste her lips again.

Just once.

He leaned closer breathing in her scent—musk and irises. Her breath hitched. She didn't move away. Instead, she watched him like a rabbit caught in a daze of bright headlights.

You promised not to go there.

Just as his lips hovered over her luscious pair, the voice in his head broke the spell. He leaned back into his chair and picked up the magazine in the seat holder.

"I'm perfectly all right," he said without looking at her, flipping the pages unseeingly.

"I know you're not all right. You've been different since you found out about Vincent. Something is bothering you. I wish you'd talk to me," she said angrily, her voice low.

"Why should I talk to you, Ijay? What am I to you apart from your client and your brother-in-law to be? You made it quite clear you don't want anything to do with me otherwise. Let's leave it that way," he spoke in a dangerously low whisper.

"Oh, you are so pig-headed. Do you think I would have given myself over to you all those months ago if I didn't care about you?" She leaned so closed to him, her warm breath whispered against his cheek with each word she spoke. Her voice still low and angry. "You want me to give up my fiancé for you and yet you're not willing to open yourself up even a little bit... I need a bit more than just sex, Paul. And Vincent will give me that—"

"The hell he will!"

Paul dropped the magazine in his hand and replaced it with a mass of Ijay's dark hair as he reached behind her neck and pulled her forward. She let out a soft gasp, her warm breath fanning his cheek as he pulled her closer and sealed their lips together.

Chapter Fifteen

You are playing with fire.

Ijay couldn't shake the thought that replayed itself over and over in her mind since they'd disembarked from the flight at Akanu Ibiam International Airport, Enugu. She gently massaged her stomach through the cool cotton of her cream-coloured sleeveless shirt. The knot of tension in her belly loosened a little as she took several deep calming breaths. She avoided looking at Paul for a few minutes.

"How is Uju?" Paul asked Amaechi, his chauffeur.

His voice sounded light and jovial, belying the tension that had sizzled between them earlier. He sat next to her in the plush soft tan leather-covered backseats of a navy-coloured BMW X5 as they travelled to her hotel.

She stole a glance at Paul. He appeared relaxed; his body sunk back into the seat, his head leaning against the headrest. One of his arms stretched across the backseats almost touching her. If she turned her face a couple of inches, his fingertips would brush her cheek.

Her skin tingled at the tempting thought, reminding her of the impact of Paul's kiss on the plane. A part of her had known the kiss was coming from the moment she'd gotten into the car with Paul on the way to the airport. The strain of emotions had rolled off his body in waves throughout their journey. From his rigid shoulders to his balled fists and of course the heat of hunger in his eyes.

Even as they'd argued about Vincent, she'd wanted to reach across and caress the day-old stubble on his dark rugged chin. She knew the short thick hairs would grate against her soft palm. She'd wanted to run her tongue along the firm edge of his lips before finally delving into the soft depth of his mouth.

"Uju is doing great. She was worried when you didn't visit Amori last week," Amaechi replied, drawing her attention back to the present.

The congenial middle-aged man dressed in a white shirt and dark trousers had greeted Paul warmly when they arrived. Ijay sensed immediately that their relationship was more than employer-employee. Now, the flow of banter between them confirmed her assumption. She hadn't sensed the same kind of rapport with Paul's Abuja chauffeur.

"You should've explained I had business in Abuja that kept me."

Ijay sensed the smile in Paul's voice, though she wasn't looking at him.

Amaechi laughed but didn't look back, glancing at the rear-view mirror instead.

"You should know my wife by now. She still chose to worry even after I explained."

Paul laughed too. The first time she'd heard him laugh since their disastrous dinner night. The sound of his laughter was like honey over toast. The temptation to close her eyes and savour the warmth spread through her body.

When she closed her eyes, she was greeted by the thunderous expression on Paul's face on the plane. And a replay of the hot crushing and branding kiss he'd given her.

The bruising press of his lips on hers, the invading sweep of his tongue in her mouth left her with no doubt as to his intent. His kiss had told her something he'd never said directly to her. He laid claim to her body in that kiss and damned anyone else who would dare to touch it.

Her body had trembled with the assault of passion. One of her hands clung onto his shoulders, the other gripping the chair arm to keep her body upright. His lips had plundered hers, his tongue delving into her mouth vociferously. There was no denying him his claim. Not that she'd wanted to rebuff him. She'd welcomed his invasion, surrendering with a soft sigh and a warm shudder.

She'd been lost in the kiss, she hadn't realised the plane was touching down until the tell-tale bump of the wheels on the runway tarmac. Paul had pulled back then, his eyes unable to hide his hunger and anger. As the plane taxied to the terminal, he'd kept silent, his body language withdrawn.

Heat spread across her cheeks as she opened her eyes and stole another glance at Paul. His eyes glittered with a warm smile as he chatted with Amaechi.

This was a different Paul. Gone was the astute and ambitious businessman. This Paul was jovial and affectionate; laughing at something Amaechi said about a girl whom she assumed was the chauffeur's daughter. It was as if breathing in the Enugu air had transformed Paul.

I love him.

She inhaled sharply and turned away to stare out of the window as the realisation hit her. Thinking of it now, she knew she'd been in love with him from their first night together in London. It was why she'd left him early the next morning. She'd been afraid to lose her heart to love another man who wouldn't love her in return.

But seeing this side of Paul gave her courage. Her mother had been right. Ijay needed to take a leap of faith. She had to give Paul a chance. Things could work out between them if they got to know each other outside of the bedroom.

Oh, she wanted to get back into his bed. To feel the passion of his kiss, his touch and his love-making again.

Most of all, she wanted the passion of his love.

That's why she had to carry on with the charade. *Let him think I still want to marry Vincent.* It was the only thing that'd keep him restrained. Paul's honour wouldn't let him touch his brother's fiancée.

When she risked another glance at his profile, Paul turned at that moment and their gazes met. The slam of her heart against her chest was so loud; she could've sworn he heard it. She gulped down the lump in her throat when he smiled at her, his lips curved in a glorious sensuous lift—inviting and irresistible. She returned the smile with gladness.

"Paul, do you have a guest annex attached to your house?" she asked conversationally, widening her smile.

He lifted his eyebrow in a query, though his eyes didn't lose their sparkling warmth. "Yes," he replied hesitantly. "Why?"

"I'm thinking I really don't want to stay in another hotel. Can I stay in your house...well, your guest annex, please?" she asked, keeping her voice sweet, her tone seductive.

She placed her hand on his thigh. His hard muscles tautened through the soft fabric of his trousers. His body heat burnt her hand. Boldly, she maintained the contact. She'd missed the feel of his firmness. That her pulse quickened and her breathing became shallow was just a hazardous side effect of her plans.

The double lines on his forehead deepened and his eyes narrowed with suspicion. "My guest annex is occupied at the moment," he said offhandedly.

His gaze travelled to her hand on his thigh. The look he gave it was similar to the one she gave a table laden with all the irresistible desserts she shouldn't eat. It was a cross between adoration and hatred. He didn't know what to do with her hand—

whether to fling it as far away from his body or allow it to caress his skin.

Now he knows what it felt like when he was teasing me at dinner!

Ijay fought to suppress the laughter bubbling in her stomach. It felt good to finally have the upper hand where Paul was concerned. "Then perhaps you have a spare room. It'd only be for three days and then I'll get out of your hair." She smiled innocently, lowering her eyelids to watch him through her lashes.

"Ijay, I don't think it's a good idea staying in my house. The Park Hotel is one of the best hotels in Nigeria. You'll be well taken care of," Paul said gruffly as the car pulled to the front entrance of the hotel set in a tree -avenue very close to Nike Lake. The lush green leaves and branches swayed in the evening breeze.

"If it helps, I'll inform Pamela to find you a short stay apartment in Abuja so you no longer have to stay in a hotel."

"Thank you," she replied immediately. Her heart sank. He hadn't taken the bait. Still she wasn't about to give up yet.

"That would be good although it's not really what I wanted. I'm sure this hotel is great. I was hoping for the convivial environment of your home rather than the cool charm of a hotel. Well, if that's what I get then I have to live with it."

She didn't hide the disappointment on her face or her voice as she turned to step out of the car.

"Wait." The urgency in Paul's voice stopped her from moving further. Her heart leapt with hope.

She hid the smile on her face by keeping her gaze out of the car window.

"Are you sure you want to stay at my house?" he asked, his voice deep and husky, his toned strained and resigned.

Her heart turned over, a twinge of guilt clamping her stomach in cramps. She felt remorse for playing this game with him. She turned around slowly to face him and met his gaze. His dark eyes studied her with curious intensity and warm tenderness.

"Yes, I want to," she replied suddenly breathless as her heart rate increased with excitement.

He nodded in response. "Okay. Stay here for a moment. I want to speak to the hotel receptionist."

Paul stepped out of the car and entered the hotel lobby. Ijay sat in the car, excitement coursed through her veins.

Yes! She was going to stay in Paul's house.

It was a high risk strategy considering they seemed unable to keep their hands off each other when they were alone. However she didn't think she'd ever get the opportunity of seeing the true Paul except in his own environment outside work. Living in his lair for a few days should reveal more to her than anything he'd tell her; if he'd ever talk to her about personal stuff.

She just hoped her plans didn't backfire, consuming in the flames that were sure to erupt when Paul found out the truth.

Paul returned to the car and instructed Amaechi to take them home. Ijay sat back in her chair, suppressing her smug smile.

"I hope I can get to see much of Enugu while I'm here. It's my first time in the city," she said in a friendly tone.

It was already dusk, the last rays of the sunshine creating an orange glow in the darkening horizon. The evening road traffic was heavy, although not as congested as rush hour in Lagos. Immediately she sensed the city's appeal to Paul. It was serene with none of the hustle and bustle that characterised living in Lagos. The roads were smooth and the sidewalks clean. The environment was green and leafy with tree-lined avenues and low shrubbery surrounding houses.

Paul looked at her, his brow lifted in a stunned query. "You would?"

"Yes. I'd love to know what it is about the city you love so much," she replied, beaming him a friendly smile.

His dark eyes sparkled as he returned the smile. He really was gorgeous when he smiled, the harsh angles of his face softened by laughter lines. "Hopefully, if we finish with the factory visits early enough, I'll get to show you the city. I spent some of my best times here as a boy and young man."

"Really? You were born here?" she asked excited that he was already loosening up and willing to chat.

"No, I was born in Lagos. My father sent me to boarding school here when I was old enough," he answered conversationally.

"Perhaps, you'll get to show me your old school one day." She knew she was pushing it. Still, she had to keep going now.

He looked at her curiously again, scrutinising her as if trying to figure out her motive for wanting to know so much. Her face heated up as she blushed under his scrutiny.

"Perhaps," he said ominously.

The car pulled up in front of wrought iron gates in a house surrounded by high fencing. Ijay couldn't make out much of the building inside. It looked large and imposing.

"Simon, open the gates," Paul spoke into his mobile phone.

A few minutes later, the gates slid back. They drove into a wide paved driveway. The car stopped in front of a portico with Greco-Roman white pillars. The house was a large modern two-storey building with white-washed walls and neo-Georgian windows.

Paul stepped out of the car and Ijay shortly followed suit. For a moment she couldn't speak and had to close her mouth wide open in amazement.

"Welcome to my home, Ijay," Paul said, his voice filled with emotion and a warm smile on his face. He appeared genuinely happy to have her there.

"Thank you," she said unable to hide the curiosity in her voice. "You live here alone?"

He frowned at her, his brow lifted in a mocking query as if she'd asked a stupid question. "With my family, of course."

His family?

A wave of nausea hit Ijay. She leant onto the car for support to hold up her wobbly legs as she fought the dizzy spell that took hold of her.

Chapter Sixteen

"Welcome, big bro."

Still stunned, Ijay lifted her head and looked up; distracted momentarily from her worrying thoughts, as the young man who'd opened the gates greeted Paul enthusiastically.

Strangely, she welcomed the distraction and shoved aside the blanket of despair that hit her mind. There had to be a simple explanation for Paul's reference to his family. Surely he wouldn't have brought her to his family home if he was married.

So she focused on the young man. He was almost as tall as Paul, lanky and looked in his late teens or early twenties, dressed in blue denim and black t-shirt with stylish trainers on his feet. He'd addressed Paul as big brother. Still, that could be just an African thing—a boy's way of showing respect to an older man. It didn't mean they were related.

"Thank you, Simon. It's good to be home," Paul answered with a bright smile as the boy approached. "How's school?"

"Not bad at the moment," the young man replied as Paul clasped his shoulder.

Ijay studied Simon's face in the fading light. The slash of his eyebrows and strong curve of his nose were similar to Paul's. He could pass for a younger version of Paul.

That wasn't possible, or was she just seeing things?

"Good. This is Ijay. She'll be staying with us for a few days." Paul turned to Ijay, his eyes twinkling with humour. He looked animated. It was the most excited she'd seen him in days.

"You're welcome," Simon greeted with a welcoming smile, drawing her attention back to him.

"Thank you," Ijay replied returning the smile.

Despite her misgivings, when two charming men were smiling down at her with such warmth, it was tough not to give in and go with the flow. She'd find out what was going on soon enough.

Simon moved to help Amaechi who was getting the luggage out of the car boot.

"Please bring the bags inside," Paul said as he extended his hand to Ijay, indicating she should follow him.

Ijay followed Paul inside the house. They walked through a wide hallway with marble flooring and original landscape paintings by Nigerian artist Kanayo Ede, hanging on the walls. He led her into a spacious living room. The marble flooring continued in here too. And more paintings on the wall with sculptures and figurines in the room corners.

One picture hanging on the wall in a focal position drew Ijay's attention. It wasn't an oil painting on canvas. Rather, it was the framed picture of a beautiful young woman in traditional Ibo attire. The woman seemed to be smiling down on them benevolently.

Curious, Ijay wanted to ask who the woman was as she studied the picture. However, she bit her tongue choosing to keep silent for now.

"Please sit down," Paul said, waving his hand to one of the tan coloured leather sofas. "I need to arrange for a room to be prepared for you."

Her shoulders stiffened with apprehension. Since Paul had announced he lived with his family, someone would have to vacate a room for her benefit. It made her uncomfortable. She sat down tentatively and fiddled with the straps of her shoulder bag on her lap.

"Should I put all the bags in your room?" Simon's cheerful voice made her look up. He stood just under the archway leading to the hallway.

The question caused embarrassment to sting her cheeks with heat. If Simon had to ask that question, then he'd already assumed she was lovers with Paul. Yet, the question also set a flicker of hope within her heart. There was no other woman currently occupying Paul room. He didn't have a wife living in this house. Nor in any other house. Slowly, she let out a breath of relief.

"No, put Ijay's bag in the adjacent room," Paul replied. "Please make sure it's decent."

"No worries." Simon left with the bags.

All of a sudden, insecurity plagued her mind. Did Paul bring women regularly to his house? Did they share his bedroom during their stay?

Bitterness rose in her throat with envy. She didn't like the idea of other women coming to Paul's house regularly.

However, she disliked the idea that Paul was putting her into a separate room from his even more.

"I'm really sorry to put you out like this," she said out loud. "If I'd known it would be such a problem, I wouldn't have imposed. I don't want to cause any problems, really. Strangely for some reason, I thought you had a wife."

Stunned, Paul's brows lifted, his mouth opened and closed. He looked at her like she'd gone mad. "A wife? What made you think I had one?"

"Well, you mentioned your family and I thought--"

"You thought wrong! You think I had a wife and I was messing around with you. Is that what you think of me?"

"I'm sorry. I don't know what came over me." Looking away shamefaced, she balled her hands on her laps. She really was making a mess of things already. And she'd only been in his house all of two minutes.

"You can't just jump to conclusions about people," he said in a low voice ringed with irritation.

"Says the man who assumed I was engaged to Frederick," she retorted sarcastically as she turned back to glare at him. "You've got to tell me who Simon is and what you meant by family."

Paul's chest rose and fell in a frustrated sigh.

"Listen. That conversation will have to wait. I'm going to make sure everything is set up for you," he said brusquely. "I won't be long." He turned and walked out of the room.

Ijay let out her own aggravated sigh. It seemed that for every step forward she took with Paul, she took another step backward. She really had to find a way of making sure he was more relaxed around her. Their constant arguments wouldn't help her cause.

A few minutes later an older dark-skinned woman walked in. She was dressed in a flowing guinea print boubou. She didn't look like the woman in the picture on the wall. And she didn't quite look old enough to be Paul's mother. Perhaps an aunty? Ijay stood as was customary when an older person walked into a room.

"Good evening, ma," she greeted the woman with a bright smile.

"*Nno nwa m,*" the woman replied smiling widely. *Welcome, my daughter.*

Ijay liked the woman instantly. Her smile was warm and genuine.

"*Dalu.* Thank you," she replied.

She rarely spoke in Ibo language these days except occasionally with her father. So it didn't roll of her tongue as easily as it used to. Somehow she wanted to connect with this woman on her level.

The woman looked really pleased that Ijay had replied in Ibo. "Well done. You speak Ibo well," she carried on speaking in Ibo to her. "Sit down." She gestured for Ijay to sit as she sat on the armchair adjacent to Ijay's sofa.

"Not as fluently as I used to. I enjoy speaking it when I do," Ijay replied again in Ibo when she'd sat back down.

"You do and that's important."

"Please, don't be angry. Paul didn't tell me about anyone here. Are you his mother?" Ijay asked. She didn't think she should carry on chatting with this woman without at least finding out her relationship with Paul. Since the woman seemed chatty, it was as good an opportunity as ever.

"No. I'm not," the woman replied, shaking her head sadly. "That's his mother's picture on the wall."

She pointed to the photo Ijay had noticed earlier.

"Unfortunately she died when he was just a boy. I'm Simon's mother. Simon is Paul's half-brother through their father. Paul is such a good boy. God will keep blessing him. He took us in after his father died and I was left destitute."

Everything suddenly made sense to Ijay after hearing Simon's mother words. The woman sniffed and swiped her eyes.

"I'm sorry to hear that," Ijay replied suddenly unsure of what to do at the woman's tears. Guilty pangs shot through her for asking the question that upset her.

"Don't mind me. I get emotional when I retell the story." Simon's mother stood up. "When Paul comes down, tell him dinner will be ready shortly. I hope you like *Nsala soup*. It's his favourite."

As Simon's mother turned to leave, Paul walked into the living room.

"Did someone mention *Nsala soup*? I'm suddenly very hungry."

As if in response, Ijay's stomach growled loudly in protest. For a moment, she cringed, wanting to hide under a rock. She clutched her stomach.

"Sorry," she said with a weak smile, trying to hide her horror.

Paul and his step-mother exchanged amused glances and burst out laughing. Surprised she gave Paul a mock glare and smiled. She hadn't been expecting Paul to be in a good mood after their heated discussion a few minutes previously. It seemed it was all forgotten. At least, for the moment.

"Aunty, you should hurry with the food before we die of hunger here," Paul said and winked at Ijay mischievously.

"Yes, I'm off to dish out the food fast then," Simon's mother said and left the room.

"Come, let me show you your room before dinner," Paul nodded toward the door.

Ijay stood and walked with him. She was glad he was back to being in a chirpy mood after her faux pas earlier. It was much better dealing with him when he was in a friendly mood rather than arguing with him all the time. She followed him up the light and airy stairwell. At the top, there was an open plan sitting area at one end and four doors leading to bedrooms, she guessed.

He opened one of the doors. "This is your room." He waited by the door, not going in. "It isn't the Park hotel but I hope it's suitable."

Ijay walked in. It was a tastefully decorated large room with an en-suite and walk-in closet. In the middle was a made-up bed with crisp clean cotton sheets and a red throw-over folded down the bottom. The room looked like a Mistress suite if not a Master suite.

"It's more than I expected. Thank you," she said breathlessly. She hadn't been expecting him to go to all that trouble.

"I'll leave you for a moment. Dinner will be ready soon, so don't be long."

"No worries. I'll just clean up quickly and come downstairs."

When Paul closed the door behind him, Ijay released a deep breath in relief. She was finally in Paul's house. And what she'd learnt so far about him proved she'd made the right decision to stay here.

It also showed Paul was a deeply compassionate and caring man despite his hard exterior.

Only a person who had a huge capacity to love would open up his heart and home to others, the way Paul seemed to have done. He cared about his family and they cared about him in return.

There was hope for her and Paul yet.

Feeling elated, she washed her hands in the en-suite sink, checked her appearance in the full length mirror on the wall and left her room to find Paul.

***

When Ijay arrived downstairs, dinner turned out to be a cosy affair set just for two. Puzzled, she looked up at Paul who was already seated when she stepped into the dinner area adjoining the sitting room.

"Is it just the two of us eating?" she queried a little disheartened. She'd been hoping to get to chat with Simon and perhaps find out a little bit more about Paul and his relationship with his younger sibling.

"Yes," he shrugged. "They seem to think you're someone important to me. And they don't want to ruin a private evening."

"They? Didn't you explain?"

"I tried. Simon claims he has a test to study for tomorrow. And his mum? Well...she claims she'd eaten anyway." Paul shrugged dismissively.

"Is it just the two of them living here? Do you have any more family I'm yet to meet?"

"Simon and his mother live mainly in the guest annex, although I've given them free access to the rest of the house," Paul said. "He's studying Law at the University of Nigeria Enugu Campus, so living here is handy for him to get to school. His mother insists she wants to pay her way, so she works as housekeeper. Really, she's more like an aunt than an employee. I love having both of them here."

The tormented shadows glazed over his eyes for a moment. Her heart turned over with love. She reached out and covered his hand with hers. He glanced down at her hand and gave her a brief melancholic smile. Then he covered her hand with his other hand. His warmth seeped through her skin. She hoped she was giving him as much comfort as he gave her by holding onto her.

"Why didn't you tell me about them before?" she asked gently.

She would've understood him better if she'd known all this about him. He was more than a hardnosed business man living a playboy lifestyle in Abuja. In Enugu, he was a responsible family man with dependants that he cared about. It was such a contrast. Yet that was Paul. An enigma.

The melancholic glaze departed from his eyes, replaced by a hard glint. He moved his hands away from hers, leaving her cold.

"Ijay, you seem to forget your place. You're my brother's fiancée. Shouldn't you be asking him all these questions? Why didn't he tell you he had half-brothers dotted across Nigeria," he spat the words at her with such force, it felt like she'd been physically hit. He pushed the chair back, the scrap of wood against marble resounding in the dining room. Without another word he walked out of the room.

Chapter Seventeen

You've done it this time.

Ijay let out a resigned sigh as she clutched her head and squeezed in frustration. She'd allowed her enthusiasm to run away with her. The result was a bad case of foot-in-mouth syndrome.

And a very annoyed Paul.

As much as she wanted Paul to open up and talk to her, she realised it might take a lot longer than she'd like. In the mean time, she'd have to bite her tongue and learn some patience. A trait she wasn't best at.

She looked at the dishes of food laid out on the table. It was her fault that Paul was not enjoying his meal. The aromatic scent of the food made her mouth water. It was unfair that he was missing out because of her.

She moved her chair back to stand up. Paul strode back into the room. Her pulse rate increased, her heart thudding n her chest.

Without saying anything he pulled his chair back and sat down again. She searched his face to figure out what mood he was in. His expression was unreadable.

She took a deep breath before speaking. "Paul, I'm sorry."

He looked up. His black gaze connected with hers—intense and calculated, heated and in control. Gone was the warm and fuzzy Paul. Back was the man-in-charge-of-his-domain Paul. She knew instantly the game was up.

"Are you?" he said coldly, his eyebrow raised sardonically.

Reaching across the table he grabbed her hand. He caressed the back of her hand, the rough texture of his callused palm sensitising the back of her hand. Sensation speared through her body. She inhaled sharply, her stare fixated on Paul, her body alert and aware of the arc of tension between them.

"I don't know what game you're up to," he said, his voice low and deep. "One minute you're insisting you're going to marry my brother. The next minute you tell me you care about me. One minute you don't want to get personal. The next you want to stay in my house and ask me personal questions."

He loomed closer, near enough for his breath to fan her cheek and neck. She inhaled his raw spice and cologne. Her skin flushed with feverish heat. She struggled to keep her body from trembling as her core melted.

"I'm trying very hard to not break a promise," he continued his gravelly whisper, his intent unmistakable. "However if you carry on with this little game of yours, then I promise you'll be screaming my name with pleasure so quickly. By the time I'm done, you won't remember the name

Vincent or your ridiculous engagement. Are we clear, sweet Ijay?"

Her face warmed up both from the heat of his breath against her cheeks and his provoking words. She gulped down the lump in her throat loudly and nodded vigorously. Her mouth suddenly dry and barring any speech.

The vision of the two of them entwined, hot and sweaty was clear and vibrant; a full high definition playback visual.

Except...right now she didn't want just an optical illusion. She wanted a full physical re-enactment. Her body came alive with arousal; her breasts got heavier, her nipples tautened and her core creamed.

"No, sweet Ijay, that's not good enough. I want to hear you say it." He continued his exquisite entrancing caress of her hand, his finger tips drawing slow circles on her sensitive skin. "Shall we play or are you still hung up on getting married?" he said insolently.

She flinched, blinking rapidly.

His words stung, like a slap on the face. He'd seen through her ruse. She'd been so carried away with her plan working well that she'd forgotten how dangerous Paul could be. He was a predator only caged by his honour. Not because she'd tamed him. He wasn't broken. The feral glint in his eyes told her as much.

She'd been deluding herself that she was in control. He was only letting her think she was. The warning was clear as day.

Yet, her body wanted to get intimate with Paul. The aching pulse at her melting core needed his strength and rigidity to sooth it.

Gosh, she'd missed him—the sexy authority of his presence, the heat of desire in his eyes and the masterful pleasure of his touch.

He was so close, his heat and spice surrounded her. Just a tilt of her head and their lips would connect. Her heart raced as her mind hovered in indecision.

Yield; have mind-blowing sex and then what? Nothing.

The sobering thought snapped her out of the steamy haze surrounding her body. She wanted more from Paul.

She tugged at her hand. He held on to it, his dark brow rose in an impatient query. "What'll it be?"

"I won't ask you any more personal questions," she whispered hoarsely, barely able to speak properly, her brain still focused on feeling, smelling and seeing Paul.

"Right." He released her hand instantly.

Her heart sank, her body bereft of his touch and warmth. A part of her wished she was brave enough to accept his challenge and play his game. Somehow, she knew she'd be the loser.

"Then, let's eat this food. Aunty won't be happy to come in and see the food untouched," he continued before washing his hands and uncovering the dishes.

The spicy smell of the food wafted around the room. Ijay inhaled deeply. The food really smelled heavenly. As Paul tucked in unreservedly, she decided to push everything else aside herself and enjoy the meal.

***

The next day they left early for the factory which was about an hour's drive from Enugu. Paul had told her to wear something more casual and comfortable than a business suit which was her normal working gear. He was dressed in navy linen shirt and trousers. She'd chosen a simple sky blue linen shift dress. She was grateful for the lighter clothing as the day was hot, the sun blazing brightly in the cerulean sky.

On the way Paul briefed her on what to expect at the factory. He was back to being serious and professional. She was grateful for the reprieve. Her close shave from last night pushed to the back of her mind.

The scenery along the way changed very quickly from cityscape to countryside, concrete buildings replaced by trees and farmland. Halfway there they got off the dual-carriage highway onto a minor tarred road that went through miles of greenery— thick vegetation of palm trees as far as the eyes could see—before they arrived at a populated area.

The factory was a large industrial building located in a massive plot of land surrounded by woodland in the countryside. It was marked by high concrete walls and a security gate. A small building next to the gate housed the security man who waved at them as the car drove in.

"This is POD Foods processing plant," Paul said when he got out of the car. Ijay's first reaction was amazement at the scale of the building; her mouth open in awe.

"Wow. I'm impressed," she said when she pulled her lips closed. "I wasn't expecting it to be this large."

A middle-aged man in grey and black Ankara print trouser and shirt greeted them at the entrance to the building.

"Ijay, this is Mr. Obi, the factory manager," Paul said. "John, Ms. Amadi is the consultant I told you about who's going to help us grow our brand image. She's here for a few days to see how we work."

"You're welcome, Ms. Amadi. I hope your time with us will be enlightening. If you need anything, please ask," Mr Obi said with a smile.

"Thank you," Ijay replied returning the smile.

"I'll take Ijay up to the office briefly, and then I'll be down to show her around the production line. I hope all is well today."Paul led the way into the building with Ijay close to him.

"There's no problem at all today. Everything is on track." The manager walked behind them.

"Good," Paul said before turning to Ijay. "This way."

Ijay followed him up some metal stairs in the hanger-type interior of the factory. At the top she looked down and saw most of the open area of the factory floor. She spotted close to twenty men and women working at different stages of the semi-automated production lines. The office was a glass-walled small space with a small wooden desk, two leather chairs and a metal file storage cabinet on the corner.

Paul sat behind the desk and indicated for Ijay to sit on the other chair.

"Do you need anything before we start?" Paul asked as he flipped through the folder of documents on the desk.

"No. I just need my notepad and pen and I'm ready to go," she said, taking out her notepad from her bag.

"Okay. Just give me a second to glance through the weekly report and I'll be right with you," he said without looking up, his attention glued to what he was reading.

She turned her gaze to the factory floor. Everyone down at each point of the chain seemed to know what they were doing. A result of robust training, she assumed. It was inspiring to watch.

A prickling sensation on her arms made her turn around. She found Paul scrutinising her closely.

Her breath caught in her throat from the intense heat of his gaze, the black of his eyes marbled with copper. A tendril of desire unfurled in her belly. He broke his stare and looked away.

"Let's walk the floor so I can show you around."

Gracefully, he unwound his body from the worn leather chair and walked to the door without looking at her. At the door he stopped. He stood rigidly, his back stiff, shoulders straight. His hands balled into fists before they slowly unclenched.

Watching his response to the tension between them, her heart clenched painfully. For a brief moment, a strong urge to throw caution to the wind gripped her. She wanted to walk to him, touch his hard back and let him engulf her body in his warm embrace.

Still, she was already set on a course and she wanted to see it through. So she exhaled a deep breath and followed him out.

"Do your employees have to come from a long way to work every day?" she asked, happy that her calm voice hid her inner turmoil.

"No," Paul replied as he kept walking. "They're all local people from Amori and the neighbouring villages."

"That's great. I'd assumed they travel in from the city."

"A healthy portion of our staffing budget goes on training the workers. One thing I didn't want to do was import people from the city to work here."

The passion in Paul's voice touched Ijay heart.

"We had a problem of all the young people disappearing from the villages once they left secondary school and moving to the cities. When I started this factory, I wanted something to keep the young people here and to help grow the local economy."

Ijay turned and gave Paul a side glance. Pride swelled her heart for him. She knew he cared about the people who worked for him by the way he'd interacted with them in Abuja.

This was a whole new side of him. His compassion and vision for his community was impressive. He wasn't just an entrepreneur out for a quick profit. By investing in the local economy, he was making sure families could take care of themselves in a sustainable way.

As Paul walked her around the floor introducing her to the staff in each section, she understood that fact even more. They interacted with him as if he was one of them—a brother or a son. She made her notes emphasising family and community sustainability as key brand points to focus on.

After the tour, Paul left Ijay in the office while he returned to meet with the manager to discuss ongoing issues. The day went very quickly afterwards and by the time they made their way back to the city, it was late afternoon.

"So what did you think of the factory?" Paul asked a few minutes into their drive back to Enugu.

"I was really surprised at how efficient the place worked. Somehow, I wasn't expecting that. I don't know maybe because of my preconceived ideas about Nigeria. Honestly, I was impressed. How did you do it?" Ijay replied, unable to hide her delight at his success.

"It's taken hard graft and a lot of money. I have to say I'm grateful for my backers who bought into my vision. And the local support of my hometown people who have helped me along the way even before I had the money to build the factory. I was given a free lease of the land. So really, it's a community project."

"What about the raw materials, the fresh foods? Are they sourced locally?"

"Most of it is sourced from local producers. The farmers have a cooperative and we also source from local plantations."

He stopped and waited for her while she scribbled a note.

"If you need to see a list of our suppliers, I can give that to you tomorrow."

"Sure, that'll be fine. So you do this weekly?"

He raised his brow in a confused query.

"I mean, visiting the factory," she added.

"Yes, except when I'm out of the country." He shrugged dismissively as if it wasn't remarkable. She certainly thought it was.

Sensing he didn't want to talk any more, she returned to reviewing her notes and making a list of things to do the next day.

***

"On your knees."

Ijay scrambled up from her lying position to do his bidding. She didn't know why but the powerful tone of Paul's voice compelled her to obey without question.

He'd previously bound her hands to the bedpost while they made love. Now her hands were free. So she leveraged her body to kneel in front of him.

He stood magnificently erect by the edge of the bed, his presence imposing, and his expression hungry. She'd seen his body all night.

Yet she couldn't get enough of looking at him— toned broad shoulders, arms and back with tight muscles that flexed each time he moved, a six-pack chest and stomach that tapered into narrow hips and powerful thighs that drew her attention to his distended erection.

Slowly, he stroked the length of his hardened shaft. A pearl of his seeds glimmered at the tip.

Consciously, she rolled her tongue along her lips. She'd never taken a man's length into her mouth. Yet she wanted to taste Paul's. Wanted to feel his strength plundering her cavernous depths.

Paul must have read her thoughts because he chuckled.

"You want me in your mouth."

She couldn't explain the powerful emotions evoked within her in his presence. With him, reserved and sensible Ijay disappeared replaced by a wanton and adventurous woman she barely recognised. She was discovering so much about herself that she didn't know she possessed.

For starters, she'd never known she wanted a dominant man in the bedroom. Yet the mere sound of Paul's deep take-charge voice had her body creaming and trembling for his touch.

Looking up, she saw the amused glint in his fiery gaze. She nodded, swallowing hard as her body flushed with heat.

"Come closer."

She shuffled to the edge of the bed on her knees, her heart ramming against her chest in anticipation. Lithely, he moved behind her and secured her hands with the silk tie. With her hands tied behind her, her breasts jutted out higher, heat and desire making them sensitive and heavier. Her core pulsed in tune with her heart pounding in her chest.

Paul combed his fingers through her messed-up hair and leaned down. His body heat surrounded her as he kissed her lips tenderly, swiping his tongue along the rim of her lips before pulling back. It always amazed her how he could be rough and ready one minute and yet be tender and loving the next. She felt beautiful and sexy, secure and cared for in his arms.

She let out a soft sigh of yearning. She would give anything for him to love her.

He straightened up. With one hand on her head, and the other stroking his rigid erection, he guided it to her eager lips. Tentatively, she licked the drop of essence from the engorged tip, savouring the slightly fruity taste exploding on her tongue.

Paul let out a low groan as she swirled her tongue around his tip again. Feeling emboldened by his response, she licked and kissed the rest of his turgid length, amazed by the feel of the satiny surface against steel beneath. She continued her caressing attention, laving his balls with her tongue before returning to the shaft.

"Open your mouth," he said, his voice hoarse with lust. "I want to feel your sweet mouth swallow me whole."

Eager to give him pleasure she opened up to his instruction. As his blunt head slid in, she opened her mouth wider, sucking him in. She bobbed her head, pumping him quickly.

"Slowly, sweet...Slowly."

Gripping her head tightly, he stopped her fast pace. She relaxed, letting the movement of his hips and hands guide her pace. Gradually she took most of him, her mouth widening to accommodate his large gait.

She relished the deep sounds of enjoyment he emitted. She was the one on her knees but she felt powerful and sexy knowing her actions brought him pleasure. She loved the heady sensation sweeping through her body, ensuring her juices ran down her thigh.

She glanced up and noted his head was tipped back, his eyes closed, and his expression tight. When his grip on her head slackened, her excitement made her rush the pace. The blunt head rammed the back of her mouth. She choked.

Tightening his grip on her hair, he opened his eyes. He pulled out. She inhaled deeply drawing air into her lungs until the stifling sensation passed.

"I told you to go slowly, sweet Ijay."

He grinned at her wolfishly before claiming her swollen lips in a kiss. This time was fierce, his tongue delving into her mouth like a marauding warrior invading a castle. When he broke the kiss, she panted in shallow breaths, disappointed and wanting more contact with him.

"Now, let me look at you properly," he said and moved back as if inspecting her body.

"That won't do, sweet Ijay," he continued, shaking his head. "When you kneel for me, I want you to part your thighs. I want to see all of you."

Her core wept with excitement as she moved her legs further apart, revealing her shaved pussy.

"Oh," he groaned. "You remind me of a confectionery of pink marshmallows surrounded by caramel. Do you want me to taste you, my sweet?"

"Yes," she gasped out, her body trembling expectantly.

Nodding his head, he knelt before her and pulled her closer. He leaned forward and separated her lower fat lips. She held her breath, waiting.

Leisurely, he swiped his tongue from her slit to her swollen nub.

"Ah." Her body jerked with riotous emotions.

That was another contradicting observation about Paul. Despite his authority—she was the one bound and vulnerable—he worshipped her body like she was his queen, the most important woman in his universe.

He held onto her thighs, flattening his tongue against her tightened bud. Sensation exploded within her body sending her closer and closer to the edge, her essence leaking from her body like a waterfall.

He didn't let up but lapped up everything she gave and gave her move. Leaning her upper body back, she arched her hips off the bed, breathing heavily and shouting, wanting more of him.

"Paul...please." She couldn't believe the rasping needy voice was hers.

"Say it," his voice sounded hoarse and alien too. She knew then he was as affected by this combustible lust as she was.

"I want you," she said in between catching her breath.

"Not yet. You're not ready," he said, his voice thick and husky, blowing air on her sensitive clit.

He plunged a couple of fingers into her, working her body to a frenzied awareness with his mouth and hands. Then he removed his fingers and breached her back passage with his finger.

She gasped as heat assaulted her body with the pain and pleasure of the alien touch.

"Damn, you're so tight," he said against her hot skin.

Gently he worked her tight passage, pumping in and out before inserting more fingers into her wet heat. She felt deliciously full as her body shot up with more dizzying sensation. She couldn't control her movements any longer as his fingers stroked her front and back and his tongue worked her enlarged bud.

Before long she flew off the edge, screaming his name. Then she was freefalling into nothingness.

With a jerk, Ijay opened her eyes. It took a moment for her eyes to adjust to the darkness of the room. She realised she was in her bedroom in Paul's house. Her body was slick despite the cool air from the air-conditioner. But he wasn't with her. It had been a dream re-enactment of their night together in London.

Letting out a frustrated sigh, she leaned back into the pillows and closed her eyes, hoping the dream would return.

***

The next day they arrived early at the factory. Everyone was gathered in a group unlike yesterday when they'd all been busy already. Mr. Obi, the foreman approached them. He looked harassed, wringing both hands together when they arrived.

"John, what's happened?" Paul asked.

"We arrived this morning to find that someone broke in and damaged some of the machinery," John replied, still twisting his hands.

"Which one?"

"The nut line. The engineer is looking at it but he doesn't think it can be fixed immediately."

"The nut line. We have an order to ship next week." Ijay detected urgency in Paul's calm voice.

"I know, sir. That's why I'm concerned."

"Right. I have to see." Paul turned to her. "Ijay, go up to the office. I'll be up later."

"Do you mind if I come with you? I'd like to help if I can," Ijay said, her heart thudding with worry. She'd only been here a day. Yet she felt like she had a stake in seeing the factory do well.

"Okay." He nodded.

Mr. Obi led them down to the production line that had been damaged.

"Oh no," Ijay gasped when she saw the damage. It looked like someone had taken a wrench and mallet to the machinery, the rubber mat surface ripped out of the conveyor belt, nuts and bolt all over the floor along with some twisted metal.

She glanced at Paul thinking he'd be angry and raging at whoever had done the damage. To her surprise he looked calm. She only realised he was perturbed by the vein ticking in his clenched jaw.

A man came out from behind the machinery. He was dressed in overalls and wiped his greasy hands on a small towel in his pocket.

"Engineer, can you fix this?" Paul asked the man.

"I think we have most of the spare parts but it will take a long time, probably a few days instead of a few hours."

"Okay, keep working. I'll be down later."

Paul turned around and walked back toward the office.

"Do you know who did this?" Ijay asked. She couldn't believe that anyone would be that mean and calculated.

"No one seems to know," Mr. Obi answered.

"I'll need this investigated. If we have a saboteur in our midst, I want to know," Paul said, his tone hardened.

"Are you going to call the police?" Ijay asked. Whoever had done the damage should be arrested.

Paul shook his head. "This is a private matter. I don't want to involve the police. At least not yet."

In the office, Paul didn't sit down. "How much of the Bide order have we processed?"

"We were scheduled to complete it tomorrow. But now?" Mr. Obi waved both hands.

"We're going to have to go to manual mode. It'll take longer but it's still doable since we're halfway through the order already. Get as many people as possible working on this. I'm going to help Engineer work on repairing as much damage as possible."

Mr. Obi nodded and left the office. Paul unbuttoned his shirt and pulled it off. Ijay gasped out softly at the sight of the hard muscles on his back. He glanced back with a lopsided grin and brow raised mockingly.

"I'm just changing my shirt, not about to jump your bones." He took an old grey t-shirt out of a drawer beneath the desk to buttress this point.

"Of course," Ijay replied with outrage, her face flaming with heat. How could he think she thought any differently? Even if she'd done so!

Paul chuckled as if not believing her and pulled the t-shirt on. She nearly threw her pen at him. She clenched her palm around it instead.

"Sorry to have to leave you on your own.   I really have to get that machine sorted out as soon as possible. We can't afford not to complete that order on time."

"Have you considered that whoever damaged the machine might be trying to stop you completing your order?" she asked the question that just popped in her mind. The damage must have a purpose.

"If they are then I can't let them win," Paul said harshly. His chest rose as he inhaled deeply. When he spoke again his voice was calmer. "Actually, I'm going to ask Amaechi to take you back to Enugu now. I don't know how long this is going to take. I may have to spend the night down here at the village."

"In that case, I'm not going to Enugu. I want to help." She wasn't about to leave him to cope of his own. Moreover, there must be something she could do here.

"You do? How? Seriously I think you are better off returning to Enugu. You're not an employee. You don't have to help."

"Paul, please. Let me help. I'll do whatever it takes. I don't mind helping the guys with the packaging or sorting through. I'm doing this not as an employee of Havers & Child. We are friends. At least, I hope we are."

He stared at her for a moment, his expression unreadable. Eventually he let out a deep sigh and nodded.

"Okay. I'll speak to John."

Chapter Eighteen

Paul's back ached when he finally headed back up to the office that night. The day had gone in a quick blur. He hadn't even stopped for lunch except when Ijay had brought him a bottle of water.

True to her words, she'd stayed on, helping to manually pack the processed cashew nuts with the rest of the staff. She'd kept working until he'd sent everyone else home late this evening. She'd still refused to be dropped off by Amaechi and was now up in the office.

He walked up the stairs. Before he walked into the office, he saw her. She was sitting on the chair with her head laid on the table against her arms. Her hair tied back in a ponytail hung down her shoulder. She was asleep, her chest rising and falling gently. She looked vulnerable and beautiful. Exquisite.

The clamp in his chest tightened with protectiveness, his body suffused with warm tenderness. She must've been exhausted to have fallen asleep on the desk. He knew she'd worked as hard as anyone else today.

The thing that got to him was that she didn't have to. It wasn't her job. It wasn't her business.

And despite the fact that she'd said she wanted them to be friends, he knew that once she married his brother, they couldn't be friends. His brother would never allow it. And Paul wouldn't blame him.

The kind of feeling Paul had for Ijay had less to do with friendship and more to do with...*love?*

A wave of dizziness passed over him at the thought. He swallowed the hard lump in his throat and leaned on the door post as he watched her prone body.

Love? It couldn't be. He didn't know how to love the way other people did. He wasn't taught to love.

Yes, you do. You don't want her to marry your brother. You want her to wear your ring.

His gaze moved to her hand with the sparkling engagement ring. His heart rammed in his chest at the sudden realisation.

Yes, he wished it was his ring she was wearing.

Still, he was also scared of hurting her. Just like his father had hurt his mother, he'd surely hurt Ijay. He didn't want to do that. He didn't want to be the source of any pain to her. He'd hate himself. He needed to stay away from her. If he didn't make promises of forever to her, then there would be no chance of him breaking them.

Maybe Vincent will do a better job.
Bullshit!

Vincent was as good as a fox in a hen's coop—cunning and deadly. Leaving Ijay to marry him would be setting her up for a life of misery. While

Paul knew he wasn't good enough for Ijay in the long run, he also knew that Vincent was worse.

He could never let Ijay marry Vincent no matter how much she protested. He just had to figure out a way to convince her to give him a chance. First he had to survive another night of having her close by and not touching her. Two nights of her under his roof in Enugu had been torture. That he'd managed to get any sleep was a surprise to him. When all he'd wanted to do in the middle of the night was take the short walk across from his room to hers and join her in her bed.

He'd stayed up listening to her movements as she'd walked around in her room. Every sound she'd made augmented his desire until it had been swollen and throbbing. Only a cold shower had helped him get to sleep eventually.

Now just watching her sleep, he knew it was going to be another tough night. Gritting his teeth, he quickly stripped off the t-shirt and replaced it with the clean shirt he'd worn that morning. He leaned over and shook her shoulders.

"Ijay," he spoke her name hoarsely, his throat clogged up with emotion.

She roused, lifted her head and looked at him blankly for a moment.

"Come on. It's time to go."

She blinked a few times before her brown eyes cleared. She rubbed her head. "Sorry. I didn't realise I was so tired," she said, her soft voice husky with sleep.

"I'm the one who's sorry for keeping you out here for so long." He grabbed his leather briefcase with one hand and pulled Ijay up with the other. She picked up her bag and he let her lean into him as they both left the office.

Her sweet scent assaulted his senses adding to his body's growing need. Perhaps the weariness of his body made his mind susceptible too. He let out a soft groan as desire kicked into his blood.

Ijay stilled in his arm and glanced up at him, her chocolate eyes wide with concerned. "Did I hurt you?" She moved to step away.

Not wanting to lose the contact, he held her soft body to him and shook his head. "No."

He didn't want to look away but he did. Otherwise they wouldn't make it out of the front door.

"What time is it? It's so dark outside," she asked, looking confused.

"It's past eight," he said as they walked outside. Thankfully, Amaechi had the car close to the entrance so they didn't have far to walk. The night air was warm and humid. He really needed a cold shower for more than one reason.

"Gosh. That's late. Are we heading back to Enugu now?" Ijay said as she got into the car. Paul missed her softness as soon as she stepped away.

You'll miss her even more when she marries your brother.

He ignored the voice in his head and got into the car. "No. We'll stay the night at my villa," he replied.

"Oh, you mean your family home." She turned to look at him, now more alert.

"No. It's just a little place I built two years ago," he said nonchalantly.

He didn't want to get into the details and was glad when she replied with "Oh, okay."

Paul waved to the night watch-men standing guard as they drove out of the premises.

"Do you normally have so many security men on duty?" Ijay asked.

"Not usually. After today's incident, we can't afford any more mishaps. So I made a request to the local youth vigilante group for more men to patrol, at least for the next few days."

"I think that's a good idea. Hopefully there won't be any more break-ins and it'll give you time to find the culprit."

"That's the idea." He leaned back into his seat, letting hot tired muscles sink into the cool leather. As usual, Ijay's scent surrounded him with intoxicating musk. He inhaled deeply, closing his eyes.

"I want to thank you for all your help today. I really appreciate it." He opened his eyes and looked at her. In the dimness of the night, her face was in shadow. He saw her white teeth gleam as she smiled widely.

"You're welcome," she said and leaned back into her seat.

The drive to his villa was a short one. It was a small bungalow set in a small fenced plot of land surrounded by dense trees. The whole place was in darkness when they arrived.

"Ijay, stay in the car until I turn the generator on," he said to Ijay as he got out of the car.

Amaechi left the headlights on so he could see to open the front door.

Paul found the large torchlight he kept by the table in the hallway and turned it on. He walked round to the back of the building to the little generator housing and unlocked the door. Luckily the generator started quickly. He turned on the switch on the fuse box and the outside security lights came on.

When Paul walked round to the front, Ijay and Amaechi were taking the bags inside the house.

"Thank you," Paul said to Amaechi. "Good night. I'll see you in the morning." Though, Amaechi was his driver and stayed in the other half of his guest house in Enugu, his main family home was in Amori. So he was always glad when they had to spend time here.

"Good night," Amaechi said before leaving them.

Paul turned to Ijay who was looking around the living room. "Sorry the place is sparsely decorated. I don't use it often except for emergencies like today. I'll definitely make sure Amaechi takes you back to Enugu tomorrow early enough."

She turned to him, her lips pulled up in a wide smile, her eyes gleaming. "I love your place."

Stunned, he reared back thinking she was joking. There wasn't much in the place. Just a couple of worn leather sofas and a coffee table. She must have seen the doubt in his eyes because she came closer.

"Really, I love it. I love that it isn't ostentatious. I mean I know how other people's villas are. Believe me I've seen a few in my village. They are grand buildings decorated to impress. This...this is just a bungalow and simple but it feels homely. Like a place I'd want to escape to on the weekends when I need some downtime from the bustle of city life." She waved her hand around. "Can you show me the rest of it, please?"

Paul's heart leapt and a smile crept onto his face. The admiration and joy on Ijay's face was unavoidable. She really did like the place. He wanted to go to her and lift her high up in the air to match how high his own heart had leapt with joy. He wanted to kiss her lips for speaking such blissful words.

Finally, something of his that she liked. Some common ground. He always enjoyed coming back here. Always enjoyed the quiet time away from everyone.

Without thinking, he reached out and took her hand. "Come; let me show you the rest of the place."

Eagerly, she followed him. He opened the door to the kitchen. It wasn't as large as his kitchen in Enugu. It had an aluminium sink/tap by the window, tall white fridge-freezer, cooker/oven and wooden kitchen wall units.

"It's basic and functional," he said.

"It's got everything you need. That's what's important," Ijay said as she followed him down the hallway.

"Unfortunately, there are no en-suite bathrooms in the bedrooms but this is the main bathroom." Paul opened the door. The bathroom had white units and wall tiles with the shower head over the bath.

"Is there hot water in here?" Ijay asked.

"There's an electric heater, if you need a warm shower." He pointed to the white panel on the wall. "Just adjust the dial from blue to red when you're in the shower."

He led her out and stopped in front of his bedroom door.

"There are two bedrooms but only this one is functional." He opened the door revealed the white walled bedroom and his large wooden frame bed in the middle. His acacia wood wardrobe stood in the corner. "You can take the bed and I'll sleep on the sofa tonight."

"That seems unfair, Paul. You've been working hard all day. I think you should take the bed and I can stay on the sofa."

He ignored her for a moment as the thoughts of her in his bed swirled in his head. He walked to the wardrobe and opened it, taking out fresh bed linen as a distraction.

"Ijay, take the bed. No arguments. Unless you want me to join you in it?" He raised his eyebrows quizzically.

He saw her throat dilate as she swallowed hard. He suppressed a smile. At least she was still as affected as he was by the sexual tension between them.

"I'm afraid I don't have any female clothing you can wear. If you need to borrow a shirt or t-shirt, then help yourself to mine," he said when she didn't reply. "I'm going to see if there's anything edible in the kitchen to make for dinner. I'll leave you to freshen up."

That he managed to walk to the door when he wanted to stay with Ijay was a minor miracle. Having her in his bedroom did all sorts of crazy things to his libido.

Before he got to the kitchen, there was a knock at the front door. He opened it. Amaechi stood there was a large food flask and a big wide grin.

"Uju said I should bring this to you," Amaechi said, holding out the flask.

Paul smiled and took the flask. "You should have told her not to bother."

"As if I can argue with her. You know what she's like when her mind is made up," Amaechi laughed.

Paul joined him, his ribs hurting as he laughed. Amaechi's wife never took "no" for an answer. She took it upon herself to clean Paul's villa and stock up his cupboards before his visit every week. He'd told her several times not to bother but she persisted. In the end, Paul had given up. He'd simply increased Amaechi's salary to compensate for the woman's time and expense.

"Tell her thank you for her work this week. The place looks great."

"No worries. See you in the morning," Amaechi said and turned to leave. Paul closed the door and took the flask into the kitchen.

He was glad he didn't have to cook anything tonight. He opened the flask. It was filled to the brim with jollof rice and grilled goat meat. He covered it back up and waited for Ijay. While waiting, he walked to the living room and called Peter. They were supposed to meet tonight for their usual catch-up.

"Old boy, are you on your way?" Peter said as soon as the line connected.

"No. I'm in Amori. We had an incident this morning."

"What happened?" Peter asked, his voice losing its cheeriness and turning worried.

"One of the machines was damaged, deliberately. I found out when I got in there this morning," Paul replied.

"That's nasty. Do you know who did it?"

"Not yet. I mean to find out soon." Paul's grip tightened on the phone. "Anyway, we have an order due and I was there late with the Engineer. I'm going to spend the night here so I can get in there early tomorrow."

"Do you need me to help with anything? Do you need another mechanical Engineer to look at it?"

"We could do with extra help. So if you have someone available, then that'll be great."

"No problem. I'll send one of the spare Engineers from the airline. He'll be there in the morning," Peter said.

"Thank you," Paul said. He really was grateful for his friends. They were a lifeline he didn't get anywhere else.

"Well, since you're on your own, try and get some sleep. Michael and I'll catch up."

"I'm not on my own. I've got Ijay here."

"Ijay? You took a girl to the villa?" Peter sounded shocked. Paul didn't blame him. He'd never taken a woman to his house in Enugu. Neither had he ever taken a woman to his village. So having Ijay here was uncharacteristic.

"Ijay Amadi is the consultant from Havers & Child," Paul said simply, not wanting to go into details on the phone, especially with Ijay not too far away.

"She's spending the night with you? How come Amaechi didn't take her back to the hotel?"

"It's a long story. She wanted to stay and help." He said dismissively, shrugging his shoulders though he knew Peter couldn't see him.

"Listen, before you go back to Abuja, I must see you and this Ijay. I want to meet the woman who bypassed Abuja and Enugu and ended up in Amori. Something no other person has achieved. I haven't been invited to spend the night in your villa and I'm your best friend." Peter joked.

Paul had to laugh. If only his best friend knew how far Ijay had gotten under Paul's skin. Ijay had already stayed in his family home in Enugu where no other woman had stayed previously. In truth the decision to let her stay there had been easy to make. That first night of seeing her sit at his dining table, had felt so natural. He'd wanted to see her there every day.

Now that she was here in Amori, Paul knew he wanted her here on a permanent basis. And that thought frightened him more than anything he'd ever had to deal with before.

Ijay had already taken residence in his heart.

Chapter Nineteen

"Where can I get—"

The melodious sound of Ijay's voice filtered through the boom of Peter's words into Paul's ears. He turned around. Ijay stood in the doorway, wearing one of his white t-shirts. It enveloped her body, skimming her curves and stopping mid-thighs. It revealed sleek long legs, buttery skin clear of makeup and long dark hair pulled back from her face in a ponytail.

He'd never seen anybody sexier in that moment. In her simple appearance, she looked young, yet so full of life. Covered in his shirt, yet so feminine.

The pulse of longing thumped to life within his body. Urgent. Undeniable. Compelled to look into her eyes, his intent gaze swept back up from her feet blue varnish-painted toes to her flawless face. He didn't miss the prominent rise of her breasts when her breath hitched. Nor the heart-thudding nip of her teeth on her lower lip. Their gaze met, her brown eyes wide and flickering with desire.

The fire in his veins spread quickly. For a moment, he forgot where he was. It was just Ijay— sweet Ijay—and the powerful, electrifying connection between them. He knew then he had to reach her. Touch her. Taste her. Nothing else mattered in that moment. He stood and took a step toward her.

"Is that Ijay?"

The voice halted his movement, clearing some of the fog of hunger from his mind. Paul nodded before he realised it was Peter talking to him on the phone. He inhaled a fortifying breath.

"Yes, hold on," Paul replied before pressing the on-hold button on his handset.

"You wanted something?" he said brusquely, his voice was roughened with desire.

Tell me you want me. Only me.

Jealousy rose in his gut, leaving a bitter taste in his mouth and darkening his mood. He looked away from Ijay, seeking to hide the bitterness he felt from her.

"Sorry, I didn't realise you were on the phone," she sounded hurt. Like she'd read his thoughts. He turned back to her but she turned away. "I'll come back later."

"Ijay, wait." He took several steps to her and took several calming breaths. He needed to stop taking out his frustrations on her. She looked back at him warily before turning to face him fully. They were only inches apart. He could smell her clean fragrance mixed with the scent of his soap. He reached out and clasped her cheek in his palm. Her skin was satiny and cool from her shower. He ran his thumb down her jaw line in a slow caress. "What was it you wanted?"

She stared at him for a brief moment, her nose flared, her mouth slightly opened as if she was going to speak but didn't say anything. Then she shook her head and lifted her hand showing him her top. "I wanted to wash this so I can wear it in the morning. I was looking for detergent."

Her functional request reminded him their relationship was purely platonic. He lowered his hand and stepped back.

"There should be a pack in one of the kitchen cupboards. I'll get it for you," he replied.

"No. That's not necessary. I'll find it myself. Don't keep your friend hanging." Her lips widened as she beamed him a gentle smile before she walked away.

His rampaging heart rate took a little while to calm down. He returned to his spot on the sofa and pressed the button on his phone to speak to Peter.

"Sorry about that," he said and kept his voice jovial. He didn't want his friends to sense the turmoil going on within his mind and body. It was unlike him to be this rattled by a woman. They wouldn't even believe it if he tried explaining how he felt.

"No worries," Peter replied. "I'm putting you on speaker. I've just been telling Michael about the babe at your villa. He wants to call out the Special Ops team for a rescue mission."

"You guys are not serious," Paul chuckled loudly.

Paul heard Peter and Michael laughing in the background. They hadn't even heard the half of his dilemma and they were laughing. They would think he'd gone mad when he told them he was in love with his brother's fiancée.

"We are very serious," Michael said. "Just make sure we see you before you head back to Abuja. We have to make sure you haven't been swapped with an alien."

He hadn't really thought about how much flak he'd receive from his friends because of Ijay. Out of the three of them, he was the least likely to want to settle down. If there was any sort of pre-ordained order it would have been Peter first, then Michael and Paul never. Peter had always been the most open and trusting when it came to women and people in general. That was a trait Paul struggled with on a daily basis.

The only people he trusted were those close to him—his best friends, Michael and Peter, followed by his family, Simon and his mother. Women generally lagged at the bottom of that list.

However Ijay had climbed a few rungs on his trust ladder. He just needed her to break things off from Vincent before they could proceed further.

His grip on the phone tightened as he quelled the rage bubbling in his vein.

"I don't know why you guys are so bothered. I'm more concerned about the factory right now than a woman in my villa," he said in a nonchalant tone, he didn't feel.

"Yes, indeed." Peter coughed in a mock serious manner.

Paul shook his head. His friends obviously didn't buy his casual attitude. He didn't blame them. He wouldn't buy it too. For now, he had to focus on getting through the night.

"I have to go now," Paul said. "I'll let you know how it goes at the factory tomorrow."

"Catch you later," his friends signed off and Paul switched off the phone.

With mixed feelings, he walked to the kitchen. He was relieved he'd spoken to his friends and they knew about Ijay. Soon he'd have to tell them how important she was to him. Still, he was troubled about Ijay. It was going to be one long night.

When his stomach growled with hunger pangs, Paul washed his hands. He took out plates and cutlery in preparation for their meal. He put them all on a tray including the food flask and a bottle of water and cups. He walked back into the living room with the tray and placed it on the table.

"Ijay, come on. The food is ready. And I'm hungry," he called out. The sooner he ate some food, the sooner he could get some sleep. All he'd have to worry about then would be dreaming about Ijay. That was relatively safer than watching her walk around in nothing but his shirt.

"I'm coming," her voice sounded from the hallway before she appeared at the doorway.

Failing to find somewhere to look on her body that didn't incite cravings he couldn't fulfil, he turned his gaze back to the meal on the table.

"That smells delicious," she said when she came round and sat on the sofa. The action placed her creamy smooth legs in his line of vision. He swallowed hard. "Don't tell me you just cooked that."

He heard the amazement in her voice and looked up at her face. "I would have to be some kind of magician or wonder chef," he joked. "Amaechi brought it. His wife cooked it." He took a plate and scooped food into it, distracting himself from staring at her.

"That's really nice of her," she said and took the full plate of food he passed to her. "That means his family lives close by."

"Yes, just a few minutes' walk from here."

"Okay," she said hesitantly.

He looked up. She bit her lip worriedly. He knew she wanted to ask something but was holding back. Inhaling deeply, he let out a sigh in resignation. He'd told her not to ask personal questions unless she wanted to get personal with him. She was adhering to her side of the bargain. He'd never met a woman who was as curious as she was. A smile played at the corners of his lips.

To reassure her, he reached out and grazed her arm lightly with his hand. "Ijay, it's okay. Ask what you want to ask. I won't misconstrue its purpose." He smiled encouragingly at her.

Her lips parted in surprise, her eyes widening. "You sure?"

He nodded. "I won't bite your head off. If that's what you mean," he joked and smiled widely.

Her eyes glittered with amusement, her lips uplifted in a glowing smile. The warmth returned to his heart and skin, wrapping around him like a blanket. He moved his hand back to his plate afraid if he didn't move it now, he wouldn't be able to later.

"I wanted to know if you're related to Amaechi," Ijay said excitedly, her fork waving in the air. The pleasure of seeing her so happy relaxed his tense shoulders. "The two of you seemed much more than employer and employee. And you seemed to know quite a lot about his family when you were chatting on the way back from the airport on Monday."

"Yes, Amaechi is a distant cousin on my mother's side of the family. We became close years ago when I had to stay with one of my uncles. He looked out for me," Paul said practically.

"It's really great to meet all these wonderful people around you," Ijay said cheerfully. "It's so obvious that they care about you—Simon, his mother, Amaechi and his family, your friends. You are loved, Paul. Not many people get that much love in their entire life."

I would swap all their love for yours.

His close gaze met hers filled with tender intensity. Yet he didn't say the words that were at the tip of his tongue and swallowed them instead. He wasn't ready to bare all to her yet. Not when he didn't know what was in her heart. Was she telling him to make do with other people's love and not look to her for it?

Fighting the disappointment gnawing at his gut, Paul looked down at his plate breaking the spell being wound around them. He focused on eating the rest of his meal quickly and silently.

Luckily, Ijay seemed to pick up that he didn't want to talk any more. She left him alone in his mental solitude. Yet the silence seemed more torturous than the velvety sound of her voice.

When they were done, he picked up the tray and took it into the kitchen.

How am I going to survive the night?

Suppressing a groan, he prayed that the weariness he felt earlier that evening would return and send him to sleep.

"I'll wash the dishes," Ijay's soft voice roused him.

His grip on the worktop tightened in frustration before he swivelled to face her. She stood so close, her clean scent invaded his nostrils and her warmth surrounded him. His hand moved up toward her face. He snatched it back in time and swiped his head with it.

"Thanks. I'll go and have a shower," he said and walked out of the kitchen in a hurry without looking back.

***

Ijay stared at Paul's retreating back and fought the urge to stop him. To walk into his arms and lift her lips up to meet his. To persuade him to sate the desire simmering slowly in her veins. From the moment she'd stepped into his villa, something had clicked between them. The intensity of the energy every time they were close to each other was growing.

Each time he looked at her, her skin came alive. When he spoke, his deep voice resonated within her body. She was barely keeping it together.

She inhaled deeply, drawing in a sustaining breath. The warmth from Paul lingered for a moment, his scent and spice still in the air.

She turned to the dishes and focused on washing up. There was no point fantasising about Paul. He still wasn't declaring undying love for her. She rolled her eyes heavenwards. Would that ever happen?

However, it seemed his hard stance had thawed a little. He'd allowed her to ask him a personal question about his family. Surely that meant they were heading in the right direction.

When she'd mentioned he was loved by so many people, the intense look he'd given her had arrested her breath. In that moment, she longed to trust him fully. To share her thoughts, her worries and her dreams with him. She longed to tell him that she loved him.

The more time she'd spent with him had confirmed for her that he was the one. Was she the one to him? Would she ever be? She wanted to find out.

When she finished washing up, she returned to the living room and sat tensely at the edge of the sofa. Tonight was really her last night to get through to Paul before the week was over. Once they returned to Enugu and subsequently Abuja, they wouldn't have the quiet secluded space and intimacy of the villa.

A prickling sensation on Ijay's back made her look up. She swivelled in her seat. He stood behind her, just inside the doorway, watching her closely. She hadn't heard him approach. Her breath died in her throat. Her mouth dried out, gluing her tongue to the roof of her mouth.

He came closer to the sofa. He was dressed only in a pair of loose charcoal shorts. His biceps rippled as he moved his arm. His dark toned chest gleamed, some flecks of water shimmering on his skin from his shower. Suddenly, he seemed taller, larger, and sexier. So masculine.

She remembered their one night together, when he'd stood above her, his arousal swollen and hard, his expression intense with desire yet filled with tenderness. Her core throbbed in tune with her heart. She squeezed her thighs together seeking relief.

"I'm going to switch off the generator before we sleep. You can use this to light the room."

The casual tone of Paul's deep voice brought her back to the present. She looked up at him distractedly. He lifted a battery-powered lamp in his hand and turned it on. His eyes twinkled with a knowing smirk.

Heat travelled up to her face in a hot blush. He knew that she'd been remembering again. With indignation, she stood and took the lamp from him. "Thank you," she said with annoyance. "I take it you don't need me to come out with you to light your way with the lamp?"

He shook his head still smirking. "No. It's not necessary. I've got the torchlight." He pointed to the table near the front door with a large black torch on top.

"Good night, then." She nodded and walked to the bedroom somewhat disappointed. She wasn't sure what she'd been expecting. Whatever it was, she wasn't going to get it from Paul. He had no intentions of relenting.

She left the lamp in the bedroom and walked to the bathroom just across the hallway. She was still in the bathroom when all the lights went off leaving just the light from the lamp in the bedroom lighting the way. She heard the sound of the side door close and lock when Paul came in.

Thinking he was now settled on the sofa, she returned to the bedroom and stood by the open window. The night was lit grey with a large full moon. Beyond the walls surrounding Paul's villa was a densely wooded area. She watched the outline of the tall trees through the moonlight. She listened to the chirp of the crickets and other night creatures. The still air had cooled somewhat.

"Are you okay?" the sound of Paul's deep voice made her heart thud loudly in her chest. She turned to find him by the doorway. Her heart rate quickened.

He came! Could she convince him to stay?

"Yes...no," she replied breathlessly.

With quick steps he strode to her, his hands reached out and cupped her shoulders. A frown creased his features. "What's the matter?" his deep voice was concerned.

"I—I don't want to sleep alone." She lowered her lashes coyly as her cheeks stung in a blush. She looked at him through her lashes.

"If you don't like the dark, you should have said. I would've left the gen on."

"I like the generator being off," she replied petulantly. Why didn't he get it? Did she need to take out a billboard advertisement?

"So what...?" his frown deepened as if he got her meaning for the first time.

She took a bolstering breath and exhaled. "I don't want you on the sofa. I want you in bed with me."

His eyes narrowed into slits as he shook his head and stepped back. His jaw tensed. He looked like she'd just hit him. Panicked, she reached out and gripped his arms.

"Please..."

"Ijay, if I stay in this bed we won't be getting much sleep. Do you understand that?" His dark gaze was grave. There was no mistaking the dangerous determination in his voice.

Heat flared from her pulsing core. Her grip on his arms tightened to stop her trembling legs from collapsing.

"Yes," she replied, her body quivering in anticipation.

"And when that happens, you won't be marrying my brother."

Chapter Twenty

Paul held his breath waiting for Ijay's response knowing that her reply would change the course of their relationship. Their lives. Their future. He couldn't remember waiting for any other thing with such anticipation. Such excitement. Such fear. His heart hammered in his chest loudly, the whooshing sound of his racing pulse resounding in his ears.

She didn't know how much he wanted to join her in the bed tonight. He'd waited months, planning her arrival. He'd spent the past week fighting his impulses, his desires, just because she'd asked him to back off. On several incidents, he could have persuaded her to yield to their mutual cravings. And she would've yielded too.

Still, he'd let his emotional feelings for her take precedent over his physical need. Now there was a chance to feed that craving. To fulfil it. Yet it was no longer enough.

More than he wanted to make love to Ijay tonight, he wanted her in his life permanently. Still, he had to be sure she understood the implications of making love tonight. He wouldn't be walking away. Neither would he let her walk away from him again. Not without fighting for her first.

Her brown eyes hardened into harsh glint as she squinted, her grip on his arms loosening. "You're back playing games again Paul." Anger and indignation laced her breathy voice. Her chest rose and fell rapidly.

"I'm not playing games, Ijay." He emphasised his words by pulling her closer, flushing her soft body against his hardness. She couldn't mistake his intent. "I've made no bones about the fact that I've wanted you from the first day you arrived in Abuja. But I won't share you with my brother," he bit out harshly.

"I'll not be a source of competition between you and Vincent," she shouted. Then her chest lifted as she paused to take a deep breath, her expression still furious. "You want me to leave him," she said in a calmer voice.

"Yes." His grip on her shoulders tightened. The idea that his brother had touched her already made his blood boil with rage. He wouldn't allow Vincent to touch Ijay again.

She winced as his grip on her shoulders tightened. He released her immediately and inhaled deeply. "You know what, have it your way. Good night." The ache in his groin pulsed. Ignoring it, he gritted his teeth and turned away.

He was at the door, when he heard her velvety whisper. "Wait...please tell me why you want me to leave Vincent?"

He had to strain his ears to hear her soft words. Compelled, he turned round and walked back to her, his need to make her understand even greater. She looked at him with smouldering eyes, her nose flared and her luscious lips parted invitingly.

"Because you're mine alone."

Tangling one hand in her hair, the other on the small of her back, he pulled her against his body. He lowered his lips and crushed her lips with his. Brutally. Vengefully. Unforgiving. She responded, her passion fuelled by her own rage. Her lips refusing to surrender even as her mouth opened to him. Her tongue duelled with his, cutting and parrying, advancing and retreating. A warrior's defiant dance.

He hated that he was reduced to this. He hated his weakness for her. Because he knew even if he'd wanted to, he couldn't resist her any longer. He hated that his brother had touched her. Any other man, he'd have lived with but not Vincent. And worse, she wore his brother's ring. It was always there on her finger, reminding him she wasn't his. Goading him. Telling him that she was offering him nothing more than her body.

Damn it! He wanted all of her. Body, heart and soul. Nothing less would do.

He lifted her, her long smooth legs wrapped around his waist as he backed her up toward the bed. Her soft curves moulded against his. His hot blood pumped around his body at an alarming rate, most of it going south. Her hard nipples grazed his bare chest through his t-shirt. A growl rumbled through him. His arousal throbbed against his shorts, pushing between Ijay's thighs. The heat from her core scorched him.

Panting, he broke the kiss and pushed her onto the bed, his body covering hers. She opened her eyes on impact, her breathing uneven. He clasped her hands above her head. Her breasts lifted into view, her hard nipples pushing through the fabric.

He took a nipple between his teeth, biting it through the fabric of his cotton t-shirt. Ijay let out a long slow moan arching her body to push more of her breast into his mouth. He withdrew his lips and hovered just above blowing warm air onto the wet spot. She whimpered.

"You're mine," he whispered in a hoarse voice. "Mine. Say it, Ijay."

Her eyes flashed defiant fire. Her pink tongue darted out and swiped her lower lip. She remained silent. Angrily, he moved back, releasing his restraining grip on her hands and standing up.

He lifted her up and flipped her over onto her belly. He pulled her up till she was on her hands and knees, her legs dangling at the edge of the bed. The t-shirt slid up her back exposing her arse and lower plump lips. She was clean-shaven. Exactly the way he remembered her. Just the way he liked her—soft and smooth.

He ran his fingertips from the cleft up to the top of the valley between her cheeks. A trail of glistening juice followed the path of his fingers. He felt her body tremble beneath his caress.

"Say the word now, sweet Ijay. Stop me before I go any further," he spoke against her back, blowing warm air against her skin. Her body's trembling increased.

He waited but she didn't say anything. Instead she whimpered and swung her hips toward him, recklessly. He knew this game well. It was a battle of wills. She was only offering her body on her own terms. This was her way of telling him, she wouldn't surrender to his.

Except, he was a master at this game. He knew the perfect way to gain her submission.

He knelt at the edge of the bed and parted her thighs wider. He leaned forward and took her tight swollen bud in his mouth. The taste of her syrupy essence fizzed on his tongue. His shaft swelled and throbbed with sweet pain.

Ijay bucked her hips again. He held onto her hips, stilling her body. He swiped his tongue around her clit, licking it several times before he sucked on her bud again. She writhed and bucked, twisted and jolted but he didn't let up. He wanted to taste all of her. Her sweetness. Her capitulation. He wanted her to shatter on his tongue. He'd waited so long for this.

He carried on his onslaught. He slid his fingers into her slit, moving them in a circular motion until she started bucking wildly. He knew her body so well. She was on the edge of climax. He stopped and withdrew his fingers.

"Paul...please," Ijay whimpered, turning her head to look at him. Her eyes were glazed with desire and pleading as she bit her lip.

"Do you want me to make you come, sweet Ijay?"

"Yes."

"I will. Only 'cause you're mine," he said before clamping his lips around her bud again. He applied suction pressure while he dipped a finger into her wet slit and played with the star of her back aperture. She bucked wilder and wilder, her body coiled with tension as she neared her peak. He slid more fingers into her and her inner walls contracted around his digits. He pumped into her several times, while applying pressure with his tongue on her bud.

"Oh...Paul!" Ijay screamed into the night.

More of her essence exploded onto his tongue as she came apart. He didn't let go of her until her body's trembling stopped and she went limp.

Then he walked to the side table and picked up his wallet. He took out two foils of condom. With one shove, he discarded his shorts and returned to the bedside. Ijay lay flat on her stomach, her head on the pillow. She looked replete, her eyes closed, her dark hair loose and spread on her back. His heart turned over with love.

Lifting her off the bed, he took the t-shirt off her body. He trailed kisses on her back along her spine, from her neck to her hips. Then he nipped and licked one bottom cheek, then the other.

He knelt behind her and nipped her shoulders. His hands caressed a path from her stomach to her breast, kneading and folding. Tweaking her breasts with one hand, he caressed her body with the other, travelling down to her slick clit. She bucked when he touched her again. Ijay moaned softly and moved her hands behind to grip his thighs. Her warm hands on his skin drove him crazy.

He let out a loud groan and got off the bed.

"On your knees."

Without hesitation, Ijay straightened her back and took the position; her hands behind her back, her thighs parted, giving him full view of her rosy juicy clit.

She remembered.

He suppressed a smile. His hard erection jutted out close to her lips. Her eyes gleamed with excitement. She swiped her bottom lip with her pink tongue. He didn't know whether to laugh or groan at her brazenness.

"You're being especially bad tonight, sweet Ijay. I'm almost tempted to go back to the sofa and leave you in this large bed alone."

Her eyes widened with surprise.

"But we know that's not going to happen," he continued. "Because you're going to say those words soon, aren't you?

She lowered her eyes coyly. He didn't miss the charged longing in their depths.

He grabbed a fistful of her hair, pulling her forward. She leaned in and swiped the blunt head of his erection with her pink tongue. She moved her tongue around his length, licking and caressing before pressing against the sensitive underside.

His hips bucked out of control surprised at her practised skill with her tongue. Their first night together, she'd been hesitant. He'd realised she'd never taken a man rigid length in her mouth before.

Yet, tonight...

He groaned out loud as she opened her mouth and slowly took him in. Gently she sucked him like a tube of lolly, gradually taking him deeper into her warm wet mouth. He moved his hips, controlling the pace with his hand on her head, mindful that she wasn't used to giving head.

When he thrust in, she swallowed and clamped his head at the back of her throat. His balls tightened with the need to spill his essence.

Damn! It was too soon.

He yanked out of her mouth, glaring at her. She looked at him with a defiant smile on her face and licked her lips with satisfaction. She'd done it on purpose, the obstinate vixen. She'd wanted him to come in her mouth.

"I don't even want to know where you learned to do that," Paul said, unable to hide his shock. He pushed the rising jealousy aside. For now he was more interested in reminding Ijay who was in control here. "For pulling this little stunt you're not going to come again until you beg for me. Bend over and keep those legs wide apart."

Instantly, her face lost its smugness. She lowered her eyes and bit her lip worried. He walked to the dresser table and picked up the bottle of baby oil. Lubricating his fingers with the oil, he put the bottle close by on the bedside table.

The sight of her round arse and glistening swollen clit had him swollen and aching to be seated deep within her. She was so pink, so juicy, so wet.

He dipped his finger into her back aperture and pushed past the tight ring. Her heat clamped around his digit. Her panting increased as he slid his finger in and out slowly. With the other hand, he played with her clit.

In little time, the sound of her whimpering increased at the sensations he knew assaulted her body. He'd learnt to play her body from their night together. He could take her any which way he wanted.

Still he didn't.

He continued to strum her body, taking her close to the edge again, feeling her muscles contract around his fingers and her hips gyrate wildly. Each time he stopped short of letting her fly off to the seven heavens, grounding her on earth with him.

"Paul...please!"

"Say it, sweet Ijay?"

"Fill me up...make me yours."

The sweet words he'd wanted to hear for so long. Her words should fill him with elation. Yet his blood bubbled with disappointment and rage. He should be happy, glad that she was finally surrendering her body to him like he'd wanted for weeks. Yet tonight it was no longer enough. He didn't just want her body. She'd given her body to his brother. Taking it back wasn't good enough. He wanted more. He wanted all of her. Still it was more than he'd ever had from her. It would have to do for now. He didn't like it. The fire in his blood wanted more. He wanted to give more too. Yet he couldn't. Not when she could still walk away tomorrow.

So he lifted her till she was on her hands and knees again. Then he mounted her, pushing into her from behind till he could go no further. Her slick walls tightened around his shaft with heat like a clamp. She was so tight, like the first time they'd been together. He had to wait for her to adjust to him before he started moving. Each time he rocked into her body, her walls squeezed him, milking him, forcing his own surrender.

With each thrust, Ijay pushed back, gyrating her hips and driving him crazy. He knew it wouldn't be long before he climaxed. He had waited so long for her. He could no longer hold back. He wasn't coming apart without her. He wanted her with him all the way. It was no longer just him or just her. They would have to find a way together.

So he stopped pumping and reached across to her lower lips. He caressed her just the way he knew she liked. She bucked back against him. Her back arched lower as her body tensed.

"You wait for me, sweet Ijay." He rocked faster. "I'm coming with you."

She screamed his name again. The world around him exploded into splinters as he surrendered to her. They both collapsed onto the bed, him on top of Ijay, both their bodies slick with sweat and heat. He took a moment to catch his breath, his chest rising and falling rapidly. Then he rolled to the side and spooned Ijay's body against his. He pushed her hair aside and kissed her neck, her skin salty.

"I'll never let you go again," he said emphatically against the side of her face. "I won't let Vincent touch you again."

He waited for her to say something. She didn't. Worried, he turned her around until she faced him. Her eyes were squeezed shut. There were tear drops on her long black lashes.

His blood went cold, his body tensed. *Did he just overstep the mark?*

"Ijay? What's wrong? Did I hurt you?"

She shook her head but didn't open her eyes.

"Ijay, look at me. Tell me what's wrong," he said gruffly. How could he forgive himself if he'd hurt her? He'd been too rough with her because of his jealousy. All he wanted to do was love her. Yet he couldn't seem to get past his rage at Vincent.

She opened her eyes, a reflective pool of chocolate he could lose his soul in shimmering with more tears. His heart flipped over with tenderness.

"Hey, don't cry, sweet Ijay," he whispered huskily before blowing feathery kisses on each eyes. "I'll take care of you. I promise. Just tell me what's wrong and I'll fix it."

She shook her head. "You can't fix everything."

"I will...I'll try. Trust me."

I love you.

He kissed her, gently this time. His lips grazed hers in a featherlike touch. He nibbled her lips, alternating between nipping and licking. The salt from her tears mixed with her sweetness. Then his tongue slid into the warm depth of her mouth and took her tongue on a slow waltz. He poured all the tenderness into that kiss, wanting her to feel the love that blossomed within him because of her. She'd made him feel things he never thought he was capable of feeling.

Surely she could hear the beat of his racing heart, feel his love in his embrace and kiss. He'd take care of her just like he took care of everybody that mattered to him. And even more.

He lifted his head and caressed her cheek with his thumb. She looked back at him with heated desire and tenderness.

Perhaps she felt a little of what he felt for her.

"Tell me why you were crying. Please." He stroked her chin gently.

"I was just overwhelmed," she said huskily, her voice filled with emotion. "No one else has ever made me feel the way you do. I didn't realise how much I needed it until now."

"I was that fantastic?" he asked with a wolfish grin on his face.

She laughed. "You were. Then again, I have no one else to compare you to."

He narrowed his eyes into slits and moved back, not sure he'd like what she was alluding to. "What's that supposed to mean?"

"It means that I haven't been with anyone else since our night together all those months ago," she said indignantly.

Paul couldn't believe her words. He hadn't been with any other woman for six months because the only woman he'd craved was Ijay. It'd been a choice he'd made. For Ijay it was different. She was due to marry his brother in a few weeks.

"Ijay, you're engaged to my brother. Don't feed me this nonsense. You don't have to lie to me," he said, his heart dropping into his stomach with sadness and disappointment.

"It's not a lie. Vincent has never touched me. He wants us to wait till out wedding night."

He looked at her suspiciously with narrowed eyes. He couldn't believe what she said. Why would she tell such a lie now? What did she hope to gain? Her eyes were clear and bore no deceit. She appeared sincere.

If Ijay was telling the truth, then what was Vincent up to? One thing Paul was certain of, Vincent was no saint. And if Vincent hadn't had sex with Ijay then something was wrong. Terribly wrong.

And Paul had to find out what.

Chapter Twenty-One

The next day Paul sent Ijay back to Enugu with Amaechi. Ijay who was still basking in the afterglow of their love-making and Paul's declaration of glorious intent, didn't want to leave him in Amori by himself. She had to agree when he told her she needed some change of clothes.

And perhaps the time apart would give her space to prepare herself for whatever Paul had in store for them.

So after a lingering kiss in the car when they arrived at the factory to drop him off, Paul stepped out of the car with what seemed like reluctant steps. She couldn't hide the smile of joy spreading over her face because he wasn't overexcited about being away from her. She wasn't either.

As the car had moved off on its way to Enugu, she relaxed back into the comfort of the soft leather seats and cool air. Paul's words last night returned in her mind.

"...You're mine alone."

He'd finally staked his claim on her last night. At first she'd thought he was back to playing games at seducing her. That he was simply trying to compete with Vincent in whatever feud they seemed to have going on.

Yet his actions had convinced her otherwise. The passion of their love-making had been thorough and single-minded, compulsive and earth-shattering. It was like six months worth of love-making exploded in one night. The heated frenzy of the first time had eventually turned into a slow tender soul-searing act.

Every part of her body had come alive with his touch and his kiss. Her lungs had been saturated with his spicy scent, her pores saturated with his heat. When she'd looked into Paul's eyes it had been filled with intensity, yearning and...*love?*

Oh, how she wished it was so. He'd made her feel special, desired, and loved. When he said he'd never let her go, she hadn't doubted him. Still, he hadn't said the words *I love you.*

Did that mean he wouldn't want her to return to London? Her friends, her job, her life was in London. She'd give them up for Paul. However, she needed to know the extent of his feelings. That it was more than sex and desire driving his declaration. Or his competition with Vincent.

She loved Paul. Not Vincent.

She twisted the engagement ring from her finger and put it into her handbag. She'd have to return it to Vincent somehow after she'd spoken to him on the phone.

She had to choose the right moment to call Vincent. After his outrageous outburst the last time, she had to brace herself for the impact of his anger. It wasn't best to say what she had to say on the phone. Yet, it was better than waiting for his arrival in Nigeria in a few weeks.

Letting out a sigh, she let her mind roam, daydreaming about Paul and what the future held for them together.

Something still disturbed her mind about Paul—his relationship with Vincent and his mother. She hadn't had time to ask Paul last night. She'd been too wrapped up in enjoying his attention to even think of anything else. Now it bothered her. And there was one person who could help her solve that mystery.

"Amaechi," she said, leaning forward to get the driver's attention.

He looked at her through the rear-view mirror and smiled. "Yes."

"I hope you don't mind if I call you Amaechi. I know that's how Paul addresses you and I didn't want to refer to you as driver," she said tentatively. The man was in his forties, so he was someone she should defer to as an older person.

"It's not a problem at all. You can call me Amaechi," he replied genially.

"Thank you and you can call me Ijay," she replied before pausing hesitantly. "Paul said you were a distant relative on his mother's side."

"Yes, his mother and my father were cousins. He's more like my younger brother than my cousin," he said pleasantly.

"Okay. He said some years ago he stayed with your family," she continued her gentle probing.

"When he was a teenager he came to stay in my father's house for a while. We became close then," Amaechi volunteered.

"Oh, why was that?" she asked directly.

Amaechi reared back and shook his head. "I'm not sure I should discuss it with you. Maybe you should ask Paul."

"I know. I've tried but he's so closed up sometimes," her frustration seeped out in her voice. "I really care about him. I just need to understand everything about him."

"You like him?" he asked. His dark eyes sparked with amusement.

"A lot." She nodded and smiled shyly. "More than you know. I think we could have a future together. But things are so complicated especially with Vincent..."

"You know Vincent?" Amaechi face lost the amusing smile instantly and turned into a dark frown. His expression wasn't as bad as when she'd first mentioned Vincent to Paul. Still, she couldn't miss the fact that Amaechi didn't like Vincent either.

Ijay nodded, not saying anything else.

"Vincent and his mother are bad news," Amaechi continued. "They made Paul's life a misery as a child. I'm thankful that despite all they did to crush Paul, he's doing very well for himself. You are better off staying away from those two."

"What did they do to Paul?" she probed. She needed to know exactly what had happened.

Amaechi shook his head and turned away, looking out of the windscreen.

"Please tell me," she said, the desperation back in her voice. "Vincent's mother said that Paul raped a girl years ago. Is it true?"

"That's a big lie. Paul never hurt that girl. I can swear it on my father's grave," Amaechi said angrily. "I'm sure Vincent did it and they framed Paul for it. Vincent was always a cruel boy, just like his mother. They connived to chase Paul out of his father's house. And they succeeded. He's not even welcome in his own father's compound in the village. Can you imagine such nonsense?"

"What? You can't be serious." Ijay couldn't believe that. In African culture, men were always welcome in their fathers' houses.

"Deadly serious. After Chief Arinze died, it turned out that neither Paul nor any of his other siblings were named in the man's will apart from Vincent and his mother."

"That can't be right?"

"It's not and Paul has refused to contest the will. In fact, it's better for him that he didn't because look at him now. He's doing so well for himself and with peace of mind too."

"If he was disinherited, then what about the villa property and land?"

"The land Paul built on is partly from his mother's people and partly from the community of Amori in recognition of all he has done for the community. Do you know how many children of Amori are on scholarship fund because of him or how many of the citizens he employs at the factory?"

"So if you really care about Paul, whatever dealings you have with Vincent or his mother, you have to break it. They will only poison you. They are venomous snakes," Amaechi concluded before concentrating back on his driving.

"Thank you," Ijay said in shock as she absorbed all of Amaechi's revealing words.

She'd known there was something odd about Mrs. Arinze when she'd found out what the woman had said about Paul. She'd been surprised by the woman stooping so low as to share something that had happened so many years ago with Ijay's family. Ijay had even tried to dismiss the woman's controlling demand that Ijay stopped working on the POD project.

But Amaechi's revelations had just put Vincent and his mother at the top of her creepy list. To think they'd been so mean as to cut Paul and Simon off from their inheritance.

To think that she'd once thought she was in love with Vincent? She hadn't known him at all. The face Vincent had shown her was the face of a lamb. Meanwhile he was a wolf, bound on destroying members of his own family.

Why were they that mean? She could understand if Paul and Vincent had fallen out in the past over some girl. What about Simon? Why wouldn't Vincent want to take care of his younger brother? Especially at a critical stage of Simon's life, when he was trying to build a future for himself.

The more she thought about it the angrier she got. How could she have been so deceived by

Vincent? After what Vincent and Mrs. Arinze had done to Paul, they didn't deserve an apology from her. Vincent was the one who needed to apologise to her for making her think he was something he wasn't.

Furiously she took the ring out of her bag intent on throwing it out of the car window. She was furious at Vincent and his mother for all they'd done to Paul. Why should she bother returning the ring to him? Vincent could go and look for it on the highway if he wanted it back.

As she slid the window down, she realised she didn't want to damage any property or hurt anyone by hauling an object out of a fast-moving car in the mid-morning Enugu traffic. So she balled her hand into a fist around the ring instead.

When they got to Paul's house, she stopped Amaechi before he came out to open the door for her.

"Amaechi, you have to do me a favour. Wait for me. I'm going back to Amori with you," she said.

"I don't think so. Paul instructions were to bring you back to Enugu. He didn't say anything about taking you with me on the return trip," Amaechi replied.

"I know. Hear me out. I want to go back. I don't want to leave him on his own. There's so much that needs to be done to get the order ready to be shipped next week. I can't sit here in Enugu while he's doing all the work down there."

Amaechi continued shaking his head. "I don't know."

Ijay reached out and touched his arm with her hand. "Amaechi, I love Paul. Help me, please," she pleaded. If that didn't work nothing else would.

Slowly a smile broke out on his face. "You love him," Amaechi said.

She nodded and smiled in return. "Yes, I do. With all my heart."

"Then I'll wait."

"Thank you so much." She wanted to hug him but restrained herself. "I'm going to pack a bag and tell Simon's mum to pack a few other things in case we have to stay in Amori for a few more days."

"While I wait I'm going to get some diesel for the generator," he said.

"Good idea. See you later."

Ijay stepped out of the car feeling much better. She had a purpose and things to do instead of just waiting for Paul's arrival in Enugu. Most of all, she'd be seeing him again soon.

When she got into the house, she found Simon's mother in the kitchen.

"Good morning," Ijay said to the woman.

"Welcome," the woman said without looking at Ijay. She seemed a bit distracted opening the cupboards to put away dishes. "Did you want some breakfast?"

"No. I'm not hungry," Ijay replied. "I just wondered if it was possible to pack some foodstuff so I can take it back to Amori."

Simon's mother closed the cupboard and turned to look at Ijay for the first time since she entered the kitchen. "You're going back to Amori again?"

"Yes, I just want to pack a few things. Paul is still there and I have to be with him."

"Aren't you better off staying here since Paul sent you back? He'd prefer not to be distracted while he's working. I know him. He doesn't like to be distracted."

Ijay paused, her face creasing in a frown. If she didn't know better, she'd think Simon's mother didn't want her to be with Paul. But the woman had been so nice to her since Ijay's arrival in Enugu. She didn't want to entertain any unpleasant thoughts. Moreover Simon's mother was a member of Paul's family and Paul trusted her.

"I know Paul will be busy. I also want to help. I really don't want to stay in Enugu doing nothing," Ijay replied boldly.

"Well, suit yourself. It's a good thing I went shopping yesterday, so I can pack some things for you. I'll let you know when it's ready."

"Thank you so much," She smiled, relieved that the woman had agreed. She turned to leave and spotted the small kitchen dust bin. She opened it and threw her engagement ring into it. Feeling much better, she went to her room to pack her bag.

Chapter Twenty-Two

Paul sat in the back seat of the car as Amaechi drove him back to the villa. The exhaustion that had threatened to overwhelm him all day finally took a hold of his body. His back and shoulders ached from hours spent either lifting heavy machinery or hauling crates of packaged foods.

Though weary he was satisfied with the progress they'd made at the factory. The damaged equipment was finally in a state where it could be used again. Though, he'd had to order new spare parts which would take weeks to arrive from the manufacturer. The engineer that Peter had sent him had helped to ensure that the production line was up and running again.

They could make their order delivery on time if they worked through the weekend. Usually the staff were away during the weekend but he'd asked some to come back to complete the order. He'd have to stay too to make sure everything was done on time and ready to ship on Monday.

His weekends were usually spent either in Abuja or Enugu. He'd hoped he'd get to spend some time with Ijay this weekend. That would have to wait. He caught a faint whiff of Ijay. His mind flashed back to this morning, her image as she sat next to him in the car kissing him, replaying itself.

She'd been warm, soft and sweet. He'd been reluctant to leave her and had missed her presence as soon as he'd stepped out of the car. Now his heart ached at not seeing her again for a few more days.

Having her at the villa had made it feel like home. Their night together confirmed to him what he'd been afraid to acknowledge before. She made him feel complete for the first time in his adult life.

He wanted her by his side constantly especially at this early stage. Yet he knew she was better off in Enugu instead of in Amori. It would be safer especially since he had a sneaky suspicion that Vincent had a hand in the damage of his factory equipment.

Things were far from perfect for them. He still had Vincent as a thorn on his side. Paul had to resolve the problem between them once and for all. For Ijay's sake.

She'd been correct. She shouldn't be the source of competition between him and his brother.

As the car neared the gates to this villa, he noted that the outside security lights were on. He assumed that the mains electricity supply was back on after yesterday. The supply was intermittent at best which was why he needed the generator to supply power.

When the car drove in and stopped in the front driveway, he noted the light in the living room was on too. His body tensed and screwed in a worried frown.

Had he forgotten to switch them off? It would be unlike him to do so but was possible.

When he got out of the car, he noticed Amaechi was smiling sheepishly. His frown deepened.

"What's going on?" Paul asked.

Amaechi shrugged. "I'm sorry but she told me not to tell you. She's one woman who knows her own mind. I couldn't persuade her to stay in Enugu."

"Ijay?" Even as he asked the question he already knew. His heart leapt before speeding into a pounding pulse of anticipation.

Amaechi nodded confirming Paul's thoughts. He took his briefcase from Amaechi.

"Goodnight," Paul said and didn't look at Amaechi. His thoughts were already in the villa, with the woman he knew he'd find in there. His steps to the front door quickened. Suddenly he couldn't wait to see Ijay again. Even though he should be angry she'd disobeyed his instructions, he only knew gladness that she was here. He hadn't realised how much he didn't want to spend another night without her until now.

Before he could knock on the door, it swung inwards. Ijay stood there, her lips curved in a tentative smile, her body covered in a pink figure hugging t-shirt and denim wrap skirt that stopped above her knees. Her feet were bare, her blue toe nails catching his attention. Her hair tied back in its usual ponytail. She was the best thing he'd ever seen. Beautiful. Desirable.

His previous weariness departed, replaced by pure pleasure at the sight of her. He stood at the doorway taking in the sight of her for a moment.

"You came back," he said, his lips broadening in a wide grin he couldn't repress nor wanted to, his voice husky with joyous emotion.

"I couldn't keep away from you," she replied breathlessly, her face lit up in a responding smile.

Her words were sweet music to his ears. He took one long step to her and lifted her body into his in a bear hug. Her soft curves crushed against his body. He could feel her hardened nipples push against his chest. Sensation scoured through his body. His heart rate rocketed skywards. His trousers suddenly felt tighter. He groaned with pleasure. With his booted foot, he kicked the door shut and with his other hand he swept the objects on the table in the hallway to the floor and sat Ijay on its edge.

It was just the right height. Her legs stayed wrapped around his hips. He looked into her chocolate eyes wide like saucers and filled with flaming desire and adoration. She looked at him with such devotion. He knew he had to tell her how he felt. Now. He had to push his need to be buried inside her warmth back for now. He stepped back, though she tightened her legs around his hips stopping him from moving further away.

He lifted her hand from his shoulder to his lips. As he brushed his lips against the back of her hand something clicked in his mind.

It's gone! Her engagement ring is gone.

The words resounded in his brain, his eyes unwilling to believe what they saw. Had she spoken to Vincent and returned the ring? Was there a possibility she loved him instead of his psycho half-brother. He looked up at her, his face creased in a frown, his brow raised in a query.

"The ring?" he asked unable to keep silent.

"I threw it away...I broke off the engagement." She lowered her eyelashes in a coy move before lifting them and flashing him a confident smile, her white teeth gleaming.

In that moment it was like the weight of the world left his shoulders and his heart leapt with joyous excitement. She'd taken it off not because he'd asked her but because she decided herself. A most wonderful gift. What he'd wanted all along. A lump clogged his throat.

"I love you," he said gruffly and swallowed the emotional lump in his throat. He blew kisses on her hand.

Her breath hitched, her eyes widening before her face broke into the most glorious smile he'd ever seen. He'd made the right decision by telling her now instead of waiting till they were back in Enugu.

"I love you too," she replied, her eyes glittering with happy tears.

He lowered his head and kissed her lips. Hungrily. Tenderly. His tongue started off swiping her lips gently, seeking to savour her taste. Yet as soon as it swept into her mouth, passion overtook him, uncontrollable sensation racing through his body. His emotions racing between pure joy in his heart and the rush of white heat in his groin.

Ijay couldn't explain the profound joy and pleasure she felt at that moment being in Paul's arms, her legs wrapped around him wanting him even closer than he was.

Paul loved her, just like she loved him. Nothing else matters. They would work through the rest of their problems together.

She closed her eyes and returned his kiss like her life depended on it for sustenance, surrendering her body to the feelings swamping her. Her arms clamped around his neck for balance and to pull him closer.

She no longer recognised the sound of her heart except that she could hear two distinct drums playing in tune with each other. Just as her tongue danced in a tango with Paul's. Their dance sensuous, thrilling and erotic.

Her body came alive with each sinuous movement. She rubbed her nipples against his chest enjoying the sensations that shot through them without the restriction of her bra. She'd taken her bra off earlier seeking some coolness in the heat of the day. Now that decision brought her pure exhilaration.

Paul lifted his head. She inhaled in short gasps, trying to get air into her starved lungs. Her hand slid down his chest. She felt his heart thudding rhythmically through his chest. A strong beat full of life and promise. She undid a button and then the next. She slipped her hand through the gap created under his shirt. He let out a throaty growl. It sounded like a wild lion stretching languorously in the shade.

She glanced up at his face. He looked at her hungrily, like he was really the king of the jungle about to claim his mate. Excitement coursed through her. Her breasts became heavy with arousal and wet heat pooled in her core.

Without a word he pulled his shirt out of his trousers, over his head and discarded it behind him on the sofa. She inhaled sharply in awe. She could never get enough of seeing his bare body especially his toned chest and arms. When he moved the sinuous muscles undulated like a flowing stream of water.

She ran the tips of her fingers across his nipples. His breath hitched in response and he kissed her again. His hands roamed her body and pulled at her top. He broke the kiss to pull it over her head. It joined his shirt somewhere on the sofa.

"I'm afraid we won't be making the bedroom," he growled before his mouth clamped on a bare breast and sucked hard.

Letting out a long moan, she curved her back as more heat coursed through her body and held onto his head. Her head leaned back against the wall. The sensation of his wet hot mouth on her breast drove her crazy. She moved her hips against his, rubbing her already soaking panties against the bulge in his trouser in desperate motion for relief. The initial slow burning ache within her raged out of control now.

"Paul, I need you now," she said huskily, hardly able to speak with her dry mouth that was concentrating more on getting air into her lungs.

In response he growled again and pushed her skirt up her thighs until it sat around her waist. Then he slipped his fingers between her thighs, hooked it onto her lace panties and ripped it. Cool air rushed around her sensitive lower lips.

When she gasped at the damage, he looked up, gave her a wolfish grin as he unzipped his trousers. "I'll buy your more of those," he said with a wink and pushed his hardened shaft into her wet heat.

She moaned as he filled her up. He slid out and rocked into her again, till she felt his blunt head hit the back of her womb wall, stretching her, filling her to the max. He worked up a fast rhythm, gripping her thighs and setting a ramming pace. Before long she was trembling with feverish heat, rushing off to her climax. He rammed into her a few more times and joined her in ecstasy.

He held her tight for a moment, their hot skins clammy together, his chin on her head, before lifting her and carried her to the sofa. Good thing because her legs felt like jelly and she wouldn't have been able to walk without his help. On the sofa he leaned back pulling her on top of him. Thankfully the overhead fan was blowing cool air and refreshed their hot skins.

"Did you speak to Vincent?" he asked, his voice sounding distant and thoughtful.

"I called. He didn't pick up as usual. I left a message for him." She shrugged.

He lifted her head up and looked into her eyes. His dark eyes looked sad.

"You do realise that you are making an enemy of Vincent by being with me. He's a nasty enemy to have. He'll never forgive you for this."

"He'll have to. It's not the end of the world when a relationship breaks. Believe me I know. I was in a relationship with Frederick for three years and I got over the split. I've only know Vincent for six months. He'll get over it too."

Paul shook his head sadly. "Unfortunately, you don't know Vincent at all. He never forgives nor forgets."

"Why do you say that? It can't be that bad." She saw an opportunity to hear Paul's side of the events from his childhood.

"Just know that he isn't a very nice person."

She leaned back and sat up. "Paul, don't freak out okay. I have something to tell you."

Paul's face wrinkled in a frown and he sat up too. "What is it?"

"I know about the rape incident."

"How?" His eyes narrowed into suspicious slits, his lips forming a hard line. "Who told you?"

He pulled his hand back. She held on, refusing to let go. She wasn't going to allow him to withdraw from her. Not now that she finally had his undivided and loving attention.

"You promise you won't freak out, right?" She raised her eyebrow waiting for him to respond.

"Yes, I promise." He nodded reluctantly.

"Vincent's mother told my mum that you raped a girl when you were a teenager."

His body tensed, his hands beneath hers balled into fists. The muscles along his jaw ticked furiously. His eyes suddenly black pools of ice.

"You believe her?" His voice was cold and flat.

"If I believed her I wouldn't be here. How could I believe her when I know differently?" she said.

"I spent the night with you in London as a stranger and yet you were the most considerate lover I'd ever had. Last week I asked you to back off and you did, even when you knew I was yours for the taking. That is all the proof I need to know that you would never take a woman against her will. I've watched the way you deal with people around you and I know you're a man of integrity."

His eyes searched her face, seeking answers only her heart could give.

"Do you mean that?" he asked.

"I do. I love you and I'll stand by you no matter what Vincent and his mother throw at us. You're not alone anymore."

He pulled her close and gave her a lingering kiss. When they broke apart, he told her about his tragic childhood; about his late father's will and about finally walking away from his father's home simply to keep his peace of mind.

She got angry about all the pain he'd suffered at the hands of Vincent and his mother. Paul kissed her and told her to forget it. They had a future to work toward. That was the most important thing.

She asked him why he'd never told her all of these things before.

He looked at her intensely for a moment before replying. "I wanted you to love me, not because Vincent was bad and I was the next best thing. But because you loved me regardless of Vincent. I don't want pity. I want your love, pure and simple."

This time she kissed him as her heart swelled with affection for him. Later she fed him the *Nsala* soup she'd brought from Enugu especially for him.

That night, they made love and talked more before finally falling asleep.

Ijay woke up in the morning to the sound of loud banging on the door. She looked out of the window. The sun was high in the sky. They must have overslept.

"I wonder who that is," she said as Paul scrambled out bed and pulled on his shorts. She grabbed one of Paul's t-shirt and followed him. She stood behind him in the hallway while he opened the door.

Amaechi stood at the door with another man she didn't recognise. He looked harassed.

"Amaechi, what's the matter?" Paul asked.

"Paul, we have a problem at the factory," Amaechi said.

Chapter Twenty-Three

"What problem?" Paul asked, his voice laced with irritation.

"There are some men from NAFDAC there to do an inspection." Amaechi said.

Ijay's face screwed up in a frown. NAFDAC was the National Agency for Food and Drug Administration and Control. She knew they controlled the quality standards on food and other substances. What were they doing at POD Foods now?

"We don't have a scheduled inspection," Paul said, answering her silent query. "Then again they can turn up for random visits. Tell John to open up and let them in. I'm going to get dressed and be there as soon as I can."

Amaechi turned to go.

"You can take the car and come back to pick us," Paul added. He waited for Amaechi to head to the car before he turned round.

Ijay couldn't shake the feeling that something was wrong. Paul headed back to the bedroom and she followed him.

"Do they usually turn up like this for unscheduled inspections?" she asked Paul as he took fresh clothes from the wardrobe.

He shrugged. "We haven't had any of those. But it's not totally unheard of."

He turned to look at her. He must have seen the concern in her eyes because he walked to her and lifted her chin.

"Don't worry about this. We have nothing to hide. So I don't mind the inspection. It's just a couple of hours of inconvenience and they'll be gone and we can get on packing the consignment ready for shipping."

"Okay." She nodded accepting his reassurance though the sense that something bad was about to happen didn't leave her. "I'm going to the factory with you. So I'm going to have a wash and get dressed."

"And I wouldn't have it any other way." He smiled at her. "You should get in there quickly before I think about getting down and dirty," he said in a deep teasing voice that had her core weeping with its suggestion.

How she would've loved to get all sweaty. Yet, her concern about the factory didn't leave her mind. They had to get there soon to know what was going on. Reluctantly, she turned toward the bathroom. He chuckled and swatted her bottom.

She turned when she got into the bathroom and stuck her tongue out petulantly. When he advanced toward her with a wicked glint in his eyes, she shut the door quickly. The hallway reverberated with his deep laughter.

"I'm going to get you for that bit of cheek, sweet Ijay. Very soon." A warm shiver ran down her spine at his erotic threat.

"Promises, promises," she replied with laughter from the relative safety of the bathroom. His punishments were sweet torture. She loved defying him just for the pleasure she knew awaited her in the end. No other man had ever worshipped her body like Paul did.

No other man had ever loved her like he did.

She washed quickly. When she came out of the bathroom, there was a tray with a cup of tea and an omelette on the bedside table.

"Make sure you eat it all." She turned to find Paul by the door watching her. "I'm not sure when we'll get time to stop for food today."

He walked to her, his stride confident and sexy, his smile even more so. He gave her a brief kiss, grazing his lips over hers and headed to the bathroom.

Ijay dressed in a simple print Ankara sundress. She ate the entire omelette, drank all her tea, took the tray back into the kitchen and washed up. Paul came out pulling on a short-sleeved linen shirt. He already had his trousers and shoes on.

"Are you ready to leave?"

"Yes," she replied.

"Okay, you can head to the car. I'll lock up and meet you there."

Ijay went to the bedroom, picked up her handbag and walked out to the car. When she got into the car, Amaechi glanced back. He had a worried expression.

"Amaechi, what is it?" she asked curiously.

"I'm worried about all the bad things suddenly going on at the factory. We've never had any incidents like this before. In the space of a few days we've had the place broken into, equipment damaged and now random inspectors. They've got policemen with them too. As if they're actually expecting to find something wrong."

"Wow, I'm worried too. Paul seems to think there's nothing to worry about, though."

"I'm hoping the same thing too because Amori can't afford to have the factory close."

"The factory won't close. Paul will make sure of it. It's very important to him to sustain the community. Don't worry," she reassured Amaechi.

Yet the knot of apprehension remained in her stomach and weighed heavily on her. When Paul got into the car. His presence soothed her for a little while until they arrived at the factory. Throughout the journey, Paul appeared calm, holding onto her hand and gently caressing it. She was glad he was unperturbed. She only hoped that his confidence would be justified.

There were several marked vehicles both of the Nigerian Police and NAFDAC officials packed in front of the industrial warehouse building. Some of the staff were standing outside.

Ijay followed Paul inside where they met Mr. Obi. He looked hassled, his brow covered in sweat beads. A man standing next to him flashed his NAFDAC agent badge and introduced himself as Mr. Savage.

"Have you completed the inspection?" Paul asked calmly.

"Yes sir," Mr. Savage replied. "Unfortunately we have reasons to believe that food packaged in your factory is injurious to health. So we'll be closing it down temporarily."

"What? That's not possible. We run a clean and safe environment here. We adhere to hygiene standard as you can see for yourself," Paul said waving his hands about.

"Mr. Arinze, the issue is not with the hygiene but rather with harmful substances found in your packaging material."

"Our packaging was approved by your people long ago. The documents are in the office. John, did you show him the documents?"

"I'm sorry I've searched for the certificates and couldn't find any of them," Mr Obi replied, looking even more worked up.

"Your manager couldn't produce any NAFDAC approval certificates for your packaging. However, we found these." Mr. Savage lifted a sheaf of papers in his hand. "They show that your packaging materials have higher mercury and silicon content than is approved for packaging food products."

Paul's expression was thunderous. "That's impossible." His gaze moved to Mr. Obi who was now visibly shaking. "You found that document where?"

"In your office. Your manager gave it to us."

Paul levelled his gaze suspiciously at the factory manager. The man couldn't meet his gaze.

"Mr. Obi, how did that get in here."

"I—I," the man stammered as more sweat dripped down his face.

Paul shook his head furiously before turning back to Mr. Savage. "Listen all this can be resolved. I know my food and packaging meet the required standards. I have the original certificates to prove it at my office in Abuja. I can get them for you. So you don't have to shut this place down."

"If you produce the items, then we can reopen the factory. In the meantime, we have to shut it down and you have to come with us to our offices in Enugu for questioning," the inspector replied.

"What? I'm not going anywhere with you." Paul let out an angry growl, his hands clenched into fists by his sides ready to smash through anything.

"Ensuring food safety is a grave issue for NAFDAC and we take any cases of violation seriously. The policemen are here to ensure that if you do not wish to accompany us quietly, you come along forcefully. Your choice."

"How am I supposed to bring the documents to you, if I'm in Enugu answering questions?" he raised his hands in exasperation.

Ijay stepped forward, placing her hand on his back. It seemed to stop his agitation as he turned and looked at her.

"I'll go to Abuja and get the documents," she said.

"I can't let you do that. I should go. I know where they are," Paul replied.

"Remember we're in this together now. I'll go. Just tell me where they are or I'll ask Pamela. I'll be back in Enugu tomorrow morning at the latest and all this will be sorted."

"Okay," he nodded and squeezed her hand. "Thank you. Call Pamela to arrange a flight for you. Amaechi will take you to the airport."

"Don't worry about a thing. Just go and sort this out. I'll be back as soon as I can."

He gave her hand one last squeeze. She turned around and went out of the entrance, her heart heavy. Amaechi's words from earlier came back to her.

"...in the space of a few days we've had the place broken into, equipment damaged and now random inspectors..."

All these things had happened since her arrival in Amori. Who was doing this? She couldn't believe that Paul would have sub-standard packaging material for his products. He wasn't that kind of a man. The factory was modern and clean. He didn't cut corners with anything else. He surely wouldn't with something like that.

Were all the bad things happening because of her? Who would want to hurt Paul because of her?

Vincent!

It suddenly dawned on her. Paul had said Vincent could be vicious. Would he really go this far to threaten Paul's business and employees?

"I need to get to the airport," she said distractedly to Amaechi who walked back to the car beside her.

"I heard Paul," he replied. "Do you want to get to the villa first?"

"Yes, I need my carry on case, as I might have to spend the night in Abuja."

He drove her back to the villa. As she packed her things and headed back to the car, her mind was on Paul. She hated leaving him by himself. At least she was on a mission to help. When she got back to Enugu with the documents, hopefully everything would be resolved and she could get on with a life with Paul.

She called Pamela and told her what was going on. Shortly after she got into the car on their way to Enugu, Pamela called back.

"I've booked you on the next flight to Abuja which is in two hours so you should have enough time to get to the airport. I've also booked you a night at the hotel. The documents will be ready for you when you get into the office later."

"Thank you," Ijay replied with relief. At least the documents were in Abuja so there should be no problem. Pamela gave her the flight booking details and hung up.

Ijay called Paul.

"I've spoken to Pamela. The documents will be ready when I arrive into Abuja," she said when he answered the call.

"That's good. Did she manage to get you a flight?" he asked in a sombre tone.

"Yep, flight and hotel. So I'll be back in the morning," she said keeping her tone cheery. She didn't want him staying upset about what was happening. Plus she felt guilty that his misfortunes could be her fault.

"Good. I have to go now. Have a safe journey and I'll see you tomorrow in Enugu."

"Thank you," she replied and added "I love you," just before the line disconnected.

The flight to Abuja was uneventful. The mid-afternoon sunshine was baking hot. Paul's chauffeur was there to pick her up and took her straight to the POD offices. Pamela handed her the plastic file folder with the documents as well as a message to call Sonia in London.

Ijay thanked her and headed to the hotel. After she checked in, she headed to the lifts. She was busy fiddling with her handbag when someone bumped her. The folder she had in her hand slipped out and hit the marble lobby floor.

"Sorry, I'm such a klutz."

Ijay looked up at the sound of the saccharin voice. Her gaze connected with that of the woman Paul had been speaking to last week right here in this same hotel. The woman smiled at her, her red lips curved. Ijay noted her eyes had none of the amusement.

"It's not a problem." Ijay held her gaze not wanting to look away first. A passing bellboy picked up the folder from the floor. The woman took it from him. "That's mine. Can I have it back?" she replied indignantly.

"Of course," her nemesis replied. "You wouldn't want someone else taking something that belongs to you now, would you? I mean if someone took something or someone important from me, I would be forgiven for doing everything within my power to get it back. I mean everything. You understand, don't you?"

Ijay frowned and snatched the folder back angrily. "What's that supposed to mean? Who are you by the way?"

"My name is Kate. Let's just say we have a mutual lover in Paul. Since he was mine first, I'm claiming him. So keep away from him or watch your back. I don't care if you're one of those bitches that like to keep two men chasing after them. I mean looking at you, no one would think that butter melts in your mouth, would they. You've had two brothers so I have to give it to you. But keep away from Paul. Or watch your back, bitch!" Kate spat out at her before swivelling and walking away.

Confused, Ijay stood on the spot watching Kate walk out of the hotel entrance, unable to quite process all the information she'd been fed in such a short time. How did Kate know about Paul and Vincent? Her face heated up at the insinuation she'd had both brothers. Her grip on her bag and folder tightened as she got angrier. She was going to call Paul and find out what was going on.

She dragged her luggage up to her room. She called Paul's phone. It was out of reach. She turned on the TV as a distraction and paced the room. Fuming, she was undecided about what to do about Kate and decided to call Sonia. She hadn't spoken to her friend since last week. They were overdue for a chat and so much had happened.

"Girl, you're having so much fun out there, you've forgotten me," Sonia said as soon as the line connected.

"I'm sorry. So much has happened in such a short time and it's not all fun and games."

"Come on, spill. What's going on?"

"Gosh, where do I start? The short of it is that I've broken off the engagement with Vincent."

"*What?*" Ijay could hear Sonia's shout and moved the phone away from her ear.

"You're in the office, right?" She asked, worried that everyone at Havers & Child would hear about her exploits in Nigeria.

"Yes, but most people have headed home. Remember it's Friday."

"Okay," Ijay said with relief. Then she told her friend the abbreviated version of what had happened in the past week. In between 'goshing' and 'ahing' Sonia listened to all she had to say.

"So you think Vincent is responsible for the problems Paul's having at the factory?"

"I do. It all started after his mother demanded I keep away from Paul and I refused and went to Enugu. Maybe it's Vincent's mother organising all these things since Vincent is in London."

"Maybe," Sonia said thoughtfully.

"On top of all that I bumped into Kate in the hotel lobby. As if I don't have enough to deal with."

"Who's Kate?" Sonia sounded confused and Ijay couldn't blame her. She was confused too.

"She claims she's Paul's girlfriend and has practically threatened me if I don't stay away from him."

"What nonsense." Sonia said angrily. "You don't believe her do you?"

"Right now, I don't know what to believe. I saw her with Paul in that very same lobby last week. She was touching him proprietarily and he didn't stop her. The thing is she knew Paul and Vincent are brothers. How else would she know that if not from Paul?"

The sound of a knock at her hotel door drew her attention.

"Sonia, hold on there's someone at the door."

Ijay walked to the door and looked through the peephole. Her body froze. An icy shiver of trepidation and shock slid down her back. Her breath hitched loudly.

"Ijay, what is it?" Sonia's words filtered into her ears.

"Vincent is here!" Ijay gasped in shock.

Chapter Twenty-Four

"What is he doing there? I thought he wasn't due in Nigeria for another couple of weeks," Sonia remarked, her shock apparent in her tone of voice.

"I know! He's not supposed to be here," Ijay replied in a low brash tone, her heart pounding in her chest with worry.

After Vincent's aggressive reaction on the phone when she'd told him about Paul, she didn't know what to expect from him this time. She'd been a little relieved that she only got his voice-mail yesterday when she'd called him. She hadn't wanted to deal with another outburst from him then. She still didn't want to deal with him.

"What am I going to do? I'm not ready to talk to him," she said biting her lower lip.

"You could just ignore him and not open the door," Sonia suggested.

Ijay nodded as she paced the room. The knocking sound persisted. "I could. He's still knocking, though. How does he even know I'm here?"

So many questions bombarded her mind that she couldn't answer.

While this was the same hotel she'd stayed in when she'd arrived in Abuja the first time, she hadn't told Vincent her room details.

When did he get to Nigeria?

The last time she'd spoke to Vincent had been the day he'd called her a bitch. She'd purposely chosen not to call him until she'd resolved things with Paul.

Had he received her message yet? If he'd been on a flight to Nigeria yesterday, that might explain why his phone had been switched off.

"Ijay, it's me Vincent. Open the door." Ijay recognised his loud voice through the door.

"Did you hear that?" Ijay said in a muffled voice to her friend. "He just called my name. He knows I'm here. I'm going to have to let him in."

"I'll stay on the line to keep you company," Sonia replied reassuringly.

"Thanks," Ijay said as she walked to the door and opened it.

Vincent stood in the hotel hallway. Dressed in a dark blue blazer, trousers and a white shirt, he looked exactly the way she remembered him—two inches taller than her, stocky and dark-skinned— handsome and harmless.

She'd always thought he reminded her of Femi Branch the Nollywood actor. Vincent's face didn't have the harsh angles like Paul's but when he smiled he could be charming. It was partly why she'd been attracted to him at first.

Now though, his smile didn't reach his eyes. They were dark and menacing, though his lips curved up. It made him appear like a snarling wolf.

In that moment, she realised so many things she thought were charming about him were false. He'd been toying with her, playing her like a pawn in a deadly game of chess with Paul.

Vincent had never loved her.

"I was wondering if you were going to open the door. Aren't you happy to see your fiancé after a week?" his deep voice used to sound soothing to her. Now it only added to her irritation. Her temper rose as she thought about how she'd been played by him. Her first response was to shut the door in his face.

Vincent raised his eyebrows in a mocking query. Then she decided she'd play along with his game to see exactly where it would end. She wasn't going to let him get the better of her.

"I'm on the phone. That's why," she said in a cool voice and raised the phone in her hand for emphasis. "What are you doing here?"

"If I didn't have a thick skin, I'd be hurt by that." He placed his hand on his heart and feigned a pained look. "Aren't you going to invite me in?"

"I'm just surprised to see you here after your rude behaviour to me on the phone the last time. Anyway, come in." She shrugged indifferently and moved away from the door.

Vincent came in and shut the door. She heard the sound of the lock going into place. Her heart jumped, pounding into her chest. She turned and walked further away afraid he'd notice her apprehension at being in a room alone with him.

If he'd raped a girl once because the girl had rejected him when he was a boy, what would he do to her now that she'd annulled their engagement?

"Did you get my message?" She gripped the phone tighter and turned back to face him, her back stiffened. She needed to know how much Vincent knew already about her and Paul.

"Which message was that?" he asked. On the outside, he appeared unperturbed, the confident smirk on his face as he curiously looked around the room. "You have a nice room here," he added casually.

Didn't he know? He acted like he thought they were still engaged. Perhaps he hadn't checked his messages yet.

"The last message I left calling off the engagement," she said, her voice rising with her exasperation. Her heart rate got higher, her hands clammier.

"Oh that. Yes, I got it." He nodded, his expression didn't change. "Who are you talking to on the phone?" he asked, changing the conversation nonchalantly.

Stunned by his seemingly calm attitude, Ijay didn't know what to say at first. Where was the Vincent that had been angry on the phone? Either Vincent had taken the news well or he was about to erupt like he'd done the last time. She shifted her stance warily.

"Sonia," she replied eventually.

"That slut!" His outburst was so sudden she didn't have time to respond before he snatched her phone out of her hand with force.

"Give me back my phone," she shouted.

"Sonia or whatever your name is," Vincent spoke into the phone, ignoring Ijay. Ijay could only watch in horror as he spoke insolently to her friend. "You haven't been a good friend to Ijay, have you? You've been the one encouraging her to fuck around while she's engaged. Well, don't call her anymore. Ijay doesn't need friends like you."

He pressed the off button and switched the phone off, putting it in his pocket.

"How dare you talk to my friend like that? You have no right," Ijay snapped angrily, her hands clenched in a ball on her side. She really wanted to hit him for that tirade. What was wrong with him? She felt appalled and ashamed. No man had even insulted her like Vincent did. Worse, he'd just insulted Sonia too.

"I have every right," he advanced toward her menacingly, his eyes glinting with fury, his hand raised. Icy terror shot down her spine. She thought he'd hit her and she backed away.

"You're my fiancé. Once we're married you won't be keeping friends like that anymore," he spat his words in her face.

"I'm not going to marry you Vincent. I told you that already," she couldn't hide the faint quiver in her voice.

Still, she straightened her spine, refusing to let him intimidate her. She could never marry Vincent now. Knowing all that she knew about him. If he treated her this way now, how would he behave when they were actually married? Would he be physically abusive?

She remembered Paul's words.

"...You'll stay with a man who is verbally abusive? What would he have done if you had that conversation in his presence? Hit you?"

At the time, she'd defended Vincent's action. Now, she knew Vincent hitting her was a strong possibility. The mad glint in his eyes confirmed it. Her body shivered with dread at what her life would've been like if she'd married him.

Vincent ignored her and walked to the sofa. Smiling, he sat down and patted the seat beside him, inviting her to sit beside him. She glared furiously at him wondering how he could switch from being so calm one minute to being violent the next.

"You'll be my wife, my dear Ijay." There was no mistaking the menace in his cold voice.

Ijay lost her temper again, leaning forward and jabbing her hand in his direction. "You have to be insane to think that I'll marry someone like you. You were pretending to be someone different in London. Meanwhile, you are devious and conniving. Look at all the things you did to Paul."

He shot up off the sofa and walked toward her. His eyes blazed with twisted rage. For a moment he looked crazed. "Don't you dare mention his name again near me, do you understand," he shouted.

Panting, he turned his back and said more calmly. "I bet he gave you a whole sob story about how I did this or that to him. Well, I don't care. He's lucky to still be alive. If it wasn't for mother, who doesn't want another blood on her conscience, I would've had him consigned to the grave years ago."

Ijay gasped in horror. "You wouldn't!"

He turned around, the cold menace back in his eyes. "Oh, I would. I've done it before. I'll do it again." He laughed out, hollow and demented.

"You see, you are no longer in London. From the moment you arrived here, I knew everything you did, where you went, whom you saw. And it's the same thing with Paul. I've known his movements for years. So getting rid of him would be pretty easy."

He snapped his fingers loudly making Ijay jump. Then, he placed his hand under his chin and tapped his lips as if thinking.

Stunned, Ijay watched him, mouth agape, not believing what she was hearing. Who was this man? Surely it wasn't the same man who had romantically wined and dined her. He'd promised her all sorts of things. She'd let him kiss her and thought about their wedding excitedly.

Yet the man in front of her was a monster if he really meant half of the things he was saying now. He'd been watching her and Paul somehow. Who was spying for him? Whoever it was had access to a lot of information and had to be close to Paul.

She racked her brain thinking about all the people close to Paul—Amaechi, Simon, Simon's mother, Pamela, Mr. Obi. She couldn't stomach the thought that one of these people that Paul trusted was betraying him to Vincent. She really had to speak to Paul. Hopefully he'd call her soon.

Then she remembered her phone was switched off in Vincent's pocket and gritted her teeth in frustration.

"You know I'm undecided between a car accident and an explosion at the factory. Which do you think will be more effective?" He turned to her excitedly as if actually expecting her to offer an opinion.

Ijay felt sick, her stomach churning. Blood drained from her head. She walked to the sofa and sat down heavily clutching her head.

Vincent was insane. A mad man. There was no other explanation.

She raised her head and looked at him again, as she inhaled in panic, her breath coming in short gasps. He stood there, looking at her and waved his hands urgently.

"Come on, which one would you choose? I'm partial to the car accident. Although I think an explosion would be spectacular."

He paced a little more. She couldn't only watch him flabbergasted, not knowing how to respond to his crazy words.

"I know, how about a car bomb. Now that's clever, isn't it?"

"You can't be serious. Paul is your brother!" she replied, unable to hold back her anger and fear any longer.

"Well, I don't want him as my brother. Neither him nor all the other bastards that claim to be my siblings," he said, looking hurt as if she shouldn't have mentioned his relationship with Paul.

"He is and it's not his fault that your father had affairs," she said, hoping a little reason might penetrate Vincent's warped mind and make him see sense.

"Perhaps, but it's his fault for being the one that my father loved. You should have seen the way my father always told me off because of him," Vincent replied, still looking pained. "'Why can't you be as clever as Paul?' 'Why can't you be as hard-working as Paul?' The old man went on and on about him every day. Well enough!"

"Vincent, I'm sorry you felt neglected by your father but killing Paul won't change it. Surely, you can see that."

Ijay could understand sibling rivalry. She had a younger sister and sometimes they competed to see who was better at some things. Although, neither of them had ever felt one of their parents was giving the other any more attention. As a child, she'd learnt to accept that her sister was younger and sometimes needed extra attention from her mother. Yet, she'd always felt special too.

Vincent obviously hadn't felt that way. Otherwise he wouldn't still be carrying a grudge against Paul, surely.

"No. What I see is that Paul keeps taking things and people that belong to me. First was my father, and then came Onome and now you. No more," Vincent replied in a loud voice, his anger unabated.

"Well I won't let you hurt him. I'm going to report you to the police." Ijay had to do something. She couldn't listen to Vincent's threats and ignore it as the ramblings of a mad man.

He laughed again. "Go ahead. What are you going to tell them? That your fiancé threatened to kill his brother after he found out you've been fucking him." He lifted her phone out of his jacket. "Here, go on. Remember this is Nigeria. You'll find that they'll be sympathetic with me. After all I'm justifiably upset and can say anything in anger. Go on, take the phone. Call them."

Ijay snatched the phone from him, her body shaking with anger. She knew he was right. Who would take her seriously? It was just her words against his.

"I won't let you hurt Paul or anybody else. There are people who depend on him. I won't let you take that away from them too," she said instead.

"So marry me and solve their problem," Vincent said in a matter of fact tone as if they were discussing the rising price of petrol or some other mundane thing.

She bit back the sharp retort on her tongue. Marrying Vincent was the last thing she ever wanted to do. She loved Paul. She couldn't imagine a life without him. However promising marriage would buy her time to speak to Paul. He'd know what to do about Vincent.

"If I agree for the wedding to go ahead, will you promise to leave Paul alone forever?" she asked boldly.

"Yes," he replied. She suppressed a gloating smile until he added, "But you're not to see him or speak to him ever again."

"That's not possible. I have the project to complete."

"No, you don't," he said sharply. "You'll tell your boss you have to withdraw from the project. I'm sure you can come up with some excuse. If I get even a whiff that you spoke to Paul—"

"I understand," she replied quickly and nodded for emphasis. "I'll marry you. Just leave Paul alone."

Her stomach churned even as she said the words. She felt sickened that she was betraying Paul by agreeing to marry Vincent. This was the wrong time for Paul to think that she'd turned her back on him when things were going wrong for him.

The alternative was even worse. She couldn't bear to see Paul get hurt or killed knowing she could've prevented it. She wouldn't be able to live with herself.

Paul alive and caring for his family and community without her was better than Paul dead because of her. And everyone else left with no one supporting them. She couldn't have that on her conscience.

"That's fantastic," Vincent's voice brought her back to the hotel room. "So you can put this back on." He reached in his jacket pocket and took out a ring. It sparkled in the light.

"How did you get that? I threw it in the bin." She recognised the engagement ring he'd given her previously.

He laughed. "I told you I knew everything you were up to. Let me have your hand."

Biting back the nausea that rose in her throat, she extended her hand robotically.

It's better this way.

He slid the ring onto her finger. The last time he'd slid it on, she'd been overjoyed and felt like she was floating in the air. Now it felt like a chain of lead dragging her down into depression and misery.

"Don't you just love it when a plan comes together?" He said with a leer. "I knew you were going to be the perfect woman for my plan when I saw you with Paul that night."

"What night?" She asked, unable to shake the creepy sensation on her spine.

"The night you threw yourself at him in London, of course."

"No!" Ijay gasped, clutching her cheeks in shock.

"Yes. I was there at the party. I saw the two of you on the balcony before you left together. I know about my brother's sexual preferences, so I know exactly what you two did together. I decided I'll kill two birds with one stone; giving my mother the grandchildren she's been nagging me about and destroying Paul for good."

"Grandchildren?"

"Oh, didn't I tell you. Once we're married I've got a clinic ready to have you artificially inseminated with my sperm. That bitch Onome did something to me so I can't fuck you the normal way, my dear fiancée."

Ijay couldn't hold back the nausea any longer and ran to the bathroom.

"When you're done in there, pack your things. We're going down to Lagos. We're booked for a registry wedding this weekend," Vincent said cheerily from the other side of the bathroom door.

Chapter Twenty-Five

Paul was in the car heading back to Enugu. The day had been quite gruelling. First was dealing with NAFDAC. He'd spent most of the day with the officials answering their questions about the products and packaging.

Then he'd had to call the customer Bide Supermarkets and warned him of a delay in shipping the products. Luckily he had a good working relationship with Bide. He'd never been late with a delivery before. The purchasing manager was happy to give him a few extra days leeway on the delivery of the goods. All he had to do now was ensure everything was sent out before the end of next week.

He scrubbed his face as he exhaled raggedly. Leaning back into the soft leather, he closed his eyes and tried to relax. He'd had to learn early in life how to cope with nerve-wracking situations.

Losing his mother as a child, dealing with a vile step-mother, fighting a nasty brother and finally being held in an unpleasant police cell for a crime he didn't commit, had all contributed to toughen his personality. So coping with a few days of hellish incidents at the factory was stressful but bearable.

His concern was about the reasons for them occurring now. There was only one catalyst for his sudden run of bad luck.

His relationship with Ijay.

And one set of perpetuators—his step-mother and his brother Vincent. They were the only ones he knew who'd be bent on exacting revenge and punishment upon him for dating Ijay.

Vincent could never live to see Paul take anything away from him. As children, Vincent had made sure he won in any fight about toys or any other items at home. If he wasn't able to acquire it by trying to physically intimidate Paul, he'd enlist his mother who would instruct Paul to give it to him.

Vincent was never big on moving on—he carried a grudge for life. He'd see Ijay choosing Paul as a great affront and do everything to punish Paul. Paul could live with Vincent's wrath. He could survive whatever his brother threw at him. He'd coped with it so far.

However, this time the incidents had hit so close to home. He'd suspected that Vincent had spies working for him for months. The break-in and disappearance of the NAFDAC approval certificates had led to sweeping out the informer in their midst. Paul had demanded the truth from Mr. Obi after the man couldn't give a proper explanation to the disappearance of documents.

Unfortunately, Mr. Obi's late confession hadn't prevented the temporary closure of the factory. Apparently, he'd been instructed to burn the papers by Mrs. Arinze and replace them with the false documents. Paul's step-mother had promised his factory manager a large amount of money and the caretaker job of the Arinze properties in Lagos.

Paul's anger rose again and he clenched his fists tightly. Suppressing a vicious growl, he inhaled and exhaled refreshingly cool air.

How could Mr. Obi be so selfish? The factory manager hadn't been thinking about his fellow employees who could lose their jobs if the factory closed permanently. The man even had the effrontery to say that he knew the factory wouldn't be closed for long. At the point, Paul had instructed the policemen present to arrest him. A few days in a police cell should hopefully make him see the error of his ways.

Paul now had to worry about hiring and training another manager. In the meantime, he'd have to appoint someone to act as the supervisor until a permanent person was appointed. At least he didn't have to worry about it for a few days while the factory was closed.

The sound of his ringing phone jarred Paul out of his thoughts. He opened his eyes, took the phone from his pocket and picked the call without recognising the number.

"Hello, Paul Arinze speaking," he spoke into the receiver.

"Hi Paul, this is Sonia from Havers & Child. I hope I haven't disturbed you," the soft tentative voice replied. Paul recognised the voice of Ijay's colleague. Ijay had explained to him that Sonia was her best friend.

"Hi Sonia, not at all. How are you?" he replied pleasantly. A warm smile broke out on his face, lifting his spirit. He was happy to speak to a friend of Ijay's. It made him feel even closer to Ijay as another link in her life was connected. He wanted to know everyone that mattered to her. Anyone who mattered to her mattered to him.

"I'm well thank you," she replied tentatively.

"How can I help you?" he asked when she didn't volunteer anymore information.

"I'm not really sure if I should be telling you this," she said, her voice hesitant and worried.

"Is there a problem at Havers & Child? Is Charles okay?" he encouraged her as he felt there was something important she felt she had to tell him. It was probably uncomfortable for her to tell him since he was technically a business client and there were non-disclosure contracts in place.

"No it's not a business matter. It's personal." She paused again and Paul waited giving her time to talk. "Have you spoken to Ijay lately?"

His hackles rose and his body tensed. Somehow he knew instantly that something was wrong with Ijay.

"Not this evening. I spoke to her before she boarded her flight to Abuja this afternoon. I'm in Enugu," he said, keeping his voice even, not wanting Sonia to pick up on his concern.

"Well, I've just been on the phone with Ijay and then Vincent turned up."

He sat up in his seat, his seatbelt tugging at across his chest. Icy fear ran down his spine. "What? Vincent turned up where?"

"In her hotel room!"

White hot rage lanced through his mind. He let out a loud growl that vibrated his whole body. Amaechi glanced back at him and looked away quickly. He must have seen the murderous fury in Paul's eyes.

Murder was too simple a solution for what he had in mind if Vincent hurt Ijay. He'd allowed his brother too many liberties in the past. Now it seemed his Vincent had overreached himself.

"Paul?" The quiet tentative voice of Sonia on the phone brought Paul back from his violent thoughts.

Slowly he leaned back into his seat. He had to understand everything that was happening before he decided on the best course of action. He inhaled several times, his regulated breathing calming his rage somewhat before he spoke again.

"Sonia, please calmly tell me exactly what happened."

"Well, Ijay called me," she began. He heard her panting breath as she narrated her conversation with Ijay. "She said she'd just arrived in Abuja from Enugu and told me what had happened in the past few days. She also told me she'd left a message for Vincent breaking off the engagement and threw away his ring. While we were talking there was a knock on her door and it was Vincent. Ijay wasn't happy to see him but had to open the door because he wouldn't go away. When he got in, he got quite angry, snatched her phone and shouted at me never to speak to Ijay again since they were going to get married. He called me a slut! Then he switched off the phone."

As Sonia told her story, Paul's blood bubbled over with rage. He could barely restrain himself. The idea that Vincent was anywhere near Ijay drove him insane. He counted mentally, keeping himself calm.

"Are you sure it was Vincent?" he asked. He had to be sure. His brother had pulled some crazy stunts before. This was new, materialising in Abuja when he should be in London. "Ijay said he wasn't due in Nigeria for another two to three weeks."

"That's what I thought too," Sonia said, her confusion apparent in her voice. "It was certainly him. I recognised his voice as soon as he spoke to me on the phone."

"Did you hear anything else? Was anyone else there?"

"No, he switched off the phone. There is something else though. Before Vincent's arrival Ijay mentioned she'd bumped into a woman in the hotel lobby who said she was your girlfriend. The woman had warned Ijay off you."

"A woman? Did Ijay tell you the person's name?"

"Yes, Kate. Do you know her?"

"I know Kate." He nodded. The jigsaw clicked into place in his mind. He'd always been suspicious about Kate's motives. Now he was absolutely certain she'd been in cahoots with Vincent from the start. She'd been feeding Vincent information about him in the past.

"She's not my girlfriend," he continued to Sonia. "I haven't dated her in almost a year. I don't know what she's playing at but I'll find out soon enough. Don't worry."

"I hope so," Sonia replied. "For now I'm more concerned about Ijay with Vincent. He sounded so angry. I couldn't think of anyone else to call apart from you and her parents. I thought you'd be the better person, since you're Vincent's brother."

"Yes, you made the right decision. Thank you for telling me. I promise you I'll make sure she's okay," he replied, hoping to reassure her. He also hoped he'd get to stop Vincent before he did anything stupid.

"If you get to speak to her soon, please tell her to call me as soon as possible so I know she's well. I've tried her number several times and it's switched off."

"No problem. I'll let you know myself as soon as I get hold of her."

"Thanks." Sonia hung up.

It took Paul several moments to calm his raging fury after Sonia disconnected.

How dare Vincent threaten Ijay?

In the past, he hadn't minded about Vincent or his mother's activities because it had been between them and him. Now that Vincent had extended that spitefulness to Ijay, Paul couldn't sit back and let it continue.

That he'd been quiet before didn't mean he didn't have a means of dealing with the rampaging pair. He'd simply chosen a path of peace because he'd made a promise to do so, no matter what they threw at him.

The idea that Ijay could get hurt by those two meant he could no longer remain passive. If Vincent and his mother wanted war, he'd give them war. And he had exactly the right weapons to bring them down.

Paul lifted his phone and scrolled through his phone numbers. When he found the right one, he pressed the dial button.

The recipient picked it up almost instantly with a gruff, "Yes."

"I need that parcel I left in your safe keeping," he said calmly.

"No problem. I'll have it ready for you. When do you want it?" the deep voice replied.

"I'll pick it up in the morning," he replied.

"I'll see you then."

Paul switched off the phone and relaxed into his seat. What he was about to unleash was extreme. The situation called for it. As he didn't know who to trust in his personal household anymore, he didn't make any other calls until he got home. He didn't want to think that Amaechi or any other person he cared about was betraying him. But if Mr. Obi could fall into the snare of Mrs. Arinze, then anyone else could too.

Moreover, someone had told Vincent where to find Ijay. Although, he could've guessed since she was staying in the same hotel she'd stayed last week. It still didn't explain how Vincent knew she was going to be there this afternoon.

He said a quick hello to Simon outside before going inside. He met Aunty by the hallway. She greeted him as usual. Something in her tone sounded off and drew his attention. She appeared to fidget with her dress.

"Is there a message for me? Did Ijay call?" he asked her curiously.

"No." She shook her head and didn't meet his gaze. Something was definitely off with her. He wanted to probe her a bit more he needed to make few more phone calls first.

"Okay, I'm going upstairs for now."

When he got into the quiet sanctity of his bedroom, he called Ijay's hotel and asked for her. He was informed she'd checked out a short time ago. The receptionist also confirmed she'd been with a man.

"Do you know where they were headed? I'm supposed to be meeting them at the airport." he added in a charming voice. He really needed to be ahead of Vincent if he was going to stop his brother.

"Yes, she mentioned something about a flight to Lagos," the girl replied in a sweet voice.

"That's great," he said pleasantly. "You've been very helpful. When I'm in Abuja next time, I'm going to bring you a nice gift. What's your name?"

"My name is Funmi," the girl giggled. "Thank you, sir"

"You're welcome. Bye."

He hung up and called Peter and Michael on a three-way voice conference.

"I need your help, guys," he said as soon as they both came online.

"Shoot. What do you need?" Peter asked first.

"I need to get on your late flight out to Lagos," he said deadpan.

"Ha. Why are you not asking Pamela to book it for you? I'm not your secretary," Peter joked.

"This is serious. I need to get to Lagos and I don't want anyone to know what's happening except you and Michael," Paul replied in a sombre tone.

"You have to tell us what's going on," Michael interjected. "You sound hassled. Why the cloak and dagger stuff?"

"I'll tell you both. First please tell your secretary to book the flight and call me back with the details. And Michael, please book a car to take me to the airport."

"You mean you don't want Amaechi to take you?" The shock in Michael's voice was loud and clear.

Amaechi was probably the closest person to Paul out of all the people that worked for him. The faintest hint of distrust would break a relationship that had existed for a long time. But Paul couldn't afford to take risks when Ijay's life was in danger.

"Right now I can't trust anyone close to me. Not my employees or people in this house," he said as sadness wrapped around him. He hated to distrust the people he cared about.

"Why?" Michael asked.

"One or more of them is passing information to Vincent and his mother." And whoever it was, Paul had to smoke them out so they didn't spoil his relationship with everyone else.

"This is serious," Peter and Michael said at the same time.

"Right. I'll sort out the flight and call you back," Peter said.

"Yes, I'll book the car. And then you can tell us exactly what's going on," Michael added.

"Thank you," Paul said and disconnected the call. His friends had his back. At a time like this it was good to know that. To beat Vincent at his own game, Paul had to call out all his resources.

Letting out a heavy sigh of relief, he went to his wardrobe to pack what he needed.

Chapter Twenty-Six

Paul had showered and changed clothes by the time the car arrived. He'd called his attorney and a few other people he needed to get his plan into action. Michael turned up in the car with his driver to pick Paul up. They'd agreed it would be better if they pretended Paul was having a night out with the guys so they wouldn't raise anyone's curiosity. He'd already dismissed Amaechi for the night.

When he left the house, he had a light overnight bag. He told Aunty and Simon he was meeting up with Peter and Michael at Park Hotel, Enugu and would be spending the night there. It wasn't unusual for him. He part-owned the business with his other friends and they met there regularly. Occasionally, he spent the night there if the need arose.

Tonight, neither Simon nor his mother acted curiously. They simply wished him a good night before he got into the car with Michael.

"You've got everything you need?" Michael asked as soon as Paul got into the car.

"Yes," he replied as they drove out of his driveway. "You know you don't have to come to Lagos with me."

"I told you already it's not a problem," Michael waved his hand dismissively. "It's my weekend with Kasie in Lagos anyway. I was supposed to get there in the morning. Catching a late flight works even better for me. Moreover I'm not about to miss out on an opportunity for a good old brawl."

Michael chuckled and Paul joined in.

"Remember the incident in school when I got into a fight with one of the seniors and you came charging in," Paul said.

"Yes, I remember it so well. You always seemed to get into trouble and we'd all end up in a brawl. We showed that guy not to mess with us, though."

"And we got punished for fighting too."

"But it felt good to defend each other," Michael said, in a more sombre tone, his expression serious. "And I'd do it again for you. It's time Vincent and his mother took a rest."

Paul nodded gravely. His brother had to be stopped finally. "I appreciate it. Thank you," he said, trying not to get too emotional.

"Plus, I've got to see the girl causing all this trouble." Michael added as an after-thought and they both broke out laughing again.

During the flight down to Lagos they caught up on their exploits as young men growing up together. When they arrived in Lagos they were picked up and taken to Michael's house in Victoria Island.

Paul made a few more calls that night to finalise his plans. That night's sleep didn't come easily. His mind was with Ijay as he wondered what state she was in and what Vincent might have told or done to her.

He thought about the way he felt about her. He must have been in love with her from the first day he saw her. It was probably why he'd been angry when she'd disappeared in the morning. But he'd allowed his pride to get in the way. Vincent had taken advantage of Paul's mistake.

Now Paul hat to fix things because Ijay loved him. The kind of love she'd shown him, no other woman had shown that to him.

Ijay had been willing to undergo discomfort and stress when the factory equipment had been damaged. She didn't have to help out but she'd done so. Even though at the time they weren't even lovers.

She'd left the comfort and luxury of the house in Enugu to return to Amori just to be with him. Then she'd volunteered to go to Abuja for the NAFDAC documents which had put her in Vincent's clutches.

She'd done all those things for him with love and gotten into trouble. Now he had to show his love and faith in her by going to her. He hoped she'd agree to his drastic plan when he told her.

His sleep was short and fitful. He woke at dawn, showered and dressed. Michael drove him first to Surulere to pick up the parcel. Mr. Lawal, his father's former chief of security handed him the package which he knew contained the DVD of his father's personal message to him as well as his last will and testament.

"I'd like to come with you," Mr. Lawal said. "I know that whatever made you request these items now is very serious. I promised your father that I'd watch your back if you ever needed me. I think that time is now."

"There's no need," Paul replied.

"Let him come with us," Michael said. "There's always safety in numbers."

"Okay," Paul replied and they headed out of the man's house. Mr. Lawal followed them in his own car as they headed across third mainland bridge to Victoria Garden City. They arrived at the leafy estate just after seven.

The night watchman opened the pedestrian gate and refused to let the car in. He told Paul the residents were still asleep. As the man talked, Paul saw two young women come out of the front door; both were in silk dressing gowns.

Paul recognised Ijay instantly in her blue robe. His heart stopped for a moment and then raced off as it recognised its love. Warm sensation suffused his body. His heart felt lighter and elated for seeing that she looked well.

The other woman came toward the gates. She looked so much like Ijay, a little younger. Paul assumed she must be Ijay's younger sister.

"What's the problem?" she asked Paul with a frown.

"My name is Paul Arinze. You must be Uloma, right?" he asked and lifted his lips in a pleasant smile.

"Oh," She cocked her head to the side and looked surprised, her brows rising in her forehead. "You're Vincent's brother," she stated boldly.

Her confident manner reminded him so much of Ijay. His smile broadened.

"Yes," he replied, encouraged by her demeanour. "Can I come in and speak to Ijay for minute, please?"

"I don't know," she said and looked behind her in Ijay's direction.

Paul's attention turned to Ijay. She hadn't moved from the spot. Her eyes were wide like saucers. She appeared petrified. Shaking her head, she gesticulated wildly with her hand for Paul to leave. On one of her waving fingers, something sparkled.

A ring! Vincent's ring?

She was wearing Vincent's ring. How was that possible? Hadn't she told him she'd thrown the ring away? Had she been lying?

White hot rage pierced his heart with pain. He gripped the gate post and leaned on it as a wave of nausea passed over him.

Had he been too late? Had he already lost her?

Lifting his gaze to Ijay's direction, he searched her face for answers. The early morning sunshine reflected the liquid in her eyes. Then the shimmering tears dropped onto her cheeks. She was distressed...ashamed? Surely she couldn't have betrayed him like the others. There had to be a chance for them. Some hope.

He loved her.

"I have to talk to her now."

Propelled by a need so strong he couldn't name it, he pushed the gateman aside and walked past Uloma toward Ijay. All he knew was that he had to get to her. He had to look into her eyes and search her soul for the answers he needed.

Each of his steps were dogged by slashing emotions—rage, fear, desperation. Everything else around him was just white noise. All he could see was Ijay.

She didn't move, as if she was frozen to the spot. Tears continued to run down her face. Watching her, it felt like someone was shredding his heart. Abruptly, he stopped in front of her. His heart jerked in his chest like he'd just done an emergency stop manoeuvre.

For a few seconds, neither of them said anything. His chest rose and fell. He tried to control his ragged breath.

She was as beautiful as ever with a clear skin and bright eyes in the morning. Yet she was agitated, her hands fidgeted with her robe. She looked like she expected the world to end any minute. He wanted to take her in his arms and tell her they'd survive today.

Then the gateman was there and broke the spell. "Madam Ijay, I'm sorry. He pushed past me."

"It's okay," Ijay said softly, her words strained. "You can go."

The gateman stood there hesitantly. He was obviously unsure of leaving his boss's daughter alone with a man who looked as fierce as Paul did at that moment.

"Go!" It was Uloma this time.

The man walked away quickly.

"Do you need me to stay?" her sister asked.

Ijay shook her head, her ponytail swinging behind her head. "Thanks but I'll be alright." Uloma walked in the front door and shut it.

"I need to talk to you," Paul said calmly, though he felt anything but relaxed.

Seeing Vincent's ring on Ijay's finger drove him insane. The little ring of metal was a symbol that Vincent had won. Paul couldn't let that happen. He couldn't give up yet.

"First, take that ring off," he bit out in a low voice.

"Paul, I can't do that. I'm not even supposed to talk to you. You have to leave," Ijay replied, some of the old defiance back in her sparkling brown eyes.

"I'm not going anywhere until I know the truth. Yesterday you told me you loved me. Today you're wearing Vincent's ring again. Tell me why."

"Paul, please go." She looked away, dismissing him in the downward sweep of her gaze.

"Tell me why, damn it!" Driven by desperation, Paul grabbed her shoulders and shook her.

"He's going to kill you," she choked out loud. "Vincent was going to kill you. I couldn't let that happen. I couldn't let him hurt you. I'm sorry."

She lowered her head and sobbed. He pulled her into his arms, wrapping his large arms and body around her. He held her tight, her head against his chest, her tears soaking his shirt. The sound of her cry tore at his heart.

She'd sacrificed herself for him. That was even more than he'd ever expected from her—from anybody. If that wasn't proof of her love, nothing was. He hoped he'd be able to live up to that love. Gently, he caressed her back. When she calmed, he leaned back and tilted her head up from under her chin.

Her eyes shone with the left over tears. With his thumb he wiped her cheeks.

"I won't let Vincent hurt you or me. After today I promise you he'll leave both of us alone permanently."

"Oh no! Don't tell me you're going to kill him?"

"Death is too easy for him after what he's put you through. I have something a bit more legal in mind but as effective," Paul said and gave her a lopsided grin.

"He's coming over later today. He's booked us to have a marriage ceremony at the registry today. I wasn't supposed to tell anybody until afterwards. He said he has people watching you and me."

Paul gritted his teeth angrily. When Ijay looked at him sharply he relaxed a little.

"Listen, don't worry about Vincent. I've already flushed out his spies. First was Kate, then Mr. Obi and I think the third person is Simon's mother."

"I suspected Mr. Obi from his behaviour yesterday but Simon's mum?" Ijay's eyes widened in shock. "Oh no! You could be right."

"Why do you say that?" His frown deepened.

"The day Amaechi drove me to Enugu, I threw Vincent's ring in the kitchen bin," Ijay said, lifting her palms to her cheeks. "Yesterday Vincent turned up in Abuja with the same ring. Simon's mother was in the kitchen when I threw the ring away. She'd also been reluctant for me to return to Amori as if she didn't want me to be with you. It had to be her that gave it to Vincent."

"You're right," Paul replied, his eyes narrowing in anger. "She was fidgety yesterday. I suspected something was up. Now you've confirmed it."

He shook his head sadly. He'd welcomed Simon and his mother into his home and heart. It was hard to swallow that the woman would betray him. He wondered what Vincent had offered her.

"What are you going to do about her?" Ijay asked, her sad eyes searching his face.

"She can't stay in my house any longer."

"Oh no. You're not going to kick them out? I feel so guilty now for splitting your family." Her eyes glittered with unshed tears.

His Ijay had such a big kind heart. Here she was worried about a woman who'd sold her out. Paul couldn't forgive the woman so easily, though.

"Don't be. I made a commitment to Simon and I won't renege on it. But his mother put your life in danger. I can't forget that. So I'll find them somewhere else to live and cover the expenses."

"Okay." Her chest rose as she heaved a sigh of relief.

"So do you still love me, sweet Ijay?" his voice dropped into a low rumble as he held her gaze and stroked her cheek with his thumb.

She blushed, her cheeks turning rouge. "Yes," she whispered in a husky voice and lowered her eyes shyly.

"Then I've got to do this." He lifted her hand and took the engagement ring off her finger. "I'm going to keep it this time and make sure it's safely disposed off." He slipped the cold ring into his pocket.

"And this."

He leaned down and kissed her soft lips passionately. She gasped and opened up welcoming his sweeping tongue into her warm sweet depth. She moved even closer, crushing her pliant body against his hardness. His hunger for her blazed to life. He reminded himself they were at her parents' and controlled his fiery urge. When he lifted his head they were both out of breath.

"Now you need to get dressed," he gave her a sexy smile and released her. Having her that close with her teasing fragrance and softness was causing havoc with his body. "I have somewhere to take you."

"You'll have to come inside and wait. Where are we going so early?" she smiled cheekily and turned toward the front door.

"We are going to beat Vincent at his own game. I'll tell you the rest in the car."

Chapter Twenty-Seven

Thirty minutes later, Ijay was in the car with Paul, Michael and Uloma heading to Ikoyi. Her sister had insisted on tagging along after Ijay narrated the events of the past few days. Strangely, Uloma wasn't surprised that Vincent had turned into some sort of psycho because of the way his mother was obsessive about him. Yet, even her wild imagination hadn't prepared her for the extent of his craziness.

Ijay and Paul sat in the back seats with Uloma in the front passenger seat while Michael drove.

"So what's this big plan of yours?" Ijay asked Paul when all the introductions had been made and Michael chatted with Uloma up front.

"After Sonia called me last night, I realised that Vincent was planning to do something crazy by turning up in Abuja unannounced." Paul took her hand, wrapping his large warm hand around it.

"Years of both of us trying to outmanoeuvre each other had taught me a few things about my brother. I realised this time he was really up to something big. So I made a few enquiries via my attorney. Vincent being Vincent played his card exactly the way I expected it."

Paul paused and held her gaze. "Do you remember filing for a marriage notice with the registry?"

"Yes, months ago," Ijay replied. "Vincent said it was best to file it as soon as possible so that there would be no delays when we wanted to register the marriage. As we were going to wed in the church I'd thought it was simply a matter of formality. Why?"

"Yes, you are required to file a marriage notice if you are going to wed in a registry and the notice is posted. It seems my dear brother Vincent had always planned to do it this way. I found out he'd scheduled your wedding for today, even before this week."

"What? He planned it that way?"

"Apparently so."

"Oh, I can't believe I was so gullible and fell for all his soft words." Ijay shook her head in anger. "He actually admitted he'd seen us together in London. He was going to marry me to get back at you."

"My brother can be very charming when he wants to be and also very devious. That night, I'd felt as if I was being watched. But it was a party and I dismissed the odd sensation."

"So what are we going to do about him?" She really wanted to get back at Vincent for using her so ruthlessly.

"Well," Paul cleared his throat suddenly looking nervous. "I'd like to ask you to marry me."

Ijay's face brightened before creasing into a frown. "Paul, you know I love you. Don't tell me your sole purpose for wanting to marry me is because of Vincent."

"No. Of course not." He looked pained. "I know this is not a very glamorous way to propose to you. But I'll be delighted to have you as my wife. I love you and a few days ago I told you I'd never let you go. I meant it."

Ijay's lips curved gloriously, her eyes sparkling. "In that case, it's a yes." She giggled. Uloma squealed in laughter.

Paul leaned across and kissed Ijay briefly.

"Wonderful. Now I can call my attorney to meet us at the Minister's house in Ikoyi."

"Minister's house?"

"Yes, we're going to get married today. This morning in fact. The Minister for Justice is the only one who can grant a marriage license without the need for a notice. We need the sworn affidavits which my attorney will do."

"Paul, I'm not dressed for a wedding. I'm not ready," she said, her heart racing in panic.

"I know. I'm sorry to have to do this. We have to stop Vincent. This is the only thing that would stop him. I promise you. He understands the sanctity of marriage and will not break it."

"I don't want to get married to you like this. Without my parents or friends."

"I totally understand. I promise we'll have another ceremony exactly the way you want it. You'll have your dress, your bridesmaids, whatever you want. But we have to survive today and stop Vincent. This is the only way I can think of."

Uloma reached across from the front seat and put her hand on Ijay's knee. "I'm here with you, Ijay. And I look forward to planning another big day with all the trimmings."

Ijay smiled tentatively. While she didn't like the idea of a secret wedding, she could understand Paul's point. And she really wanted to get back at Vincent for deceiving her.

"Us getting married would really be a slap in Vincent's face, wouldn't it?"

"Yes, it will."

"Then I'll do it. I still want my big fat Nigerian wedding too," she said and they all laughed.

***

Two hours later it was all done. Ijay walked out of the Minister's residence in Ikoyi feeling light and elated. Uloma and Michael kissed them both congratulations as they left the man's home in Ikoyi.

"How does it feel to be Mrs. Arinze?" Paul asked with a glint in his eyes.

"It feels fantastic," Ijay said. Considering she hadn't wanted a quickie ceremony, she was overjoyed at being married to Paul. Now she felt nothing could break their union. Certainly not Vincent or his mother. "So where do we go now?"

"Now we go to see Vincent and his mother."

"You mean we're going to their house?"

"Yes. It's my house too as it happens although I haven't seen it as home for years. It's not that far from here, so we'll be there in a few minutes."

Paul waited for her to get into the back of the car. Michael already knew the route to the Arinze's family residence in Ikoyi. When they arrived, he parked the car in front of the gates obstructing any cars from leaving the premises. Mr. Lawal parked his car behind Michael's.

Just as they stepped out of the cars, the gates opened and a blacked-out Lexus SUV drove to the exit. Ijay instantly recognised Vincent through the windscreen. He stepped out of the car.

"What's going on here?" he shouted at Paul. "You're not allowed here. Get out."

"You'll find that this house is as much mine as it's yours Vincent so I have every right to be here," Paul said calmly.

Ijay stepped out of the car and Vincent's eyes widened in shock and then narrowed suspiciously.

"What are you doing with him?" he shouted angrily. "I told you not to talk to him." He walked to Ijay and grabbed her by the arm.

Paul swung a right hook that connected with Vincent's chin and he staggered back onto the bonnet hood of his car. His security men came round and pulled him up.

Paul looked at Ijay, pulling her closer to his side.

"I'll kill you for this," Vincent spat out, waving his clenched hand at Paul. His henchmen stood behind him.

Michael stood beside Paul and Mr. Lawal on the other side.

"I don't think you will. If you ever get tempted to, you see what Michael has in his hand?" Paul nodded in Michael's direction. Michael raised his hand revealing a mini-camcorder.

"Don't you just love technology? Everything you say and do is captured instantly for posterity. Well, if you ever decide to make good your threat, there are witnesses and a recording that'll make sure you pay for your crime this time."

Vincent sneered but said nothing.

At that moment, Mrs. Arinze stepped out of the house, followed by a woman Ijay recognised as Kate.

"What's all the noise about?" Mrs. Arinze said. "Ijay, I didn't see you there." She smiled at Ijay.

"I came to see you but Vincent won't let us come in," Paul said.

"Mum, he hit me. Can you imagine?" Vincent said angrily. He sounded like a sulking little boy complaining about his playmates beating him up to his mother. Ijay couldn't believe he was a man in his mid-thirties.

Mrs. Arinze glared at Paul before turning back to Ijay and smiling. "You can all come in."

Paul stopped for Ijay to go in after Mrs. Arinze. Ijay walked past Kate who glared at her. Ijay bristled and turned just in time to see Kate put her hand on Paul's chest.

"It's so good to see you again, Paul," Kate purred.

Ijay was so angry, she swung her arm mimicking the move Paul played on Vincent right on Kate's cheek in a slap. The hit was so hard her palm stung afterwards. Kate staggered backwards falling into Vincent standing behind her.

"Keep your filthy hands off my husband!" Ijay shouted at her. "Bitch." She used the same word

Kate had used on her in Abuja. Except this time Ijay thought the right female dog was being labelled.

"Huh!" the sound of gasps resounded in the Arinze living room. Vincent's mother turned pale and sat heavily on a sofa.

"What did you say?" Vincent shouted.

"Yes, we thought we should share the happy news with you guys first," Paul said his gaze sweeping the room. Vincent and Kate stood together in a corner. Michael was behind them. Paul and Ijay stood in front of Mrs. Arinze. "Ijay and I were wedded by the Attorney General this morning."

He pulled Ijay beside him and smiled down at her before looking around the room again with a victorious smirk.

Vincent laughed. "You must think I was born today. You can't be married without giving twenty-one day's notice. And I know you didn't because I'd given notice already and they notified me weeks ago we could get married anytime within three months."

"The Attorney General of the country does not need a notice to wed couples. And he did. We've got the certificate and wedding rings to prove it."

Paul reached in his jacket and took out the marriage certificate. Vincent lunged for it but Paul put it out of reach and shook his head. "I'm not giving it to you."

"I want to see it," Mrs. Arinze said calmly.

Paul gave her the certificate which she perused and returned to Paul, her eyes darkening with sadness and anger.

"So Ijeoma, you decided to marry a rapist," she spat out at Ijay who gasped at the harshness of the woman's words. "Do your parents know you've married him? I'm sure they don't know because they would never approve it."

Ijay looked away shamed-faced. It was true. She was married and her parents didn't know. Even though she wanted to be married she couldn't help feeling guilty about it.

"Don't talk to my wife like that," Paul said coldly, his body tensed with anger, his hands balled by his sides.

Ijay lifted her hand and touched his back. He relaxed a little.

"Mrs. Arinze, you're right. I didn't tell my parents I was getting married today," Ijay said softly, stiffening her back muscles and standing straight, her gaze connected with Mrs. Arinze's furious one.

"It's not because I'm ashamed of Paul. I'm not. I love him. He's kind-hearted and generous. Above all he's honest. He's the fulfilment of my dream of what my husband should be and I'm very proud of him. As soon as we leave here, we'll go straight to my home and tell my parents."

"Yes, whatever," Mrs. Arinze waved her hand dismissively. "So now that you've told us. Congratulations. You can go."

Paul turned to Ijay and mouthed *I love you* silently before turning his attention back to Mrs.

Arinze. "We're not done here. The main reason we came was to make sure you and Vincent leave us alone to live our married life in peace."

"Of course we will."

"Well," Paul shook his head. "Somehow, I'm not quite ready to take your word for it yet. You see Vincent has already threatened to kill me this morning. I just want to make sure you leash him."

"What? *Do* you see how he's insulting me, mum," Vincent raged. "I'm not a dog to be leashed."

"Sometimes you behave like a rabid dog. If rabid dogs can't be caged and treated, they're put down." Michael said with a wink. Paul smiled but didn't say anything.

"Grrr," Vincent growled, rushing toward Michael.

"Enough," his mother shouted. Vincent froze on the spot. "Go and sit down."

Vincent walked to the sofa and sat down with a sulking expression. Kate joined him seating on the other end also looking flustered. Ijay and the rest remained standing.

"Sit down, please." Mrs. Arinze said in a gentler tone.

Paul nodded at Ijay. They both sat near each other with Michael in an armchair. Mr. Lawal stood behind them.

"So what exactly do you want?" Vincent's mother asked.

"Before our father died, he made a recording and sent it to me. At the time, I wasn't talking to him so I didn't watch it until after his death to my regret.

However, I think it's time we all watch it because it concerns all of us."

Paul took the parcel from Michael and opened it removing the DVD box. "I know exactly what's on this DVD and I highly recommend that everyone here watch it calmly." He gave a protracted look at Vincent before continuing. "Should I play it?"

"Go ahead," Mrs. Arinze said.

Paul put the DVD in the player and turned on the TV. He sat down next to Ijay and squeezed her hand. He had mixed feelings about watching that video again. About being in this house again.

When he'd left he'd promised himself he'd never return after the traumatic events he suffered here and the fact his father sent him away. Now he understood his father's reasoning though he didn't agree completely with them.

His father came on screen—light specks of grey hair on short hair, a square face with strong features softened by age lines around the eyes and mouth, serious dark eyes. Immediately Paul was transported to being a little boy again. He remembered his father's eyes sparkling with laughter as he told Paul a story.

Unfortunately the fun memories with his father seemed few and far between. As an adolescent boy he hadn't spent much time with his father. He only remembered his occasional visits when Paul was in boarding school. Those were the only one-on-one time he'd had with his father. By then a deep resentment of his old man had set root, for not curbing Vincent and his mother.

Paul sat tensely in his seat, his shoulders bunched and hurting. He didn't like that seeing his father's image again brought back some painful memories.

Ijay placed her warm hand on top of his. Her soothing heat settled his restless mind. He relaxed back into his seat, turning to look at her. She smiled encouragingly at him. It was as if she understood his troubled mind.

His heart lifted with joy, a warm sensation spreading through his body. He grinned at her in return.

He loved her so much. And to think he'd nearly lost her because of this own arrogance. Now she was his wife. He intended to live a very long life with her, hopefully.

He turned his attention back to the TV screen and noticed that Mrs. Arinze composure was slowly disintegrating as she watched the screen.

"...so my son," his father's deep voice resounded in the room. "I know I'm not perfect but I've always tried to do the right thing for my family. You have a right to be angry with me. I just hope you'll put it aside for the sake of our family. While you are a determined and ambitious man, I also know that you have your mother's kind and generous spirit.

This is why I give the responsibility of taking care of your siblings when I'm gone in your capable hands. I know that your step-mother hasn't always been easy on you. For the sake of our family, I want you to seek peace. Forgive her. I let you down as a father. I should have curbed her excesses in time. I didn't and now it's too late."

"I know you didn't rape that girl so many years ago. It was why I bailed you out and paid reparations to the girl's family. I finally wrung a confession out of your brother Vincent. He confessed to raping the girl to get back at you. I can't believe a child of mine could have such hatred in his heart for his siblings. It saddens me. I couldn't bear to see Vincent in jail so I didn't report it. But I wanted you to know.

"So finally, I'm dying. I've been diagnosed with prostate cancer. Ironic isn't it after the life I've lived. It's aggressive and has spread quickly. I've been given a short time to live and wanted to say my goodbye just in case. I love you, son and I hope you'll one day forgive me."

"Now that's out of the way, we can get on with legal matters. I have made provisions in my will for you and your siblings—"

Paul tuned out of the rest of the words. It was his father bequeathing his estate and businesses to all his children and his wife. He didn't really care about those words. The ones that had got to him were his father confessing he loved him. While he'd been alive Paul couldn't remember his father saying those words to him.

His one regret was that he hadn't seen the DVD before his father died. He would've gone to see him. His father had been in hospital in the UK and neither Vincent nor his mother had notified him that Chief Arinze was ill until he died.

312

It was only then he'd sat down to watch the DVD and had been even more torn apart. Now with Ijay beside him giving him the love he didn't think he deserved, he finally felt able to shed the pain.

"This doesn't change anything," Vincent remarked, pointing to the TV screen. Paul shook his head at the stupidity of his brother's words.

"The video changes everything," Paul said calmly. "For starters, it shows quite clearly that our father made a will that covered all his family not just you two. It is grounds for challenging your version of the will in court."

"That's rubbish," Vincent spat out angrily.

"Secondly," Paul ignored him and continued. "It also shows that you Vincent are guilty of raping that girl and framing me. At the most you can be charged with assault and rape. At the least with perverting the course of justice. You could spend a very long time in prison."

Vincent's expression paled. For the first time he looked cowed. His eyes widened, his hands gripped the arm of the sofa.

"What do you want," Mrs. Arinze asked in a low voice. She appeared pale, her skin drawn tight on her face.

Paul's squeezed Ijay's hand again. "I want you and Vincent to leave us alone. And I want Simon's trust fund reinstated. He's entitled to his share of father's estate when he gets to twenty-one years."

"Fine. Agreed. I'll speak to the lawyer about sorting it out," Mrs Arinze replied.

"Mum, you are just going to cave in to their demands?"

"Shut up, Vincent. If it wasn't for you and your stupidity we wouldn't be in this situation. Why you had to rape that girl, I don't know."

Vincent turned away shamefaced, his knuckles white as he clenched his hand.

Paul stood up. "And in case you think about reneging, I've given instructions to have this tape delivered to the attorney general himself if anything happens to me or Ijay.

"You have my word," Vincent's mother said calmly.

"And Vincent?"

"He'll be leashed."

Paul nodded. He extended his arm hand and pulled Ijay up. "Then we're done here. Quietly they walked out of the house. When they got to their cars, Paul turned to Mr. Lawal.

"Thank you so much for standing by me."

"It's the least I could do for you and your father. Congratulations again to you and your wife." He beamed a smile at them before getting into his car and driving away.

Michael clapped Paul on the back. "Well done. You showed them. That went better than I anticipated." He smiled and got into the car leaving Ijay and Paul alone for a moment.

Uloma gave both of them a brief hug before joining Michael in the car.

"Phew. I've never been through such a thing before. Talk about dysfunctional family," Ijay said, utterly relieved that she didn't have to see Vincent again.

"Do you regret marrying into it?" Paul asked, his brow quirked up, his stare intense.

"I'm blissfully delirious that I married you and not your psycho brother." She'd had a very lucky escape from marrying the wrong brother.

Paul chuckled. "In that case, welcome to the family. Now let's go and tell your parents."

***

Later that night, Ijay looked at her reflection in the mirror of the hotel suite Paul had booked them into for the night. Since it was officially their wedding night, he'd insisted they mark the occasion in some way. So after they'd had an impromptu celebration at her parents' home, Paul had booked them to stay the night at the luxury hotel. He called it a mini-honeymoon.

Her parents had taken the news of the marriage very well. Her father still insisted that the traditional wedding occur. Paul agreed they could still use the original date booked. After all it was still an Arinze wedding an Amadi. They would just have to revise the name on the invitation cards.

She lifted her hand and looked at the glittering gold band on her finger. It was Paul's mother's wedding ring. He'd used it because of the short notice and told her she could have her own if she wanted. Ijay wanted to keep it. It was a family heirloom and had brought her good luck so far. She imagined the future would be bright with Paul.

"So are you ready for me," she called out to Paul who was in the bedroom.

"I've been ready for you since this morning," he drawled in the deep sexy voice that always melted her insides. She giggled at Paul's provocative words. She loved that their relationship was based on hot passion as well as deep friendship. She couldn't see a life without Paul.

Drying her suddenly clammy hands on a towel, she fluffed out her hair, letting the dark waves cascade down her back. She picked up Paul's blue tie and hung it around her neck. Then she stepped into the bedroom.

Paul laid on the bed in nothing but his stretchy boxer-briefs. She could see the tent of his erection. His eyes widened before a slow sensuous smile curved his lips.

"Where did you get that from?"

"I packed it to take to Amori but we never got the chance to use. Now seems to be the best time. Do you like?"

He knelt on the bed, pulled the tie off her neck and wound it around his hand.

"I like it a lot. You know our mutual friend Kate told me once I'd die alone. If I die today, I'll be a very happy dead man. I love you."

He pulled her in for a kiss.

"And I'm going to spend the rest of our lives showing you how much, sweet Ijay" he said as he bound her hands over her head.

"You're not alone anymore, my love. I look forward to spending forever with you," she managed to say, letting out a soft contented sigh before he started showing her with his body, heart and soul.

Thank you for reading. If you enjoyed this story, please leave a quick review on the site of purchase.

There next story in the Challenge series is Worthy and it's out now.

I offer my mailing list subscribers the chance to read previews of upcoming books before the release date. Make sure you don't miss out on the free reads, giveaways and news of upcoming book events by visiting my website www.kirutaye.com and signing up for my mailing list.

Until our next fictional adventure,
Kiru xx

OTHER BOOKS BY LOVE AFRICA PRESS

Unravelling His Mark by Zee Monodee

Healing His Medic by Nana Prah

Pharaoh's Bed by Mukami Ngari

A Place Called Happiness by Diana Anyango

One More Night by Rosemary Okafor

CONNECT WITH US

Facebook.com/LoveAfricaPress

Twitter.com/LoveAfricaPress

Instagram.com/LoveAfricaPress

www.loveafricapress.com

LOVE AFRICA PRESS
Home of African Love Stories